Revenge at

Sea

A NOVEL
BY
BRIAN O'SULLIVAN

BIG B PUBLISHING

B

Novels by Brian O'Sullivan

Short Stories

Acknowledgements:

To Julie Mendelsohn, who generously bankrolled the Audible version of *The Bartender* and has been one of my biggest supporters.

To Jim Kostoryz and Nick Cuneo, two good friends who read my "in dire need of an editor" first drafts, and instead of laughing, give me valuable feedback.

As always, to my editor Therese, who makes these novels presentable. And to Liz, my fabulous cover designer.

This novel is dedicated to my social life. It died during the writing of this novel.

This is a work of fiction. Names, characters, places, and incidents either are the product of the author's imagination or are used in a fictitious manner. Any resemblance to actual persons, living or dead, events, or locales is merely coincidental.

REVENGE AT SEA
Copyright @2020 **Brian O'Sullivan**
All rights reserved.
ISBN: 978-0-9992956-6-3
Published by **Big B Publishing**
San Francisco, CA

PART I: WHITE LIES

1.

I became a journalist, at least originally, in hopes of achieving some form of immortality. That was getting less likely with each passing day.

Unless, in the not too distant future, crime-beat journalists for small-town newspapers are idolized like Hemingway.

I wasn't holding my breath.

"Maybe the next forty years will be better," I told myself.

That seemed unlikely, considering I was spending my fortieth birthday in a hospital bed. With stitches in my head. Talking to myself.

"Quint, your old ass can't handle me," my friend Dugan said. His first name was Gerald. No wonder he preferred to be called by his last name.

Maybe if I hadn't had four beers, three cocktails, and two shots throughout the day, I wouldn't have made that one awful decision.

But my friend since childhood was calling me out. With eight of my friends there for my birthday. Including my ex-girlfriend. I couldn't stand down.

So at 10:00 p.m. after a long day of drinking, I met Gerald Dugan in the middle of the Kingfish Pub & Cafe, an Oakland staple. It was a dive bar with a popcorn machine, shuffleboard, and bathrooms that looked like they hadn't been cleaned in years.

And now, the site of an ill-advised, impromptu tussle between friends. I was 6'3" and 190 pounds but still dwarfed by Dugan. No, this wasn't my best idea.

I put my arms around his shoulders, but this wasn't going to be a dance. We started grappling, and for a brief second, I had the upper hand. But then, less than five seconds into the looming disaster, Dugan swung me around like a rag doll and sent me careening toward a wall.

The Kingfish's walls are replete with framed photographs of famous Bay Area athletes. If I'd had all my faculties about me, I could have slowed my momentum as I flung toward them. But I didn't and went in headfirst at full speed.

Glass exploded into my forehead and cut me up pretty good, blood gushing everywhere. Some of the girls started screaming. I, for some reason, was laughing.

I raised my hands in the air, blood dripping from my face, and yelled: "This is forty!"

A few minutes later, I was being driven to the hospital.

I was given a bed at Summit Hospital in downtown Oakland. Another patient lay on the opposite side of the room, with a partition between the two of us. I took it as a positive sign. My rationale being that if you have a "roommate," you're probably not that badly hurt.

A doctor entered. He was also fortyish, with wire-rimmed glasses and a smirk on his face.

"Looks like someone thought wrestling in a bar was a good idea," he said.

Obviously, he'd been apprised of the situation.

"I almost won, Doc."

I could be a smart-ass at times. His smirk turned into a half-smile and he looked down at my sheet on his clipboard. "Quint Adler. Robert Shaw's character in Jaws was named Quint."

"My parents saw it on their first date. I was named after him."

"Great movie. Your forehead looks like you wrestled a shark."

"Couldn't resist, could you?"

He continued smiling at me. "We'll get someone in here to stitch you up. You're going to be okay, Quint, the shark hunter."

"Thanks."

He did a double-take on the piece of paper.

"And happy birthday!"

A different doctor came and sewed me up. It took fourteen stitches. They gave me a little mirror to look at my forehead.

"This is forty," I said again, with much less aplomb. For the first time in my life, I looked old. Of course, the drinking and the stitches didn't help matters.

I'd been shocked to learn Robert Shaw was only forty-seven when he played my namesake in Jaws. He looked like he was seventy.

Maybe aging early just came with the name.

My favorite sarcastic doctor walked back in. He looked me over. "They did a good job sealing you back up."

"Can I go now?"

"We usually let patients leave after inserting the stitches. However, we both know you've had a few adult beverages tonight, so I'm going to suggest you stay a little longer. Sleep it off for a few more hours."

That didn't sound so bad.

"I think the party is over anyway," I said.

"You've got a few friends here. I'll tell them I'll release you at 1:00 a.m."

"Thanks."

I nodded to the doctor and leaned my head back on the pillow. I was asleep within seconds.

I woke up a few hours later to the sound of two men talking on the other side of the room. Really, it was less talking and more reprimanding. One guy was pissed at the other.

I could see silhouettes, but not faces.

"Are you a fucking idiot? You don't come to a hospital after a job like that."

It may seem counterintuitive, but the man seemed to be yelling and whispering at the same time. Maybe it was just the intensity of his voice. And although twenty feet and a partition separated our two sides of the room, I could hear him perfectly.

"I didn't voluntarily come. I crashed my car, and the ambulance brought me here."

"Well, let's go. We are getting you the hell out."

I heard rustling from behind the partition and could tell someone would be walking past me at any moment. Something told me I didn't want these guys seeing me awake, so I closed my eyes as footsteps came around the partition. Soon after, I heard them heading away from me and down the hall of the hospital.

The investigative journalist in me—and yes, I use that term loosely—was suspicious by nature. Every sideways glance, every misleading answer, every suspicious activity, set my mind jumping to conclusions. This was no different.

In reality, I worked for a small-town paper named the *Walnut Creek Times*, covering local crime; car break-ins and the occasional bank robbery were usually as violent as it got. I also covered high school sports and anything else deemed newsworthy. Jimmy Breslin, I was not.

I slowly made my way out of my hospital bed. I went to the other side of the partition, and as I expected, the bed was now unoccupied.

I reached in my jeans and felt for my cell phone. Luckily, they hadn't confiscated that. I pulled it out and took pictures of the hospital bed, not sure how these could help me. But then I realized there was something that just might.

At the front of the room, a slot for each patient had our basic information. Address, age, etc. Anything else would have been off limits. I took out his sheet of paper.

Griff Bauer. 1841 7th Avenue. Oakland, CA. 94606.

I took a picture. "Car accident" was listed in the reason for admittance. "Severe concussion" as the diagnosis.

I slid the paper back in the slot and walked to my bed.

A few minutes later, my favorite doctor made his way into the room. "Shit," he said.

"What is it?" I asked, casually.

"Looks like your roommate flew the coup."

"Didn't even notice. I was still passed out. Does that happen often?"

"Yes, when you drink too much."

"I meant fleeing the room."

"I know." He laughed.

"You're a good doctor for a comedian."

"As they say, laughter is the best medicine. Per your question, more than you think. People think if they leave, they won't get stuck with their hospital or ambulance bill."

"Doesn't work that way?" I asked, trying to lead him on.

"No Quint, it doesn't," he said, grabbing the piece of paper from the slot. "This is written in pen, not pencil."

"Actually, it's printed," I said.

"Touché."

I wanted to ask a few questions about the room's other inhabitant, but no need to arouse suspicion. Plus, I had his address and knew he was admitted for a concussion following a car accident. Not much else the doctor could tell me.

"I'm feeling better," I said instead.

"Yeah, we're prepared to let you go. Just give me a minute on the paperwork, and I'll return."

"Maybe I'll still be here," I said.

The doctor smiled.

He returned soon after with the paperwork. "You've got someone waiting for you in the lobby."

"Thanks for all your help."

"Stop fighting with glass," he said.

"I'll take your advice into consideration."

Cara Hudson was waiting for me when I arrived in the lobby. I should have expected it. She was one of the eight people who had been at the Kingfish, but more specifically, my ex-girlfriend.

I'd screwed up many times throughout our relationship, but she still had a soft spot in her heart for me. In fact, I think she still loved me.

She was 5'9" with perpetually tanned legs that never seemed to end. She had short brown hair, almost to the level of a pixie cut. The hairstyle fit her striking features perfectly. Every man was immediately taken with her.

And while she was no doubt beautiful, I was attracted most of all to her intelligence. Her mind worked exceptionally fast, and it sometimes took me a few seconds to get her references. I had to be on my toes with her, and I loved that challenge.

When we were together, I'd lived with many "You out-kicked your coverage" jokes. I always took them as a compliment.

I approached her.

"Hey, Quint. You've looked worse," Cara nonchalantly said.

I figured she was trying to downplay my appearance.

"Women still dig scars?" I asked.

"At twenty-five, yeah. Forty, not so much."

"Oh well, can't change that."

She leaned in and gave me a hug, then traced her finger on the outside of the stitches. "How does it feel?"

I looked around and realized we were the focal point of the lobby. A lot of eyes were on us. Most people here undoubtedly waited on news much worse than a few stitches, so I nudged Cara.

"Let's talk outside."

We walked out of Summit Hospital into the warm mid-summer air.

"I feel okay," I said, finally answering her question.

"You didn't say that with much enthusiasm," Cara said.

"Well, I'm forty years old today. I'm single, in a somewhat dead-end job. And I've got fourteen stitches in my forehead. Sorry if I'm not jumping with joy."

"You're wrong."

"Oh yeah, about what?"

"It's not your birthday anymore," she said.

I smirked. Cara had always made me laugh more than any of my previous girlfriends. She never held back. I loved that about her.

"It's funny, yesterday I was thinking about how I was going to make a concerted effort to start my forties off with a bang."

"In your defense, there was a bang when your forehead hit that glass."

A doctor and an ex-girlfriend spending the night busting my balls.

"You always said I didn't open up to you. Now I'm trying, and you're making joke after joke."

"I'm sorry," Cara said, but she could tell I wasn't actually mad. "Here, my car is this way."

She took my hand and led me in a different direction. I had to say, even just feeling Cara's hand in mine felt good.

We'd had great times together, but I'd been a jackass many times over the years. Nothing egregious, and nothing hurtful, just being a lazy boyfriend. And she still stood by me.

We walked in silence for the next few minutes until we arrived at her car. I'd made many jokes over the years about her prized Prius. Now, I was just happy to have a ride. There would be no poking fun this time.

Cara drove the fifteen miles east from Oakland to my apartment in Walnut Creek. A year earlier, I'd have invited her up. Probably even six months ago. But we'd decided a clean break was better for us. It was the right decision. Or so I thought. If I was being honest, I'd been pretty lonely lately without her.

But today wasn't the day to try and rekindle our love.

We approached the Avalon Walnut Creek apartment complex. Right off Interstate 680, my place stood a stone's throw from the Pleasant Hill BART (Bay Area Rapid Transit) station. It gave me a great way to get to Oakland or San Francisco without dealing with the traffic.

The complex held three separate four-story apartment buildings, a Peruvian restaurant, a spot for ramen, and a Starbucks. It wasn't self-contained, but if you wanted to be lazy, you could stay within the perimeter of Avalon Walnut Creek for a few days.

Cara dropped me off out front and paused. I could tell she half expected me to ask her up. But I wasn't going to. Not today, at least.

"Are you going to be okay, Quint?" she asked.

My carefree, happy-go-lucky attitude of the day had given way to a form of moroseness. And she could sense it.

"I'll be fine. I'm not one to dwell on things for long. One night of sulking over the fact that I'm not doing shit and forty years old. I'll be fine tomorrow."

"Anytime you need to talk."

"I know. Thanks, Cara."

I leaned over and kissed her on the cheek. It was friendly, not romantic.

"Let's get a coffee soon," she said.

"Of course."

I got out of the car and headed toward the light brown facade of my building. I used my fob to get inside and took the elevator to the fourth and top floor, where I walked the long hallway to my apartment.

When you entered, you had a kitchen to the immediate right and a washer/dryer and bathroom to the left. Ten feet into the apartment was a "living room," which had a couch, a T.V., a table, and some artwork on the walls. My bedroom was to the left of that.

It may not have been fit for kings, but it was clean, spacious, and I liked it.

I walked to my balcony overlooking the BART station and sat down on an old leather chair I'd positioned there.

I started thinking about the day and my life in general. I wasn't often an emotional guy, but everything got the best of me.

My eyes started to tear up. I could say I didn't know why, but I'd be lying. I hadn't accomplished much in forty years. No kids. No wife. No million-dollar company.

I just had a decent apartment and a job as the local crime writer for a city where a burglary was considered big news.

"This is forty," I said for the third time that night, this time between a few tears. "I hope the next forty are a lot more exciting."

I wiped my tears away and grabbed my phone from my pocket. Little did I know a picture on that phone would bring me a lot more than just excitement.

Careful what you wish for.

2.

Against all logic, a bang to the head ensured I'd feel better the next day. If I hadn't run into the glass at the Kingfish Pub, I almost certainly would have continued drinking for a few more hours and had a worse headache. As it was, I didn't have a hangover, just some stitches on my forehead that didn't give me too much pain.

Maybe this was twisted logic, but I was trying to think positive on the first full day of my forties.

I made myself a bowl of cornflakes and sliced a banana on top of it. I took breakfast to my balcony and started eating on the leather chair. There would be no tears today. The sun was rising, and my spirits with it.

It was Sunday, and while crime never took a break, I usually worked on a strict Mon-Fri schedule at the *Walnut Creek Times.* We produced five papers a week, with Friday's being the weekend edition. So Saturday and Sunday were generally our downtime. Occasionally, if something really important happened during the weekend, I'd get called in to write an article for our website, but that happened rarely.

I appreciated the extra day to heal before my co-workers got a look at my forehead.

As I ate my cereal, I grabbed my phone. I intended to look at some drunk pictures from before I'd smashed my head, but the first photo, the last one taken that night, got my attention.

Griff Bauer. 1841 7th Avenue. Oakland, CA. 94606.

"*Are you a fucking idiot? You don't come to a hospital after a job like that!*"

I remembered the menacing voice from the night before.

After a job like that…

Somehow, I didn't think he was referring to selling Girl Scout Cookies. Something illegal, or at the very least, shady—there was no other way to interpret it.

I looked back down at my phone. With a small sense of foreboding, I read the name and address a second time. From my extremely limited interaction (really, just listening), I knew the two men were up to no good.

But that wasn't going to stop me.

This was the first day of the rest of my life.

I picked up a coffee at my local Starbuck's, then made my way to the elevator and down to the basement to pick up my car. But I didn't arrive unscathed. A fellow Avalon dweller remarked on my stitches as the doors closed.

"What happened?"

"I decided to start the first day of my forties with a trip to the hospital."

"It was your birthday?"

"No fooling you."

In full disclosure, I didn't say that last line. But boy was I tempted.

I was a good human being, and generally a nice guy, but I could be snarky at times. And I had a feeling I was going to get a lot of questions about my forehead in the days to come. I considered a few stories:

- *A shark bit me (thank the doctor for that one).*
- *I fell down an elevator shaft.*
- *Tom Brady punched me for sleeping with Gisele.*

All terrible. Maybe I was more hungover than I thought.

I reached my car and set off for Griff Bauer's house.

Oakland was a different animal than Walnut Creek. A crime writer there had actual work to do. The frequent murder in Oakland trumped the rare bank robbery in Walnut Creek.

And while 1841 7th Avenue wasn't the worst part of the city, it wasn't going to appear on any brochures extolling Oakland's virtues.

What had once been a nice area had become run down. Dilapidated would be putting it too strongly, but it was headed in that direction. The businesses that weren't open were all boarded up. That's never a good sign.

I parked my gray Honda Civic, that of the 117,338 miles, a block short of the address. I realized I had absolutely no plan.

I sat there for twenty minutes, only furthering my opinion that I was ill-prepared.

Maybe Griff Bauer would leave the house with the man who'd reprimanded him, walk by my car, and toss me a note telling me the job he'd been working. Maybe not.

I decided to take things into my own hands. I exited my car and walked toward Mr. Bauer's house. It was a sleepy Sunday, and there weren't many people on the street. Probably for the best. I didn't want some neighbors asking me pointed questions or remembering my face.

I looked up at the numbers and realized I was approaching Bauer's house. The majority of the homes had experienced readily apparent wear and tear. Mostly small, probably two bedrooms, with tiny backyards enclosed by chain-link fences, they all looked similar, with a new paint job differentiating each from the rest of the block.

It made me grateful for my apartment back in Walnut Creek. No, it wasn't a house, but I'd prefer living there to one of these ratty old homes in a run-down part of Oakland.

There was no doubt about it; I was being a judgmental prick. Sue me.

Should I walk by his house or just knock? What the hell was I going to say? Would Mr. Bauer recognize me? No, he'd never seen my face, thanks to the partition in our hospital room.

Of course, with stitches covering my forehead, it wouldn't be crazy for him to assume I'd been at the hospital as well. This was one shitty plan.

I could say I was a reporter doing a story on this specific decaying section of Oakland. It sounded legitimate enough, and I thought it might work. I decided to go with that.

Checking for a house number, I realized I was standing right in front of Mr. Bauer's.

I immediately knew something was wrong.

The door jamb had been splintered, leaving a four-inch gap between the frame and the front door itself. I looked around, and seeing no one, walked up the three stairs to the door.

I turned around one more time, making sure no one was staring in my direction. The streets were empty.

I peeked through the hole in the door.

On the floor, there was a body. It was unmistakable. A human head had been bashed in, and blood caked the floor surrounding him.

I pulled my eyes away from the door and rubbed them.

Had I really just seen that?

I peered back through the hole. There had been no mistake. A man, with half of his brain beaten in, was sitting on the floor of the home. The assailant had taken special attention to bash his face beyond recognition.

It looked like a melon had been hit by a hammer. Repeatedly.

His right arm was splayed out, and his wrist curled upward.

The man was white, but that's about all I could deduce.

I'd seen a few dead bodies before, but never one as mangled as the one in front of me. I stepped back and drew in a big breath.

"Hey, you!"

I turned around.

"You're not trying to break in, are you?" a man approaching seventy said to me from the sidewalk.

"No! Of course not."

He eyed me suspiciously, but I was standing in front of the crack in the front door.

If he saw that, he'd be more than just suspicious.

"Alright then," he said. "Just keeping an eye on my neighborhood."

"Totally understand. I'm going to call my friend's cell phone right now. I'll be gone soon."

That seemed to placate him, and he continued down the street.

He was gone, but I did look suspicious standing there, poking through a hole in the door.

I knew not to touch it. This was going to be a crime scene sometime soon.

Against my better judgment, I decided to walk around the perimeter of the house. I didn't see anyone else on the street, so I put my shirt over my hand and pushed open the chain-link fence that ran parallel to the house. I was making some odd decisions. But why leave a potential fingerprint?

I walked along the side of the house and looked in the first window I saw.

I had a better view than from the front door. The body was even more mutilated than I'd first realized. It was impossible to tell where the neck ended and the head began. A large hammer rested in the blood next to the body.

My first impression was that it seemed staged. Not the death obviously, but who leaves the murder weapon two feet from the victim?

Unless it was a crime of severe passion. Or made to look that way.

I went into full-on reporter mode, not thinking of the potential repercussions. I pulled out my phone and took pictures of the crime scene through the window. I walked around the house and found a back window that offered a different angle of the body and snapped more pictures.

For a split second, I considered trying a door, but I knew that would be going way, way too far. I was smarter than that. Although, in the moment, I certainly didn't make many intelligent decisions. Trespassing on a crime scene, even if it was the back yard, was a serious crime.

What I did next was as well.

As I headed back toward the gate, I saw his recycling bins. I grabbed several pieces of mail and some assorted pieces of paper and slid them down my pants.

As I shut the gate and walked out on the street, I didn't see a soul.

At least not wandering around.

But down the street, there a car sat at a stop sign, not moving. A few seconds became five, and the car still hadn't moved. I was standing there, looking guilty as all hell. I decided to head toward my car, keeping an eye on the unmoving vehicle.

Mercifully, the car sped away in the opposite direction. It was probably nothing, but considering my actions, inevitably I was going to be suspicious.

I half walked, half ran to my car. When I arrived, I grabbed the papers from my pants and threw them on the passenger side.

I drove away, full of excitement and regret in equal measure.

By the time I returned to Avalon Walnut Creek, regret had gained the upper hand.

What the hell was I thinking? Taking pictures of a crime scene? Not immediately calling the police? Stealing the dead man's mail?

I'd made several decisions in the span of a few minutes, and not one of them was the right one.

I could have rectified that, obviously. I should have called the police then and there, telling them I went a little crazy after hearing a weird conversation at the hospital.

That didn't seem like a great plan, either. I'm sure the Oakland police wouldn't take kindly to my actions, no matter what my rationale.

While debating what to do, I got a text from Jan Kingston, my editor at the *Walnut Creek Times*:

Couple of errors in your piece on the recent rash of bike thefts. We'll talk tomorrow.

The dichotomy between my menial job and the crime I'd just witnessed hung in the air.

I didn't want to keep writing about bike thefts. I needed to work a real case. Do some actual reporting.

And while my actions were a little murky, it's not like I'd killed the guy. I was just going to follow the case, and hopefully be a step or two ahead of the police.

This could be my break. Certainly, reporting about the latest Schwinn to be stolen wasn't going to do the trick.

I wasn't going to call the cops.
I was going to ride this thing out.

3.

I went into work on Monday morning and was greeted with a few "Happy Birthday"s.

"Forty! You dinosaur, you."

"Now you can collect Social Security!"

"Were you and Keith Richards rehashing the old days?"

Yes, most of the greetings were based on my age.

Those were followed by comments about the stitches that took up a good three-inch space on my forehead.

I told them the truth about what happened. A few shook their heads, but they were all entertained by the story.

They especially like that I screamed, "This is forty!" with blood spilling down my face.

The office of the *Walnut Creek Times* was located in a bright red stucco building on North Main Street. Despite the fun I poke at the city, Walnut Creek does actually have a nice downtown area. Some great restaurants, a few good bars, and tons of shopping. If that's your thing. Newsflash, it's not mine.

The stucco architecture stood out next to the plain offices that sat to our left and right. The building itself was two stories. I'm not sure if they meant it to serve as a two-tiered hierarchy from the beginning, but that's what it had become. The editor and upper management (really just three people) operated from the top floor, while the reporters had their desks on the first floor.

The elevator was never used, everyone choosing to take the stairs up and down. The stairs went right up the middle of the building, and the office had a very open feel to it. We had a view of the top floor and they looked down on us. Always literally, sometimes figuratively.

I'd heard some of "upper management" refer to the stairs as The Stairway to Heaven, but my fellow reporters and I had a different name for it: The Walk of Shame.

It was so named because if you were asked to come upstairs, it usually meant something had gone wrong. They didn't like your idea for a new article, or it needed to be highly edited. You felt like a condemned prisoner walking up those steps, just waiting to be chewed out.

That said, it was a pleasant environment to work in. We all played well together. Our editor, Jan Kingston, got along famously with all the reporters even when taking her red pen to our articles.

Like she did on this day.

"And you actually should have used a semi-colon as opposed to a comma here," she said, after I'd made the Walk of Shame upstairs.

Even an experienced writer like myself wasn't above making an error or two. Or three, as was the case with this article. Although Jan did say she liked the piece.

"Thanks," I said. "I think it's my favorite stolen bike piece of the year."

"This isn't the *Wall Street Journal*." She laughed.

My mind couldn't help but return to what I'd witnessed the previous day.

"Thanks for your help, Jan."

"You got it."

I walked back downstairs and made a point of finding an Oakland paper. One nice part of working for a newspaper is that we had subscriptions to approximately ten other papers. A few small local ones, *The San Francisco Chronicle*, *The Los Angeles Times*, and several national ones.

I'd worked for the *Walnut Creek Times* for nine years, and it was sad to no longer read the papers that had vanished over the years. A fear permeated our office, and I imagine it was the same for many newsrooms across the country. The fear that our jobs lived on borrowed time.

And I admit, calling our little office a newsroom was a stretch. There was only seven of us. The reporters were: Trent Buckley; most news stories. Crystal Howell; sports, entertainment. Greg Alm; special interests, weather, obituaries. Myself; crime, some sports, local business write-ups.

Upstairs, we had Jan the editor, and the husband and wife team of Tom and Krissy Butler, who owned the paper and made all final decisions. They published the paper as well as running the website. No one worked harder at the *Walnut Creek Times* than Tom and Krissy.

As bosses, they were almost always fair, but that didn't mean they lacked tempers. They were known to drop an F-bomb or three when things fell behind schedule or we'd put out a paper not up to our standards.

In their younger days, Tom had made an obscene amount of money in the financial sector, and Krissy had raised their two children. In 2011, they launched the *Walnut Creek Times*. Tom had enough money to last a lifetime and they were recent empty nesters, so they'd decided to start a paper in the city where they'd grown up. They'd been high school sweethearts and together for over forty years.

Since inception, they'd kept to their plan for a daily paper from Tuesday to Friday and then a "weekend edition" covering Saturday, Sunday, and Monday. As I mentioned, this allowed the staff to generally work a strict Monday to Friday schedule. The paper was short, usually around ten pages from Tuesday to Friday. The weekend edition held more like twenty-five.

Walnut Creek, population 69,000, lay about twenty-five miles east of San Francisco. While it wasn't technically a small city, when you're surrounded by well-known cities like San Francisco, Oakland, and Berkeley, you get that little brother feel.

And there were times when a city our size couldn't provide enough news to support a full paper and we needed to fill it with a little fluff. A recent article about a dog giving birth to six puppies came to mind.

But usually we managed to fill it with substantive articles.

Tom and Krissy had been ahead of the curve when it came to marketing. It allowed them to make a relatively small-town paper successful. Tom seemed to know everyone who mattered in the city and all coffee shops, most bars, and several restaurants carried the *Walnut Creek Times*. At the restaurants, a stand outside usually sold the papers, but coffee shops and bars always had them lying around. The green and white of the *Walnut Creek Times* was ubiquitous around Walnut Creek itself.

Tom and Krissy knew that paid subscriptions had lost their importance. The number of eyes that found their way to the paper was what mattered. And that's why they could charge steeper advertising rates than larger papers.

The Butlers were also a step ahead when it came to their online edition. They charged a small fee, but with that came discounts to local businesses, raffles into concerts, and things of that ilk. The paper personified the city of Walnut Creek and that made it a must-read for all locals.

We put forth a good paper, but if it weren't for the genius of Tom and Krissy Butler, it probably wouldn't have lasted as long as it already had.

The first person they had hired was me. Jan came next, less than a week later. Followed by Trent, Crystal, and Greg, all within the first year.

And there had been zero turnover since.

Pretty impressive, although the fact that the Butlers were rich and paid us more than your average reporter had a great deal to do with that. The prevailing logic around the newsroom was that we were paid handsomely for a relatively easy job, so why rock the boat?

I'd written for my high school paper and then at *The Daily Northwestern* during college. Known for its journalistic programs, Northwestern provided its graduates with some esteem, and I got a writing job right out of college for the *Chicago Sun-Times*. It didn't last, as they had to make cuts. I had three more writing gigs from Chicago to Las Vegas before coming to California and being hired by Tom and Krissy. The 2000s were a tough time for papers and I was wondering if I'd chosen the right career with all the turnover I was going through. So once I joined the *Walnut Creek Times* in 2011, I knew I'd be crazy to leave.

But I had always wanted just a little more, and that's what had led me to Griff Bauer's house.

Not to say I didn't enjoy my job; it just wasn't as fulfilling as one would hope. My writing muscles were assuredly not being flexed. More like becoming atrophied.

But the camaraderie made it worthwhile. Trent was the kid at heart, not above setting down a whoopee cushion for an unsuspecting individual. "In a state of arrested development" would probably most accurately describe him.

Crystal was a hard worker, often staying longer than any other reporter. When she had first joined the paper and we were both single, Tom Butler noticed me flirting with her one day. He walked over and simply said, "Do you like working here?" He didn't have to say anything else. Two employees dating in a small little newsroom was a recipe for disaster. I stopped hitting on Crystal soon thereafter.

Greg and I had gone out for beers a few times and liked to talk about our beloved Golden State Warriors, but he was recently engaged, and I didn't see him as much anymore.

Jan was pleasant, and we got along great inside the office, but like a few of the others, I didn't socialize with her much outside of it.

I knew Tom and Krissy Butler the best. I'd been to their house many times for work BBQs, and I'd brought a few girlfriends on double dates with them over the years. But they'd always tell me the women never stacked up to Cara. Like everyone else in my life, they didn't understand why we weren't together at all times.

I'd also have dinner with just Tom and Krissy about once a month. They were my bosses, but they were also good friends. The twenty-year age gap didn't matter. We had a great back and forth.

Overall, it was a solid group of people, and I was lucky to work with them.

I found the Oakland paper. It was formerly the *Oakland Tribune* but now known as the *East Bay Times*. It had been a rough couple of years for the city of Oakland. The Warriors moved to San Francisco, and the Raiders moved to Las Vegas. And their most well-known paper no longer carried its name.

I scrolled through it, looking for any mention of what I'd seen yesterday. I couldn't find anything, though I hadn't really expected to. More likely I'd see an article the following day. The body would definitely be decaying at this point, and the smell would likely make its way out to the street. If someone saw a broken door jamb and smelled something funky, they'd probably call the cops.

Although in that area of Oakland, you never know. A lot of people liked to keep to themselves and not become involved with the police.

"Don't read that paper, Quint! You're going to get jealous of all the crimes being committed," Trent Buckley said.

"Some cities have all the luck."

Trent laughed.

And then, as if on cue, Tom Butler walked down the stairs. "Quint! We've got something for you."

"Oh yeah, what is it?"

"A murder in Oakland."

That got my attention. "Oakland? We don't cover Oakland."

"We do when the victim is from Walnut Creek. Come up and I'll give you the info."

Tom made his way back upstairs.

Trent just looked at me.

"Creepy timing," he said.

It was creepy for more than just the timing.

I walked up to Tom's office, half hoping it would be a different murder, one I wasn't already slightly involved in. But no such luck.

Tom told me the deceased was a man named Griff Bauer. He'd been born in Walnut Creek and attended a local high school named De La Salle, famous nationwide for having the longest winning streak in high school football history.

He graduated in 2010 and was now twenty-eight years old. His last known job was as a truck driver for a company known as Rick's Rigs.

Tom gave me the address. I remained stone-faced.

He sent me on my way, and I set out for a house I'd visited twenty-four hours earlier.

As I headed to Oakland, I told myself this was my last chance to come clean with the cops. But I knew I wasn't going to exercise that option.

I would instantly lose my job and possibly land in jail. Nope, this was now mine to own.

I arrived in Oakland and parked on the street, twenty feet from where I'd been the day before. Trent Buckley's "creepy" comment re-entered my mind.

It was indeed creepy, down to the fact that I walked the same steps. Yellow police tape surrounded the house, and some officers milled on the street, probably waiting on the medical examiner to finish.

As I approached, I got dirty looks from a few of the officers.

"Can we help you?" one asked.

"I'm with the media. Just trying to get information on the deceased."

"What paper?"

This was always a tough selling point.

"The *Walnut Creek Times*," I said.

"Never heard of it," said the oldest and gruffest of the officers. He looked like he was nearing retirement. You didn't see many graybeards on the force anymore.

I'd probably gotten his response a hundred times over the years when I mentioned the name of my paper. I had three rehearsed lines.

If I felt disrespected, I'd say, "*It's amazing we've managed to survive without your knowledge of us.*"

If I were mildly offended, I'd go with, "*Doesn't mean we don't exist.*"

And if I couldn't risk offending anyone, I'd say, "*We're a small paper with our own little niche.*"

Which is what I decided upon. The Oakland Police Department had bigger fish to fry than me, and if I pissed them off, I'd surely get the cold shoulder.

"Well, unless your niche is murder, I'm not sure why you're here," the older officer said. It was apparent he ran the show.

"I've been informed that the deceased is from Walnut Creek, where our paper is based. And yes, in fact, I do write about crime."

"Crime and murder are two different things, Walnut Creek. A head bashed in is different than writing about some burglary."

"Oh, it's never anything that big. Usually just stolen bikes," I said.

His fellow officers laughed. I'd managed to kill them with kindness.

"You're alright, Walnut Creek. Let me see what the M.E. says, and maybe I'll give you a little information. A very little."

"Thanks for your help," I said, deciding gratitude was the best course of action.

I loitered around, keeping my eyes on the house, but occasionally glancing back toward the street. If the old man who'd seen me by the door had alerted the police to my presence, I'd have some difficult questions to answer.

A few people lingered across the street, and I wanted to ask if they had ever met Griff Bauer. With the police still around, and not wanting to step on toes this early, I decided to wait.

To kill some time, I took out my phone and googled both Griffin and Griff Bauer. It wasn't too common a name, so I was able to find him pretty quickly. I clicked on his Facebook page. 121 friends. No posts from him in six months. And no posts grieving his death, obviously. The M.E. would have to confirm his identity before telling his immediate family. The only people who already knew he was dead were the killer (or killers), the police, the M.E., and me.

His bio said his hometown was Walnut Creek and that he currently lived in Oakland. It listed nothing else, and with very few posts, I wasn't going to learn much about Griff Bauer from his Facebook page.

I couldn't find an Instagram or a Twitter that belonged to him.

Something appeared in the corner of my eye. As I looked up, the door opened, and the M.E. wheeled a body bag out of the house on a gurney.

I remained stoic, but it hit me that this guy was alive thirty-six hours ago and sitting in a hospital bed about twenty feet from me.

What happened to you, Griff Bauer?

A few minutes later, the older officer headed in my direction. By his badge, I realized he was a detective. He stood about the same height as me, with the beginning of a potbelly, but still in good shape. Probably only in his mid-fifties, which wouldn't be old for almost any other profession. But it was for a cop.

"Walnut Creek!"

"My name is Quint, let's go with that," I said.

He smiled, proving he wasn't quite as gruff as I'd initially perceived. "You got it. We'll be canvassing the house in a few minutes, but I've got some basic info for you."

"Thanks," I said.

"Griffin Bauer, known as Griff, was born on August 19th, 1991, making him twenty-eight years old. He was born in Walnut Creek and attended De La Salle High School in neighboring Concord."

"No offense, detective, but this is all stuff I could easily find out."

He had a knowing smile on his face. "This is why I don't like dealing with the media.".

I felt a rush of pride. I'm not sure most people would consider the *Walnut Creek Times* a legitimate part of the media.

"Looks like I came out here for nothing," I said.

I pretended to start walking away.

"Hold on," he said.

I turned back.

"The M.E. thinks he was killed sometime late Saturday night or early Sunday morning. It was blunt force trauma, and the killer was also blunt in his savagery, if you catch my drift."

I did. I'd seen what was left of Bauer's face a full day earlier. And if the timeframe was right and he'd been killed on Sunday morning, I might have just missed his killer.

My mind went to the car that hovered at the stop sign, but I tried to stay focused.

"Could you name any suspects?" I said, intentionally overstepping my bounds.

"Nice try. I wouldn't name any if we did, but obviously, we don't have any this early on."

The detective would never give me a suspect, but he'd answered a question of mine just by denying there were any suspects.

Something else could be helpful information to me. "Do you know of his whereabouts leading up to the murder?"

"Another question I wouldn't answer even if I knew. But the answer is no. We literally got this call two hours ago."

"How did you find out about the dead body?"

"I won't comment on that."

Did you know that I was within twenty feet of the deceased on both Saturday night and Sunday morning? Not that I was going to ask that question.

I knew there wasn't much more I was going to get.

"Thanks for taking the time to talk to me."

"You're okay, Walnut Creek," he said, ignoring my Quint suggestion.

"What was your name?" I asked.

He pointed at his badge. "Detective Ray Kintner. Is this your first murder case? No offense, but you seem a little green."

I'd probably worked one murder every few years in Walnut Creek since joining our paper, so he wasn't far off. But if he wanted to think this was my first, I was fine with that. He seemed to enjoy talking down to me, and it helped me get information.

"As I said, usually bike thefts. I'm a little out of my league here."

I played the small-town fool to perfection. Not that Walnut Creek was all that small, but compared to Oakland, it sure felt like it.

He handed me a business card. "Call me tomorrow," he said. "Maybe I'll have some more info. But stop asking about suspects and motives. You're never going to get those out of me, and it's one sure way of losing my trust."

"No suspects. No motives. I got it. Thanks again for your patience, Detective Kintner."

"Call me Ray. See you around, Quint."

"Ahh, you did hear me."

"I'll deny it under questioning."

I laughed.

We left on good terms.

I walked back to my car and waited. And waited. Almost two hours later, the officers all left, and I made my way toward the house. Actually, to its neighbors. I decided to knock on some doors.

I would introduce myself as Quint Adler, reporter. Unless I encountered the man I'd seen the day before. Then I'd be Bob Smith.

The first door I knocked on went unanswered.

The second door was answered by a squirrelly young woman who didn't want to respond to my questions. Said she "hadn't never heard of no *Walnut Creek Times.*"

I didn't get a chance to mention she'd accomplished the rare triple negative before she shut the door in my face.

My third house proved more beneficial. The door was answered by a black man who looked to be deep into his eighties. Despite his age, he was sharp as a tack. Not always the case when I dealt with the elderly.

"My name is Quint Adler, and I'm a reporter with the *Walnut Creek Times.*"

"I like Walnut Creek," he said. "A lot safer than here in Oakland."

It seemed to be a recurring theme.

"I'm Clarence, by the way," he added.

"Nice to meet you, Clarence. Did you know your neighbor, Griffin Bauer?"

"I know they took him out of here on a stretcher a few hours ago. And not the stretcher you get up from."

"You're right about that. They are saying it was blunt force trauma," I said, hoping to elicit a response.

"Can't say I'm surprised," he said. "This area has just gotten worse over the years. When I bought this house in the 1970s, this was a nice place to live. Raised four kids here. Married fifty-one years to the same woman until she passed away a few years back."

"Sorry about your wife. But fifty-one years is a long, long time," I said. I meant it. I was forty and single, while this guy had been married fifty-one years. I wanted to ask his secret, but this wasn't the time.

"Lots of ups and downs, but I wouldn't change a thing," he continued.

"Life's a roller coaster," I said. "So, did you have any interactions with Mr. Bauer?"

"He's two doors down, so yeah, I've had some interactions with him. Probably be better if I hadn't."

"How's that?" I asked.

"The young man was a jerk. No one liked him on this block. He'd yell at people if they were talking outside of his house. He'd have people over at all hours of the night, being loud."

"Sounds like a black eye for the neighborhood.". The irony hit me as I said it. Describing a white guy using a derogatory term that had "black" in it. Talk about unfair.

Black market. Blackballed. Black hat. Blacklist. Blackball. Black cat. Blackmail. Black eye. And the list doesn't end there.

Clarence didn't remark on my faux pas.

"You can say that again. It's funny; this neighborhood started going downhill when some of these poorer white punks moved in and started selling meth or pills or whatever it is they sell these days. But because it's majority black, we get the blame. I'm not saying we don't have to do better, we do. Men need to stay with their women. It's killing our families. I'm just pointing out that when things go bad, black people are always accused of causing it. But don't worry, I'm not blaming you. You seem like a very nice young man."

"I just turned forty, not sure I still pass as young."

"Forty sounds mighty young to me, sonny boy."

I laughed. "I think saying 'sonny boy' gave away your age."

It was his turn to laugh.

"Not to get all sentimental," he said. "But this is how it should be. An old black guy and a young white guy getting along just fine. Too much hate in this world."

"No doubt about that," I said.

We both soaked in the moment.

"Listen, I'll let you be, Clarence, but I had one more question."

"Sure."

"Did you see anyone go into his house on Saturday night?"

"What time you talking about?"

I did some math in my head and reasoned he left the hospital around 12:30. "12:30 a.m. or later."

"You've got me confused with someone who stays up past 8:30."

I smiled. "How about Sunday morning?"

I had to ask, even with the chance he might have seen me.

"I was at church."

"Okay. Thanks, Clarence. It was a pleasure talking to you," I said.

"The pleasure was mine. Drop in if you're around this neighborhood again."

"I will."

We shook hands, and I left. This world could be a tough place, so I tried to soak in the moments that made for nice memories. My brief interaction with Clarence was one of those.

4.

"Quint, you've got a letter!" Krissy Butler shouted from the second floor of the office.

Sometimes when she or Tom were busy, they wouldn't walk down the stairs. They'd just give us a yell. Today was one of those times.

Krissy was an attractive woman in her late fifties. She had blonde, spiked hair and probably could have passed for her mid-forties. Tom had been a senior in high school and she a sophomore when they started dating. I'd accuse him of robbing the cradle from time to time. Krissy always enjoyed that.

I made the walk of shame upstairs and Krissy handed me an envelope. On the front, large typed letters read QUINT ADLER. There was no return address, and as I turned it over, I noticed the back of the envelope wasn't sealed.

Krissy read my mind. "It wasn't mailed. I found it under the mail slot this morning when I arrived."

"Okay, thanks."

"You've got a secret admirer," she said.

"Secret? I thought that *Playboy* Playmate had made it public."

Krissy shook her head. "Bye, Quint."

I walked back downstairs and sat at my desk. Getting personal mail wasn't all that uncommon at the *Walnut Creek Times*. Usually it was something that would benefit the sender. *Can you do a write-up on my brand new business?* Or, *You just included me in your latest crime beat, I'd like to tell my side.* Things of that nature.

This one had a different feel. Maybe it was the lack of a return address. I'm not sure exactly why, I just knew.

I leaned back in my executive chair and removed the sheet of paper from the envelope. I unfolded it and turned the written side toward me.

I read it once. And then a second time. And finally, a third time.

Mr. Adler, if your dream is to remain at the Walnut Creek Times *for life, you can stop reading right now. If you aspire to something more, I have some information that might help you get there. One caveat. If you tell anyone about this, these letters will cease. And believe me, I will know. I'm a man who knows things. And one of those things I know is who killed Griff Bauer. You should start investigating a man named Dennis McCarthy. But be subtle. He will not take kindly to being investigated. That's it for now. If you keep this to yourself, you can expect another letter in a week or so.*

I looked around the office unnecessarily. It's not as if Trent, Crystal, and Greg could read my mind. Or a piece of paper from across the room.

But the letter had my attention.

I spent most of the day writing a first draft of an article on the murder of Griff Bauer. It seemed like things were changing quickly, but I could always make updates in future articles. Tom Butler wanted a preliminary one, just summarizing the case.

A few minutes before I was slated to get off work, Tom walked by. "Quint, can you come upstairs?"

"Yeah, I'll be right there."

The anonymous letter was still on my desk, so I stuffed it in a drawer, putting old mail on top of it so it wouldn't be the first thing visible.

I then headed up the stairs, where Tom motioned me into his office.

"Have a seat, Quint."

I did.

He looked at me quite seriously.

"What is it, Tom?" I asked.

"You haven't had a proper murder case in a few years, have you?"

I tried to think back. "Probably that home invasion off of Ygnacio Valley Road. It's been a long time."

"Well, I don't want to get your hopes up, but I've heard some interesting news."

I sat up in my chair.

"We're a small-town paper, but that doesn't mean I don't have connections in law enforcement."

It was true. Tom seemed to know everyone. Usually, it didn't mean much because you couldn't invent crime out of thin air, but when the big case did come up, he knew who to put me in touch with.

"I know you are friendly with a great many people," I said.

"I am. And one of those people gave me some compelling information this morning."

He paused for dramatic effect. Then continued.

"There was a double homicide in Oakland on Saturday night."

"Okay," I said, not sure where this was going.

"They just found the bodies this morning."

"And you want me to look into it?"

"It's possible you already are," he said. "Griff Bauer was in a car crash on Saturday night. He was admitted to the hospital, but apparently left soon thereafter. The double homicide took place two blocks from where he crashed his car. And the authorities think he might have been involved. If not, it's a pretty big coincidence to crash your car a few blocks from a double homicide and then be murdered a day later."

Many thoughts churned in my mind. This had become way too complicated. I couldn't tell Tom I'd been in the same hospital room as Mr. Bauer on Saturday night. And I certainly couldn't tell him I saw his dead body before the police did.

I was worried. Confused. And even a little excited.

"What makes them think he was involved with the murders?" I asked.

It was a dumb question he'd basically just answered, but my mind was racing, and I just needed to keep the conversation moving.

"One, crashing so close to the murders. Two, he winds up dead a day later. And three, the detective I know told me Mr. Bauer had a bad reputation. That he might have been involved in some illegal activities. Add those factors together, and I guess I can't say I blame them."

"Makes sense."

"I've got the names and the address for the double homicide. But I just want to make sure you want to investigate this case. The only real affiliation to Walnut Creek is that Mr. Bauer was born here."

"With respect, Tom, if it turns out Mr. Bauer was a killer, that would absolutely be of interest to our readers."

He smiled coyly. "And you'd get to work an interesting case for once."

He read me like a book.

"Well, there's that too."

"I don't begrudge you that. I know your job can be boring most of the time."

"Doesn't mean I don't enjoy working here."

"I know, Quint. Listen, we all think you've got a great talent you don't always get to show off. Maybe this is the case."

"I'll be sure to give you a shout-out when I win the Pulitzer Prize," I said.

"You better. Listen, don't step on too many toes. Reporters don't need jurisdiction like the police do, but people from Oakland might not be as willing to work with someone from Walnut Creek. So tread lightly."

"You know me," I said.

"I do. That's why I'm worried."

We shared a laugh.

He handed me a sheet of paper.

244 Oakland Ave. Deceased: Aubrey Durban, 23. James Neil, 26.

"Thanks, Tom. I'll keep you updated."

"Yes, you will. Traffic there and back would be terrible right now, so why don't you head over early tomorrow morning? Get a read on the house. I don't expect you to solve anything, but it can't hurt to see the neighborhood and get the lay of the land."

"Of course. I'll drive there first thing in the morning."

"This could be a big one for the *Times*, Quint."

I nodded.

I always thought it was ridiculous to shorten our paper's name to just the *Times*. It brought to mind the *New York Times* and we were never going to be confused with them. But now wasn't the time to share that opinion with Tom. I was going to be working a real case for once.

Albeit one that I'd already gotten myself tangled up in.

I walked back down to the reporters' floor and everyone wanted to talk to me. Greg lamented how he'd had to watch the recently concluded NBA finals without the Warriors in them. Crystal wanted a restaurant recommendation. And Travis asked what Tom wanted to see me about.

"NOT RIGHT NOW!" I wanted to scream, but couldn't.

My mind was moving at 100 m.p.h. as I was being bombarded by questions from my co-workers. Not ideal timing.

I was able to give them enough monosyllabic answers that they realized I had work to do. I went back to my desk and looked at the two sheets of paper, the one from Tom Butler and the one from my secret admirer.

The investigation into Dennis McCarthy, whoever that was, would have to wait. My paycheck was signed by Tom. I would spend my working hours on the double murder in Oakland.

And if the letter was correct, these two cases would intersect at some point anyway.

5.

I woke up the next morning and quickly realized it was June 21st. I knew it had been approaching, but it still hit me like a ton of bricks. The toughest night of my life had occurred exactly one year ago to the day.

My father, Arthur Adler, was killed in a robbery. Some reprehensible soul, who they never caught, mugged him in San Francisco and stole his wallet. Apparently that wasn't enough for the bastard, as he had to stab him to death as well.

SFPD still listed the case as "unsolved." I'd talked to some detectives about the case and they literally have zero leads.

If he'd been a police officer or a lawyer or a publicly elected official, I would have been suspicious of the death, fearing an ulterior motive. But my father had been a high school teacher with literally zero enemies in the world. And I mean that sincerely.

The only suspicious thing was his being in San Francisco at 6:00 p.m. on a Friday. And I guess suspicious wasn't even the right word. "Unexplained" would be a better fit. There're a million reasons he could have been there, we just didn't know which one applied. And it had always bothered my mother and me.

He was seventy years old, but in perfect health. I'd been deprived of at least ten or fifteen more good years with my father.

He loved his job as much as anyone I'd ever known. While most teachers retired in their early sixties, or even late fifties, my father just kept on going. He probably would have taught forever, but due to my mother's urging, he decided to retire once he turned seventy. So when the school year ended in May of last year, my father had taught his final class.

My mother hosted a huge retirement party and probably a hundred of his former students attended, no matter how far they had scattered around the country. He was that well liked. Even some old students from his time teaching in Seattle made it. My father took that as a great compliment.

The only criticism ever leveled at him was that he was too nice a guy. Some people thought my mother wore the pants in the family. And while I'd seen him fired up at different points in my childhood, the characterization wasn't all that far off. But if that's the only accusation they can throw at you, you've lived a pretty honorable life.

He was well read and could talk about any subject you wanted. History (his primary teaching subject), the arts, sports, even pop culture. At his funeral, several of his students went up and told stories and said that Arthur Adler was their favorite teacher of all time.

Many of them had attended his retirement party less than a month earlier.

There weren't many dry eyes in the house on the day they laid my father to rest. Certainly not mine.

He had been buried in a cemetery about twenty miles from where I lived. The morning of June 21st, I called my mother and asked if she wanted to go see him. I already knew the answer was yes. I told her I'd pick her up around seven.

My mind remained on my father as I made my way to the scene of the double murder in Oakland. It was a weird thought to have, but I knew my father would be happy. He and my mother were my greatest cheerleaders, and while they loved seeing my name in print, they thought I was meant for greatness. And to my father, greatness wasn't the *Walnut Creek Times*.

He wasn't wrong.

He'd also been extremely fond of Cara. More than any of my previous girlfriends. He was always disappointed when we broke up and ecstatic when we got back together a few months later.

So if there is an afterlife, of which I have my doubts, my father probably smiled down knowing I had a murder case to report on. While at the same time pleading for me to get back together with Cara.

I chose to concentrate on the positive and hoped he saw me working on something substantive.

My daydreaming about my father almost led me to drive past the house. But I pumped on the brakes when I suddenly saw 244 Oakland Avenue out of the corner of my eye.

It was a much more prosperous area than the one in which Griff Bauer was killed. The big houses all seemed to have yards. The paint jobs were generally new and not cracking. Also, this neighborhood lacked the chain-link fences that framed each yard in Bauer's. The absence of them alone made a big difference.

To my surprise, I saw the crotchety detective Ray Kintner standing outside of the house. He saw me pulling up, so there was no denying it or speeding off.

"Jeez, Walnut Creek, you're ubiquitous."

"Maybe you should write my next article. That's a big word."

He snorted. "I guess I shouldn't be all that shocked. Word has gotten around that we're a little suspicious of Mr. Bauer. Might even suspect him for this," he said, pointing toward the home.

"That's the word around the campfire," I said.

"I did a little research on the *Walnut Creek Times*. Tom Butler is a good guy to know if you're trying to get leads."

I started to wonder if Detective Ray Kintner was the connection that Tom Butler referred to.

"He's got a lot more connections than I'll ever have, Detective Kintner," I said.

"I told you to call me Ray. And use those connections. You think I had snitches of my own when I first got on the force? It took me a long time."

I didn't mention that I'd worked at the paper for nine years. I'd already decided if he took pity on me because he thought I was new, I was fine with that.

"Thanks for the advice, Ray. It was his suggestion that I head over here. You got anything for me?" I smiled, once again overstepping my bounds.

"It makes the Bauer murder look like a picnic," he said.

"You're kidding me?" I was genuinely shocked.

"This is not fit to print, but they were tortured before they were killed. Bauer was defaced with a hammer, but it probably ended quickly for him. These two were meant to suffer."

"Was the killer trying to get information from them?"

"I'd say that's a fair guess," he said.

"Any idea on what kind of information?"

"No and no."

"That was only one question," I said.

"No, I don't know what kind of information. And no, I wouldn't tell you even if I knew."

"Ahh, that kind of no and no."

"Get used to it," he said, half smirking.

"We've got a lot in common. People don't want to help the police and the police don't want to help the media."

"Lot of truth to that, Quint."

"Every time I want to think poorly of you, you remember my name and show you care."

"Like I said a few days ago, don't tell anyone."

"So what brings you back to this crime scene? I'm assuming you've already been here," I asked.

"I have. Probably the same thing that brings you here. The potential of seeing something that stands out. A clue that I missed. Or the unlikely event that I find evidence that links the two murders together."

"Wouldn't DNA help do that?"

"DNA is indispensable, but it's not always on the same clock as me. It runs at a slightly slower speed."

"Understood," I said. "Would you ever give me a quote for my upcoming article? Obviously, I wouldn't mention your name."

"You want me to be 'a source in the Oakland Police Department'?"

"That's exactly what I want."

"A few ground rules, first," Ray said.

I tried to withhold my excitement.

"First, you can never use my name in print. If you do, I'll never speak to you again. About anything. Second, you can't say something like 'a senior police detective.' I'm old. There are only so many senior detectives."

I laughed. "Anything else?"

"You have to give me any information you come across. I can tell you're going to be a fly buzzing around this investigation, so if you see or find anything, you have to come to me first. Police detectives aren't infallible. I'm not above receiving a tip from a journalist. Even one from the *Walnut Creek Times*."

"Low blow," I said.

"So we have an understanding?"

"We do."

And while I would never use his name in print, it was going to be impossible to tell him everything I already knew. He'd be putting my hands behind my back and slapping on the cuffs.

"Alright, here's your first quote. A source in the Oakland Police Department has said that it appears the two murder locations might be related."

It was a valuable quote. Obviously I wanted more, but I had to tread lightly. I couldn't risk losing the only inside information I had.

"Thanks, Detective Kintner."

"For the last time, call me Ray. If we're going to be doing business together."

"Ray and Quint. Much simpler than Detective Kintner and Walnut Creek."

That got the gruff old guy to smile. "You might be asking yourself why I'm helping a small-town newspaper man."

"It crossed my mind," I said.

"I've known your boss for a long, long time. I throw him a bone now and then."

"I began to suspect that when you brought him up out of the blue. Is that why you helped me out at Griff Bauer's murder scene?"

"Do you think I usually help out the media?"

The question was rhetorical.

"I should have realized it then. You were a little adamant in your denial of having heard of the *Walnut Creek Times*," I said.

"I was a little over the top, wasn't I? Well, there were other officers around and we all have our own private connections. Don't need them knowing all of mine. Anyway, as long as you don't fuck me over, I'll keep you abreast of the investigation."

"Thank you, Ray. It means a lot."

"You're welcome. We'll talk soon."

I started heading toward my car but turned around.

"Just how bad was the crime scene?" I asked.

"I wasn't able to sleep last night. Pliers. A blowtorch."

"Jesus!"

"With a crime like this, it makes you wonder if he really exists."

Even though I was just using Jesus as an exclamation, his point was taken.

I drove back to the office. Tom wasn't in, so I decided to do a deep dive into Dennis McCarthy, the man the letter pointed to. I had to be subtle, and I turned my computer screen to where none of my co-workers could see it.

It wasn't easy to find much information on him. Most of the talk online was hearsay, three times removed. But one very useful article had been published in 2004 by the San Francisco Chronicle. The writer's name was Vern Coughlin and he claimed to have grown up with Dennis McCarthy.

It lent some credence to his story.

Vern Coughlin was shot and killed outside of his San Francisco home less than a year after the publication of the article. The murder lent further credence.

Apparently, you didn't want Dennis McCarthy on your bad side.

He was born in 1952 in the Sunset District, an almost exclusively Irish section of San Francisco back in the '50s and '60s. His father was a part-time bartender and a full-time gambler. It landed Millard McCarthy in trouble with the wrong type of guys. And indirectly, it put a young Dennis McCarthy in touch with them.

In 1967, most people in San Francisco were embracing the Summer of Love, but a fifteen-year-old Dennis McCarthy embraced gambling, loan sharking, and other non-love-related things.

It was basically the story of *A Bronx Tale*, where the son of a hardworking but flawed man began looking up to the local crime boss, in this case the local bookie. Dennis McCarthy didn't want to be the one placing bets like his schmuck of a father, he wanted to be the one taking them. As a very young man he understood intrinsically just how big an advantage the house had.

A bettor could win for a week or two, maybe even a few months, but in the end, the bookies always won. You could grow rich by basically doing nothing but taking a lot of bets. The more bets you took, the more money you would make. And Dennis McCarthy knew this better than most bookies three times his age.

I continued with the article by Vern Coughlin and brought up a different webpage to read about his death. I switched between the two, mesmerized.

In early 2005, Coughlin was leaving his home in the Sunset District when someone emerged from a car and shot him twice in the chest. The killer got back in his car and sped away. Two witnesses across the street said the license plate had been covered by duct tape.

Immediately, Dennis McCarthy became one of the suspects. Not for the actual killing, but ordering Coughlin's death. The police had nothing concrete tying him to the crime, however. They assumed the car was immediately taken to a chop shop and disposed of. The gun and the bullets were fairly generic, and the investigation, although garnering a lot of interest, never really went anywhere.

And this is the guy I want to investigate? I thought to myself.

I went back to reading the article by Coughlin, while in the back of my mind imagining him getting shot to death outside of his house.

Dennis McCarthy started accumulating people to bet through him by time he was twenty-one years old. He knew this was an illegal business that would likely lead to shakedowns, breaking kneecaps, and other unpleasant business, so he tried to get as many degrees of separation between him and his subordinates as he could.

He treated his business as a pyramid scheme. He'd hire a few people he trusted implicitly to be his right-hand men. They would then hire people who would take in bettors. And on down the line. The genius of the plan was twofold: First, it kept Dennis McCarthy far removed from the day-to-day operations. The people below him dealt with their own clients, using any collection methods they felt necessary. Second, they all owed a percentage to the people above them on the pyramid scheme. So McCarthy would just sit at the top and collect money.

In his article, Coughlin hypothesized that over 80% of people placing a bet in San Francisco were betting through a subordinate of McCarthy's.

And on the rare occasions the SFPD made an arrest for an illegal bookmaking operation, the chain of command always stopped before it reached McCarthy. People below him on the totem pole knew if they talked to the police there would be hell to pay.

And if, by some chance, it got near the top, McCarthy was protected by three people who would gladly take a pinch for him. There was no way the police could ever get to the top of the chain of command. Even though they all knew who sat there.

It appeared to be the same with the murder of Vern Coughlin. Even if they had been lucky enough to catch the perpetrator, he would have been so far removed from McCarthy that nothing would have ever gotten back to him.

And considering they never even found the man responsible, charging McCarthy was an impossibility to begin with.

I finished the article and leaned back, trying to take it all in.

I was a bit in awe of Dennis McCarthy, I had to admit. He'd enacted a business plan and made it virtually impossible to penetrate. Even if you somehow broke the small guy on the totem pole, it's not like he'd ever worked with McCarthy. He had nothing to give to the police. And the further up the ladder you got, the less likely you were to get any cooperation.

Murders like that of Vern Coughlin would just make people all the more wary of Dennis McCarthy. For good reason.

I wondered if the murders I was currently enmeshed in were really his doing. As the letter said. And if they were, was investigating the guy really in my best interest?

I needed to do some soul-searching.

"Let's get that coffee," Cara said.

I was on a break when she called. Cara was old school and liked to talk on the phone whenever possible. Texts weren't her style.

"When?"

"Tonight when you get off?"

"Sure. 6:00 p.m. at the Starbucks by my place."

Cara worked as a fourth-grade teacher and did some Uber driving on the side to make extra money. It infuriated me that teachers had to have a secondary income to make ends meet. What could possibly be more important than teaching our country's youth?

I'd told Cara many times I didn't think she should drive for Uber at night. I told her she was too beautiful to have men alone in her car with her. You can imagine how that went over. Usually, I'd add that I didn't want to have to write about her in the crime section. That's when I'd get a dirty look and the conversation would cease.

She much preferred to talk about her students, anyway. It's one of the factors that contributed to my father liking Cara so much. They could talk for hours about their love of teaching.

A few minutes before I left to meet Cara, Tom Butler returned to the office. I told him about my morning meeting with Detective Ray Kintner.

"Ray Kintner. The name rings a bell," Tom said and smiled coyly.

"My lips are sealed."

"We won't mention him again. But maybe someday I'll tell you how we became friends."

"I'm looking forward to it."

That was how quickly we acknowledged and then intentionally forgot about our friend in the police department. I left a minute later and headed off to Starbucks.

Cara sat at a booth in the corner. I was a regular at this particular Starbucks, it being a stone's throw from my apartment. When I needed to do some writing, and I wasn't at work, I preferred to write outside of my apartment.

Since I got my morning coffee there every morning, I knew the majority of the staff fairly well. The baristas all knew my drink of choice. A half-caf Americano. With as many cups of coffee as I drank a day, if they were all fully caffeinated, I'd be bouncing off walls.

I said hello to Kevin, a barista I'd talk poker with from time to time. Hope and Leslie came out and said hi as well.

The baristas weren't the only ones who knew my order. I remembered that as I saw Cara sitting in the corner with two drinks. She looked as beautiful as ever, wearing a yellow sundress. It reminded me that summer was officially here. June 21st, the summer solstice.

"Thanks for the drink," I said.

"You're welcome. How have you been?"

"Busy. After the shenanigans of my birthday, I've been on the straight and narrow this week."

"What made you think you could take Dugan in the first place? The guy's a beast."

"All the drinks I'd consumed."

Cara laughed. "Liquid courage isn't all it's cracked up to be," she said.

"How do you think we met? If I was sober that night, you think I would have approached you? I would have thought you were out of my league."

"You know I hate when you say that?"

"I do."

"And that's why you keep doing it?"

"Something like that."

She smiled. We always kind of pushed each other's buttons in a playful, flirting way. It's probably why everyone thought we still belonged together. I'd be lying if it didn't cross my mind occasionally. Okay, more than occasionally.

"What's that movie with Jack Nicholson where he plays a cop and has that bandage on his nose?" she asked.

"*Chinatown*. But he's actually a private eye."

"That's how I've imagined you lately. Going around town asking questions with those stitches visible to everyone."

"Comparing me to one of the most famous actors of all time. I can live with that."

"Not that you're investigating the all-time biggest crimes, but you get what I'm saying."

With the exception of my mother, Cara was probably the only person in the world I'd have said the next sentence to.

"What if I told you I might actually be working something big for once?"

"In Walnut Creek?"

"Not exactly. Took place in Oakland, but peripherally, it involves Walnut Creek."

"I'd say it's about time. You're meant for bigger."

"You sound like my dad."

"You know he always liked me."

"Oh, I know. 'Where's Cara? How's Cara? When is Cara coming over again?'"

She smiled knowingly. "And I loved him too. And still love your mom."

"Thanks. I'm going to pick her up after this."

"Oh yeah, what for?"

I hadn't planned on bringing it up, but couldn't avoid it anymore. "It's the one-year anniversary of Dad's death."

"Oh, I'm so sorry, Quint! I knew it was coming up, but didn't realize it was today."

"Thanks."

She leaned over and gave me a long hug.

"You don't talk about him as much anymore," Cara said.

"It's not for lack of thinking about him."

"I know how much you cared."

"Thanks, Cara. I'd rather not discuss it right now. Will be tough with my mother tonight."

Cara tried to find something to change the subject. "So, anything you want to tell me about this new case?"

My mind suddenly returned to the image of Vern Coughlin being shot outside of his home. I didn't want to involve Cara, even in the most roundabout way. "No, not right now."

"You tease," she said.

"Probably shouldn't have told you in the first place."

"You can't undo it."

"Reminds me of an old joke," I said, dying to change the subject.

"I'm listening."

"What's the difference between a pregnant lady and a lightbulb?"

"You can unscrew a lightbulb," Cara said.

"Can't get anything past you."

"We've dated off and on for nine years. I've heard all your jokes."

I smiled. "I need some new material."

"I'm here for it."

"So did you want to talk about anything specific, or just hear my lame old jokes?"

"I never said they were lame."

I looked at her.

"I could just tell you were a little down on Saturday," she continued.

"That was the booze talking."

"They say that's sometimes when you speak the rawest truth."

"There's something to that. But I assure you, I'm fine."

"I believe you. You don't stay down for long."

"I cried that night," I blurted out.

"Really?"

I looked down at my coffee. "You put some truth serum in this thing?"

Cara laughed again. "No, but I would have if I'd known you'd be this forthcoming so soon."

"It was just a couple of stray tears. I was sitting out on the deck and rehashing my life thus far. Got the best of me for a moment."

"Forty years old is a big deal," Cara said.

"What do you know about it, Ms. Early Thirties?"

"I'll let you know in eight years."

"Damn, I forget how young you were when I first approached you in that bar."

"Twenty-three. Fresh out of college."

"Eight years was a big age difference back then. The older you get the less it matters. Seventy and sixty-two? Who cares?"

"So you're saying we're going to grow old together?"

"If we do, it will be with twenty stops and starts in between."

As we both laughed, Cara spat up a little of her coffee.

"Glad you're enjoying my new material," I said, and she spat up a little more.

"Stop!" she said playfully.

This was us at our best. If we could bottle this type of conversation, we'd have lasted forever.

We went our separate ways a few minutes later with a promise to meet up again within a week.

Next stop on the never-ending day was to pick up my mother, Linda, and head to my father's gravesite. She lived in a two-bedroom house in the city of San Ramon at the end of a small cul-de-sac. San Ramon was only fifteen minutes from Walnut Creek, so I was able to see my mother a great deal.

My parents met in the summer of 1975. Arthur Adler was twenty-five and Linda Murphy was twenty-three. He had just finished his first full year of teaching and she'd just graduated from college at the University of Washington. And they met at a library, of all places.

In this day of online dating, I always liked hearing old-school romantic tales. My parents' was one of those.

My father saw a cute girl reading *Moby Dick* in the center of a library and was immediately enamored. Being a teacher, he gravitated toward smart women who liked to read. Not that reading *Moby Dick* ensured you were intelligent, but it was a good start.

So Arthur Adler walked over to Linda Murphy and said, "If you like stories about the sea, there's this new movie out called *Jaws*. I'd love to take you sometime."

Probably the quickest ever invitation for a date: literally the first words my father ever said to my mother.

She looked him over and said, "Does this usually work for you?"

"I don't know. First time I've tried," my father said.

"Why me?"

"Because I'm a teacher and I get captivated by women who read substantive novels. Plus, you're cute."

At that, my mother laughed. "Alright, I'll go on that date with you. You better be normal!"

"I'm far above normal. But I'm not weird, if that's what you're suggesting."

"I'll be the judge of that," my mother said.

They continued talking for an hour and agreed on a time to see *Jaws*. In the summer of 1975, the movie took the nation by storm. My parents often told me that they'd never seen an audience more invested in a movie than the time they saw *Jaws*.

Apparently, they loved it, because five years later, they decided to name their only child after one of its main characters.

I asked them why many times. Their stock answer had become something like, "We loved Quint's intensity. How he was singularly preoccupied with the shark. He knew why he was alive and he reveled in his decision to be a man of the sea. Plus, Quint is just a cool-ass name!"

I'd tell them the story of how they met was far more entertaining. They'd always laugh.

Still, *Jaws* had kicked off their nearly forty-five-year romance, so I was just fine being named after a character from the legendary movie.

My parents had been in love from the moment their first date started. Maybe even that hour talking in the library. They told me they became inseparable.

They were married two years later and then my mother gave birth to me in 1980.

They'd planned on having more children, but her ovaries wouldn't oblige. It was a subject we didn't touch on much, but I know it had created sadness early in their marriage.

At some point, they accepted their fate, and were just happy to have a healthy, young boy to raise.

And they continued loving each other up until the very end. Truly a romance, if a tragic one.

After my father died, I worried how my mother would cope. But she seemed to be taking it as well as she could.

She was still prone to the occasional woe-is-me outburst, asking why it had to happen to her beloved Arthur, who wouldn't hurt a fly. I couldn't blame her.

My parents had been in the Bay Area for the last ten years, moving from Seattle once I settled in California. They didn't like living too far away from their only child.

Bay Area prices were a lot higher than in Seattle, so they'd settled on a cozy two-bedroom home. It was quaint and cute. The spare bedroom was small, but if someone came to visit, at least they had a place to sleep.

When my father passed, my mother decided to remain there. At this point, small size became an asset and she didn't feel like the house was too much for her.

She stood outside waiting for me as I approached. She wore all black, for an obvious reason. My sixty-eight-year-old mother only started showing her age since my father passed, partly because she stopped dyeing her hair and had gone all gray.

I parked the car, walked over, and gave my mother a kiss and a long hug.

"Thanks for this, Quint. I think it's right that we go there today."

"Of course. I wouldn't have missed it, Mom."

She was holding a bouquet of flowers and a bag. I grabbed them both, putting the bag in the back seat and the flowers in the console cupholder.

"What's that?" I asked as I set the bag down.

"Some of your father's stuff. I figured I'd let you rummage through it and see if there's anything you want to keep. If not, just toss it. It's still too hard for me to look at it."

"I'll go through it. Thanks, Mom."

We both got in the car.

"You ready?" I asked.

"Ready as I'll ever be."

I started the car and we set off to pay our respects to my father.

We made it to the Sunset Cemetery in around fifteen minutes. It could take a half hour or more in prime traffic times, but after my coffee with Cara and my subsequent drive to pick up my mother, traffic was waning.

I'd been to my father's gravesite three times since he was killed and knew where to park. I came around to the other side of the car and took my mother's hand before we walked toward the gravesite.

The cemetery itself was well-kept, with beautiful trees and shrubs surrounding it. There was a nice view of the valley below. For what would always be a sad occasion, they did their best to make it peaceful.

We approached my father's headstone and my mother removed her hand from my grasp. She took the flowers and set them in the vase that sat in front of the headstone. And got down on her knees to pray.

I stood back and let her mourn by herself.

She started to cry and I couldn't stop myself from doing the same. Our father was so beloved and the way he died shocked us both. One year hadn't taken away much of our grief.

His headstone was simple.

Arthur Adler. February 22nd, 1949 - June 21st, 2019. Loving husband of Linda. Proud father of Quint.

I was willing to give my mother as much time as she needed, but after a few short minutes, she gestured for me to come over.

I went to the headstone and got down on my knees. I was what would be considered a lapsed Catholic, but that doesn't mean I didn't pray when it felt appropriate. I said a prayer for my father and thought about how much I loved him and how thankful I was that I'd had so many great memories with him. Part of me would always regret how he died, but I tried to focus on the positive. I remembered some very personal moments we'd had over the years, knowing if he somehow heard my thoughts, he'd be smiling at them as well.

Finally, I said aloud, "I love you very much, Dad."

My mother hugged me and we shared a few more tears. We remained in front of his gravestone several minutes longer, neither one saying a word, but both deep in thought.

I stood up. "Take all the time you want, Mom."

"Just a little longer," she said.

More great memories from my childhood: the time I was given a golden retriever puppy for Christmas. A huge bow over a hand-me-down car on my sixteenth birthday. But more than the gifts, just the time we had together. Watching sports. Talking about life. Discussing politics.

My mother struggled to stand up and I extended my hand to help her get to her feet. She was getting older every time I saw her.

"Did you have a nice visit?" I asked, immediately regretting my choice of words.

"I just thanked him for all he did for our family."

"I did the same," I said.

We hugged one more time and then headed to my car, sad and uplifted at once.

As I drove my mother home, we exchanged stories about my father. We agreed to grab lunch in the next week or so. She still had a few tears in her eyes as I readied to go.

"It's going to be okay, Mom. You've still got me."

"I know, Quint. And I love you dearly. But I still miss your father very much."

"So do I, Mom. So do I."

At home, I decided to try and focus on the case.

I spent an hour on Facebook, finding the accounts of Aubrey Durban and James Neil, then reading the posts dedicated to their deaths. They seemed to be pretty straight arrows from what I could gather. When you hear about a gruesome murder of two people in their twenties, you wonder if it might be drug related. None of the posts or comments hinted that they were involved in drugs. This wasn't conclusive, but it did give me pause in assuming they were wrapped up in something sinister.

After reading about Dennis McCarthy earlier that day, I looked for gambling as well. But I couldn't find a post by either James or Aubrey that mentioned gambling or even anything about sports.

From all I could gather, these were two all-American kids who happened to be in love with each other. Aubrey worked in tech and James was a sous-chef at a local Oakland restaurant. They lived together, but were not married. They'd both posted pictures of them moving into the house back in February.

While learning about James and Aubrey, I also searched Facebook with hopes of finding someone willing to talk to me about them.

After sending countless messages to people I'd deemed close to them, I got a few responses. Some cajoling helped me pin down two meetings for the next day with Tricia Knox, a close friend of Aubrey's, and Teddy Raye, an uncle of James's who lived in San Francisco.

I went to sleep that night, dreams of a Pulitzer Prize dancing in my head.

"*A small-town reporter followed three murders and through investigative brilliance, found ties to a longtime San Francisco menace named Dennis McCarthy, taking him down in the process.*"

And the Pulitzer would be dedicated to my father.

6.

The next morning started with a quick trip to the *Walnut Creek Times*, where I informed Tom that I'd secured interviews with a friend and a relative of the double homicide victims. He looked at me like a proud father. Any information on the murders in Oakland would be a coup for his hometown newspaper.

He told me that Greg Alm was going to cover crime in Walnut Creek for the next few days and I had free rein to work on my current case. Grateful, I told Tom I'd keep him updated and set out for San Francisco to meet Teddy Raye.

Which ended up amounting to absolutely nothing. We had a drink at a coffee shop on the Embarcadero, overlooking the Bay Bridge, surrounded by water.

The view was brilliant, the company less so. An obese, sweaty man of around fifty, Teddy Raye asked me within two minutes if his name was going to be in print. And whether he should give me his bio.

I told him I was just looking for information on the death of his nephew, which turned out to be a lie as well. Teddy claimed to be James's uncle, but the more he explained it, the more I suspected he was just some distant cousin.

I could have lived with all of this if he'd had any insight into the death of James Neil. He didn't. I brought up drugs and gambling and Teddy just looked at me with a blank face. He couldn't confirm or deny a single detail in answer to my questions.

Finally, I asked when he'd last seen James, and he admitted it had been a few years.

I sipped my coffee a little quicker after that, excusing myself a few minutes later.

"So you'll let me know if I appear in the paper?" he said as I walked away.

I headed back over the Bay Bridge toward the East Bay, hoping Tricia Knox proved to have more information than Teddy Raye.

We met at my second coffee shop in an hour, this one down by Lake Merritt in Oakland. It was a bustling area, with restaurants, bars, and hundreds of people always running or walking around the lake. One of the more beautiful parts of Oakland.

She had described what she was wearing and I recognized her right away. It didn't hurt that I'd seen her picture on Facebook. In her mid-twenties, she had long, braided brown hair and a tie-dyed shirt on. Hippyish, without question.

She was a bit standoffish, and seemed to be measuring her words as I introduced myself.

"Nice to meet you, Tricia."

"You too," she said.

As a journalist, I encountered this all the time. People are suspicious of my profession, fearing they'll be mischaracterized in print. Or, if they have been up to no good, fearful they'll be portrayed correctly.

Tricia Knox seemed nervous, but I didn't think it was for either of those reasons. Selfishly, I hoped it was because she had pertinent information on the death of her friend.

I ordered our drinks and we set off for a corner of the Peet's Coffee. Truly a free agent when it came to coffee, I didn't play for one team. I could drink at a Starbucks in the morning, a Peet's in the afternoon, and a local cafe at night.

Although we had a small corner table, we didn't have any privacy. A couple sat right next to us.

I could read the concern on her face. "Would you rather walk around outside?" I asked.

"Yeah," she said succinctly.

We went out and headed toward the water. Although tons of people milled around, the park benches could give us some privacy.

There was one available, and we sat down, facing the lake.

"Nice view," I said.

"Yeah, it is," she said quietly.

"Listen, Tricia, I can tell you're nervous, but I'm not the police. I'm just a reporter trying to find out why your friend was murdered."

"I know. I've just been a little anxious since Aubrey was killed."

"Do you know something about it?" I asked.

This certainly hadn't taken long. We were jumping right in.

"Not exactly. But I do know she was scared."

"Scared?"

"She told me that she and James had seen something they shouldn't have."

My juices were flowing. This was more than I could have ever expected. "Did she say what it was?"

"No. She told me it was better I didn't know."

"Tricia, I read all the posts dedicated to Aubrey and James, and the comments on them, and I never saw anyone mention this."

"Because I'm the only one she told."

"How do you know that?"

"Because I was her closest friend. And she told me I was the only one."

"That's a big burden to put on you."

"I know. I told her the same thing."

I'd already blurred the line between a reporter and an active participant on this case, but it was time to do the right thing. "Have you gone to the police?"

"No."

"Why not? That's very important information, Tricia."

"Look at me. I'm scared to talk to you. Imagine me talking to the police."

"You didn't do anything wrong. And it might help them catch your friend's killer."

Tricia broke down and started crying. I patted her shoulder. It was a weak gesture, but I didn't know what else to do.

She wiped her tears with the sleeve of her shirt. "I'm sorry."

"Don't be."

"Alright, I'm okay now," she said, and gave me what amounted to a smile.

"I have to ask, Tricia. Why would you meet up with a reporter who messaged you but not be willing to going to the police? It's a bit odd."

"I hoped maybe you could relay the information to them."

"I can do that, but they are certainly going to want to talk to you personally."

It finally seemed to hit her that talking to the police was inevitable.

"Okay, I'll meet with them."

I'd done the right thing. I would call Ray Kintner and set up a meeting with Tricia. But that didn't mean I didn't want to get the information first.

"I'll put you in touch with a detective I know. But right now, Tricia, I'd like to know exactly what Aubrey told you."

"She didn't tell me what she saw."

"I understand that. But did she tell you the circumstances? Where they were? What night it was?"

"Are you going to use my name in the article? I don't want these people to know who I am."

I could tell Tricia was on her way to breaking down again. I tried to comfort her. "I will not use your name in any article I write. I won't say '*a friend of Aubrey's*'. There will be nothing mentioned that ties you to anything."

"Okay, thanks."

I hated being a jerk, but I wanted her to stay on point. "Listen, Tricia, this is very important."

She snorted and wiped her eyes one more time. "She called me Saturday. Said that she and James had just seen something they weren't supposed to see. She wouldn't tell me what, but one thing she said chilled my bones at the time. And scares me even more now."

"What was it, Tricia?"

"She told me that it involved one of her neighbors. They were walking into their house and saw something they weren't supposed to."

"Did she call you right after it happened?"

"Yes."

"Why?"

"My guess is she wanted someone to know in case something happened to her."

It was my turn to shudder. What could one possibly see that would make killing you the only option? Not just that, but to torture you first?

And if Tricia was telling the truth, and she was the only one Aubrey told, she was definitely in harm's way.

"Tricia, give me a second."

I walked about twenty feet away from the park bench, keeping my eye on Tricia. I pulled out Detective Kintner's business card and called him.

"Ray Kintner."

"Hi Ray, this is Quint."

"How are you, Walnut Creek?"

It wasn't the time to acknowledge our running joke. "I have a woman with me who might have some information on the murders of Aubrey Durban and James Neil. Can I bring her in?"

"Of course. Do you know where the main office of the OPD is located?" he asked, meaning the Oakland Police Department.

"I do. We'll be there in fifteen minutes."

I walked back over to her. "This is going to be tough to learn, Tricia, but hear me out. Aubrey and James were tortured before they were killed. If it was to get information, she might have mentioned you. I know it's horrible to think about, but it's a possibility you have to consider. I think you should come with me to the police station and tell them what you know. Did you walk or drive here?"

"I walked," she said, her face taking on a ghost-like quality.

"I'll drive you to the police station. Are you okay with that?"

The tears returned, but she agreed to go with me.

We walked to my car and headed toward the OPD.

7.

I got a call from Ray Kintner early the next morning.

"Hello."

"I've got some tragic news, Quint."

I knew it before he said it.

"Tricia Knox is dead."

"My God. What happened?"

"After you dropped her off, we had an hour-long interview with her. Things went well and she seemed to be happy to get things off her chest. We had a patrol car drop her off at her apartment complex near Lake Merritt in Oakland. The officer drove around the block repeatedly for an hour. He then parked outside the complex, planning to stay until midnight. If anyone wanted to do anything to Ms. Knox, they'd see a police presence. The officer went up to check on her at 8:00 p.m. When there was no response, he entered the apartment and found her dead. We fear that the offender was already in the apartment complex, or possibly in the apartment itself. Quint, you're not going to like what else I have to say."

"Can it get any worse?" I asked.

"Yes, it can. We didn't catch the guy and Ms. Knox was tortured. While the officer was downstairs, a few hundred feet away, she was upstairs getting tortured. You know what that means, right?"

"They know she went to the cops," I said.

"Well, there's that. They also likely know that she met with you."

I tried to say something, but nothing came out.

"Are you there, Quint?"

"I'm here," I finally said.

"We need you to come in to the station."

"Of course. I'll head over now."

I hung up the phone and called Tom Butler, informing him I wouldn't be at the office until later in the day. I'd explain everything when I got there. He could tell something terrible had happened and didn't press me.

After a one-minute shower, I looked at myself in the mirror and didn't like what I saw. The stitches were starting to improve, but everything around them appeared older. It had only been five days since my fortieth birthday, but I'd aged five years. I'd always looked young for my age and several people had seemed genuinely astounded when they found out I was forty.

Then I hit the glass with my forehead. And overheard something I now wished I hadn't. Having someone you'd just talked to end up dead surely accelerated the aging, too.

I said a quick prayer for Tricia Knox and locked my apartment behind me. It was a small little lock that even the most novice lockpick could break into. You theoretically needed a fob to get into Avalon Walnut Creek, but Door Dash drivers and Amazon delivery guys always just followed a tenant into the building.

If someone wanted to get in and do me harm, it would be simple. I walked toward the elevator. My mind started imagining a gunman appearing out of nowhere. The hallway was long, like a hotel's, and I'd have nowhere to run. Then there was the parking garage. Probably the easiest place to kill someone and just walk or drive out onto the streets of Walnut Creek, never to be seen again.

My mind raced and I didn't like it. Although, after what happened to Tricia Knox, I didn't think I was being overly cautious. These people, whoever they were, weren't fucking around. Four people had been killed in less than a week. I didn't want to be the fifth.

I arrived in the parking garage and made it to my car without incident. I spent the whole time looking over my shoulder, however.

My car roared to life and I sped out of the garage, heading toward Oakland. A city I was getting quite sick of.

The Oakland Police Department had several different locations, but the main branch was in the western part of the city, barely a mile from the Bay Bridge that took you into San Francisco. The ugly, squat gray and white building had vertical lines shooting from the base to the top. It reminded me of someone trying to make themselves look taller. It didn't work.

I walked through the metal detectors and headed to the third floor, where I'd brought Tricia Knox the day before.

Ray Kintner was talking to a few colleagues as I approached.

"Mr. Adler," he said, trying to be as impersonal as possible with his fellow officers around.

"Detective Kintner," I said, playing along.

"We've got you set up for Interrogation Room #3. Follow me."

I followed him and he opened the door to a standard investigation room. One large table in the center. One seat where I'd be located and two seats for the detectives who would be interviewing me. Usually, my seat was meant for a suspect, but I was just there to confirm what I'd talked about with Tricia Knox. At least, that's what I assumed.

I took the seat and Ray said he'd be back in a few minutes. He returned with a young cop, likely still in his twenties, who'd spent a little too much time in the gym. His arms were each the size of a Mini Cooper.

Ray took the lead. As the senior detective, he obviously carried more weight than his partner. In the metaphorical sense only.

"Mr. Adler, this is Detective Marks and I'm Detective Kintner. I'm sorry this interview is for such a sad occasion."

"Me too."

"You've been investigating the recent murders in Oakland for the *Walnut Creek Times*?"

A lot of these answers were going to be superfluous, but I understood they were necessary. "That's right," I said.

"How did you come in contact with Tricia Knox?"

"I went on Facebook and read the tributes to Aubrey Durban and James Neil, contacting some of the people who'd posted them."

It was time for the other detective to chime in. "And you just messaged random people on Facebook?"

"Not exactly. I messaged people who had left heartfelt messages about the deceased. There were scores of likes and comments, but I wanted to talk to someone who knew them well, so I focused on the longer, more in-depth posts."

The detectives looked at each other, confirming they thought it was a smart idea. Not that they'd acknowledge it directly. More likely, they thought I was stepping on their toes and doing work meant for the police.

"How many people did you message total?" Detective Marks asked.

"Maybe eight or nine."

"And how many responded?

"Four or five. But only two agreed to meet with me."

They looked surprised.

"You met with someone else?"

"Yeah. Some guy named Teddy Raye. Claimed he was James Neil's uncle, but turned out he was just a distant cousin. He kept asking if he could get his name in the paper. He didn't know anything. And then I went to see Tricia. Who obviously did."

"Tell us everything that Tricia told you." Ray had retaken the lead.

"We met at a Peet's Coffee down by Lake Merritt. Immediately, I could tell she was nervous and didn't want to talk with people around her. So we left the coffee shop and made our way to a park bench, where it was just us. I asked her about Aubrey and she obviously knew something. Apparently, they were best friends, and Aubrey had called her before she was murdered, saying she and James had seen something outside of their house. Tricia said it involved one of their neighbors."

The detectives looked at each other and nodded. It confirmed that Tricia had told them the same thing.

"Anything else?"

"That's when it occurred to me that Tricia might be in danger and I thought it was best to call you. I asked her if she'd walked or driven to the coffee shop. She said she'd walked, so I offered to drive her here. Which I did. After I dropped her off, I went to work and didn't think anything more of it until I got your terrible call this morning."

"And we appreciate you coming in, Mr. Adler. We just wanted to confirm that she told you the same things she'd told us. There's now been quite a few murders over the last week, so we preferred to get it on record here at the station."

"I understand. Anything I can do to help."

"You can tell us when you talk to potential witnesses," Marks told me.

Ray shooed him off. "We're not here to prevent you from doing some investigating. Just make sure you keep us abreast of any news you might hear."

"That's all I was saying," the buff, rebuffed detective said.

"Of course," I said.

"Is there anything you can add about Ms. Knox?"

"Just that I'm very sad. She was a nice young woman. I'm crushed."

"We all are. The Oakland PD did all we could to protect her and it wasn't enough."

"Did you ask her about her whereabouts the last few days?" I asked.

"Why?" Ray asked.

"It's just that whoever this killer or killers are, they seem pretty ruthless. If they tortured Aubrey Durban to find out information, and she gave up Tricia Knox, why did they allow her to live for a few more days?"

"It's a fair question."

"I didn't have time to ask her, but it wouldn't shock me if she was staying somewhere else the last several days."

"It's information we'll be looking into," the younger detective said, but what he meant was: Don't tell us how to do our jobs.

"Just trying to help," I said.

"Thanks for coming in, Mr. Adler," Ray Kintner said. "If you remember anything else, please be sure to call me."

"Of course."

I walked out of the Oakland Police Department and started thinking back to my birthday. I'd hoped the next forty years were going to be more exciting than the first forty. Mission accomplished, in the worst way possible.

But whether I'd make it another forty years, or even forty days, was very much in the air.

"I've got enough to write a basic article on the murders," I said to Tom Butler once I arrived back at work.

I'd explained all that had happened since meeting Tricia Knox the day before. He expressed his remorse.

"I figured you were getting close. I've been weighing our options. Do we post an article every few days with minor updates? Or do we wait until this all plays out and publish a 10,000-word report, summarizing everything?"

It's something I had been wrestling with myself. "It's a tough call, Tom. I can write a *Who, What, When, Where, How* article today. Obviously, I'm hoping to eventually find out the Why. But that could be weeks, or even months away. Our readers would probably like to read about the case in the meantime. I'd recommend we publish something."

I could feel him weighing his options.

"Alright, I'll let you write an article today. But I want it to be in the passive voice. I don't want you mentioning your having met Tricia Knox or how you've become immersed in this case. That can wait until we're ready to publish a longform article."

"Sounds good, Tom. I can have something for you by the end of the day."

"Good work, Quint." He peered up at me. "And those stitches are starting to look better."

"Thanks," I said.

Just then, Krissy Butler walked out of her office. "Oh hey, Quint, I didn't know you were here. I've got another letter for you."

She returned to her office and emerged with a letter. I put it in the backpack that I brought to work every day.

"Secret admirer?" Tom asked.

I wasn't ready to tell them what the first letter had said. "Of course. Can I bring her to you guys' next barbecue?"

"No, we like Cara," Krissy said.

"You and everyone else in my life," I said.

They smiled, knowing not to press it.

"If you must know, we have been getting along really well lately," I said.

"I like hearing that," Krissy said.

"So do I," Tom confirmed.

"Before this deteriorates to a talk on my love life, I'm going to head downstairs and start writing that article."

They both laughed.

"But your love life is so intriguing," Krissy said.

"Not lately," I said. "I've been a monk the last several months."

They didn't respond.

"Well, this is awkward," I said, although we were all enjoying ourselves.

"Get writing, Quint the Monk."

"Yes, sir," I said, and headed back downstairs.

I spent the next hour writing the article.

Oakland Murders Have a Walnut Creek Link
by Quint Adler

One of the four tragic murders in Oakland over the last week has a sad connection to our fine city. Griffin Bauer, born and raised in Walnut Creek, was found murdered on Sunday morning on 7th Avenue in Oakland. Bauer was born in 1991 and spent his childhood in Walnut Creek, although he attended high school in Concord, going to De La Salle.

His death came a day after the as-yet unsolved murders of Aubrey Durban and her boyfriend James Neil on Oakland Avenue. Although their bodies weren't found until a day after Bauer's, the police and the medical examiner have determined the deaths of Durban and Neil occurred on Saturday, before the death of Bauer.

A source in the Oakland Police Department has said that it appears the two murder locations might be related.

Adding to the devastation, Tricia Knox, a friend of Aubrey Durban's, was tragically killed on Thursday night. Authorities are tight lipped, but they aren't denying that the Bauer murder may be related to the other three.

Mr. Bauer had attended Diablo Valley College after De La Salle, but there is no record of him having graduated with a higher education degree. His last known job was at Rick's Rigs, a trucking company based out of Oakland.

Bauer is survived by his parents, Betsy and Terence, who still live in Walnut Creek. Funeral arrangements have not been announced.

The four murders have brought Oakland's total to fifty-seven this year. After years of a declining murder rate, 2020 has proved to be particularly violent. In both 2018 and 2019, exactly seventy-four people were killed in Oakland. We are currently on pace for more than a hundred in 2020.

These murders have Oaklanders on edge as it's been the deadliest week in the city since January. Anyone who has any leads on the above cases is asked to reach out to the Oakland Police Department. Their phone number is 510-555-5920.

It was short and to the point, just what Tom was looking for.

"Good work, Quint. I imagine it was tough not throwing in some personal details of the case."

"If I'm going to get help from the OPD going forward, I better keep my articles pretty vanilla."

"Don't worry, down the line I'll let you add chocolate, strawberry, or any other flavor you want."

"Thanks, Tom. It will be a Neapolitan ice cream sandwich by time I'm finished."

Tom laughed, then confirmed the article would be in the weekend edition.

I felt guilty. Here I was, making a silly ice cream joke, while Tricia Knox was dead. A young life taken for no reason. Something was going on and it was not a laughing matter. People were systematically being killed.

I somberly headed home.

8.

I woke up on Saturday, a week removed from my birthday.

So much had happened and yet I didn't know exactly what my next move should be. The mystery's solution lay in finding out what Aubrey Durban and James Neil saw, something that was going to be next to impossible.

My initial fear of being a marked man was starting to wear off. When Detective Kintner told me I might be in harm's way, I didn't know what I was going to do. Move? Buy a gun? So many options, none of which I looked forward to, flooded my head.

But as I thought more about it, I came to the conclusion I'd be safe. After torturing Tricia, they'd have realized she didn't know what Aubrey and James had seen. So she couldn't have given me any crucial information. Furthermore, she had gone to the police. There was no need to kill me when the information had already been passed on to the authorities.

So I felt better about that. But my mindset was a different story. I was trying to be clinical and rational, which belied all the violence occurring around me.

I used Tricia being tortured as a justification for why I'd be safe. The utterly inhumane nature of her death should have told me that anything was possible with these people. Or person.

I spent a few more minutes mourning for Tricia Knox. A young woman whose life was taken in the most vicious way possible. What a tragic, unnecessary loss.

I knew I'd done the right thing by taking her to the police. But that didn't mean that I wouldn't be riddled with moments of guilt. I said another prayer for her.

Murder. Prayers. Crying.

That seemed to sum up the week since my birthday.

And then it hit me: I hadn't opened the second letter that Krissy Butler had given me.

I fished it out of my backpack, trying to touch as little of the envelope as possible, just in case we needed it checked for fingerprints down the line.

I pulled out the letter itself and started to read.

I should have known you were a small timer. I point you in the direction of Dennis McCarthy and you don't do shit with that knowledge. No mention of him in your pathetic article. So this will be your last letter unless I see you actually doing something. And trust me, I will see. Investigate Paddy Roark. He manages a grocery store on Geary Street in San Francisco called Boyle's. But it's just a front. He's McCarthy's henchman and if a murder was necessary, it would have been Paddy. Get to work or our communication is over.

I set the piece of paper down.

This was all becoming too much.

I got back in bed and tried to go back to sleep. To no avail.

I pondered if it was time to go to the police. Undoubtedly, yes, but was I willing to? If I admitted to everything, I'd almost certainly be fired from the *Walnut Creek Times*. Scratch almost. I'd undoubtedly be fired.

You couldn't have a reporter admitting to appearing at crime scenes before the police. And to withholding evidence. Tom and Krissy would have no choice but to let me go.

And then what? I'd be persona non grata in the journalism field.

You hear about that guy from the Walnut Creek Times? He withheld information from the police and tried to become a part of his own news story. What happened to journalism in this country? I hope he never gets another job.

And then there'd be the police themselves. They could charge me with a host of crimes.

I hated my decision, but I couldn't find any way around it. I wasn't going to the police. I would continue going rogue.

For better or worse.

And in all likelihood, it would be for the worst.

"The funeral for Tricia Knox is this coming Friday. But it's just going to be friends and family." Ray Kintner said.

I'd been walking in downtown Walnut Creek, heading to get some lunch, when he called.

"Probably for the best," I said.

"I'm sure they know it's not the police or the media's fault, but I don't blame them for not wanting us there."

"I think about her a lot," I said.

"Me too. Oh, and you were right about something."

"What's that?"

"Tricia had been out of town. She visited a sick grandfather in Portland. It's probably why she wasn't killed immediately after Aubrey Durban was tortured."

"Thanks."

"You've got a pretty good eye for detective work, Quint."

"Thanks again. I've always thought there were similarities between our two fields."

"Without question."

I wondered why he was buttering me up, and my answer came soon thereafter.

"If you have any other ideas about the case, I'd love to hear them," he said. "I feel like I might be missing something obvious."

My mind immediately focused on the possibility of a way out for me. If I could tell Ray I had some "inside information," maybe he'd be willing to let me off the hook for my transgressions. And work out something with Tom Butler. I valued my job and couldn't afford to lose it.

"Of course," I said. "Let's talk soon."

"Sounds good."

The rest of Saturday was relaxing. I'd decided I needed a Quint day. It had been a high stress week, to say the least. I soaked in the peace while I could. I took my first bath in months, listening to some Frank Sinatra and trying to forget about everything, despite knowing it wouldn't last long.

Turned out the calm lasted less than a day. I woke up early on Sunday morning and decided to give the letters I'd received some attention.

I didn't know where they were coming from or who'd written them. It could have been some crackpot for all I knew. But I couldn't just ignore them. For my inquiring mind, that was impossible.

I called Boyle's Grocery Store on Geary Street.

"Is Paddy Roark going to be in today?"

"Yeah, Paddy is here. Would you like to talk to him?"

"No, I'll surprise him. Thanks."

I set off for San Francisco.

Boyle's Grocery Store was on Geary Street, six blocks from the ocean. If this had been the '50s or '60s when Dennis McCarthy grew up, this area would have been 90% Irish. It was technically the Richmond District and not the Sunset, but back then, the Irish monopolized both parts, being that they were contiguous.

I noticed a few Irish pubs as I got closer to Boyle's, but there were also several Chinese and Russian restaurants. The area was no longer a stronghold of the Irish. Funny how the bars were always Irish and the restaurants some other nationality. I don't know if that's a judgement on their proclivity for drinking or their poor reputation for gourmet food.

Not wanting to bring attention to myself, I picked up a cart at the front door with the intention of buying a few things. Boyle's had three aisles that went back about thirty feet each. You could get your basics, but this wasn't a Whole Foods or even a Trader Joe's.

The inside was painted green and orange, a nod to its Irish roots, and there was an aisle dedicated solely to foods from Ireland. No question as to who this grocery store catered to.

I looked around, but didn't see any sign of Paddy Roark. No, I had no idea what he looked like, but if he'd really been Dennis McCarthy's longtime henchman, I knew he wasn't going to be a young man. And I only saw a few checkers in their twenties and a woman in her forties.

There weren't many customers. I hoped to blend in, but instead I was standing out.

I picked up a loaf of Irish soda bread. It was huge, but I could massacre that thing in two sittings. I picked up some eggs and slid them into my cart.

Just then, a man in his mid-fifties started walking down the aisle toward me. His face was a weathered mess. It looked like leather. His intense stare almost caused me to look away, but instead I offered a quick "Hello."

"Can I help you find something?"

I hadn't been expecting that.

"I was thinking about making a corned beef dinner." It's what popped in my mind, being the only Irish dish I could think of. Maybe that's why they didn't have many restaurants.

"Follow me," he said.

He took me down a different aisle and pointed in the direction of some corned beef briskets. They looked delicious, I had to say.

"Thanks," I said.

"You from around here?" he asked.

"No, why?"

I was already on the defensive. How had this happened so quickly?

"We're a store of regulars. Always happy to see a new face, though," he said, but his own face belied that statement.

He looked anything but happy.

"Thanks. Just decided to stop in."

"Oh yeah, where do you live?"

"Just down the street." I realized I'd used "just" in back to back sentences. A sure sign of being nervous.

I suddenly wanted to get out of Boyle's and away from Paddy Roark. There was no name tag, but I had no doubt it was him.

"Which street?"

He moved in a little closer.

"Just a few blocks further up Geary," I said, using "just" a third time.

"A second ago, you said down the street. Now you're saying up the street. Which is it?"

Was my life going to end in the middle of a grocery store on a Sunday morning? It certainly seemed to be trending that way.

"Is this how you treat all your customers?" I asked, trying to regain some footing.

"Only the ones who call ahead and ask about me." He was likely just fishing, but my expression must have given me away. "I'm going to ask you again: what are you doing here?"

"I was just coming to get some corned beef, but I'm obviously not wanted here, so I think I'll leave."

All of a sudden, he grabbed me in a tight bear hug. He reached down into my jeans and grabbed my wallet. It all happened so quick, I wasn't prepared.

He took out my driver's license.

"Quint Adler. 7001 Sunne Drive, Apartment 4044. Walnut Creek. It's nice to make your acquaintance, Mr. Adler."

He pulled out his phone and took a picture of my license.

And then, just as quickly, he put the driver's license back in my wallet and handed it to me.

"Don't let me see you here again," he said, his face having become a dark shade of red.

"You won't," I said.

I left my cart in the middle of the aisle and briskly walked out of Boyle's. I ran down the street, jumped in my car, and sped off.

I was just happy to get the hell away.

How had Paddy Roark known?

Obviously, my face had given me away when he'd mentioned calling ahead. But how had he suspected me in the first place?

An employee probably told him someone had called asking about him. If he was truly a henchman for Dennis McCarthy, then he was probably a suspicious guy to begin with. He'd have asked the age and the sex of the caller. And when a forty-year-old male whom he'd never seen before walked into his grocery store, he got suspicious. He was probably telling the truth that it was a store of regulars. I'd stood out like a sore thumb, especially with very few other customers.

And then when I couldn't answer where I lived, he figured he'd found his guy. My face betraying me solidified it.

It made sense.

I hoped I'd never see Paddy Roark again. He was more intimidating than just about any man I'd ever met.

I felt happy to get out of there with all my limbs in place.

But then I remembered he now had my name and address.

Fuck me!

9.

On Monday, the inevitable happened.

It was my first uneventful day at work in a week, and as I was packing my stuff to go home, I got a call from Cara. She invited me to have drinks with her and a few friends. She wasn't teaching since it was summer, so a Monday night happy hour was in the cards.

After saying no three different times, I finally agreed to come out for one drink. And one drink only. Well, you know how that ends up.

I had to get my stitches taken out after work, so I was the last to arrive.

There were five of us, three girls and two guys. Not a moment of awkward silence ever fell, and everyone got along famously.

Cara was eyeballing me early on. She talked to the other guy for extended periods and then she'd look in my direction and wink or smile.

People might think Cara played a game, but it wasn't like that. She was always polite and this guy seemed to take a liking to her. She didn't know how to get out of a conversation. But I could tell she was thinking about me.

Cara wore another one of her favorite sundresses, this one red with white flowers. She looked sexy and feminine, without intentionally playing to either.

It was an intoxicating mix.

Shockingly, no neck injuries occurred despite the number of men who reflexively looked in her direction.

While other guys might be jealous, I took it as a badge of honor. That's probably one of the reasons she was attracted to me. I didn't have a jealous bone in my body. Well, that's not true, but my jealous bones were reserved for my professional life, not my personal one.

My one drink ultimatum had lasted about a half-hour. By time the sun was going down I was three drinks and a Cuervo Gold shot deep, with no chance of leaving early. Unless it was with Cara.

I don't know if it was her pretending to play hard to get or how beautiful she looked. Or whether it had just been awhile since I'd had sex. But whatever led to it, there was a point where I knew we'd be going home together.

And that happened around 9:00 p.m. Mark, the last one standing besides ourselves, had become slightly inebriated and a little bit touchy.

I sensed Cara getting uncomfortable and I said, "Might be time this night comes to an end, Mark."

We were about to find out his true colors. Would he realize his mistake or turn into an asshole?

"Yeah, you're probably right, Quint. Think that last shot did me in. Sorry if I was a bit much, Cara."

"No problem," she said.

I shook his hand and Mark was gone a minute later.

"Last two standing," Cara said.

"How'd you rather be doing something horizontal as opposed to vertical?"

"You are so romantic," she teased and we kissed each other in the middle of the bar.

From there it was just a matter of time, and we left about fifteen minutes later.

It had been close to eight months since we'd been together, the longest stretch in almost a decade. Most of our breakups lasted for weeks, not months. But we more than made up for it. We had sex twice that night, marathon sessions both. And we added one more for good measure the following morning.

"I hope this doesn't complicate things," Cara said.

I didn't trust myself in the moment. The ecstasy of being with her could cloud my judgement. I knew that.

"Let's play it by ear," I said.

"I like ears," she said. She came over and started subtly nibbling mine.

It was 8:30 and I didn't have time for any more hanky panky—an old-school word my parents had used. I'd always found it humorous.

"I'll call you in a few days, but I have to get to work."

"Maybe I'll drive Uber for a few hours. Hopefully some passengers will ask me how my night went."

"And what will you tell them?"

"I'll ask them if they've seen *9 1/2 Weeks*."

I laughed. We'd seen the erotic, lusty, anything-goes sexual thriller a few times together. We'd never approached the brashness of Mickey Rourke and Kim Basinger's characters, but it had become a running joke with us.

"And it's spot on for the amount of time our relationship usually lasts," I said.

"Then let's not get back together. We'll just call each other on nights we get a little lonely."

"You know how that ends, Cara!"

"Yeah, but what a ride."

She said *ride* in a seductive way, but I really didn't have the time. That's what I kept telling myself.

"Speaking of rides, want me to drop you off at home?"

"Fine," she said and put on an intentionally pouty face.

I got out of bed, sans clothes, and headed to the shower. I passed by the bag of my dad's possessions in the corner of the living room. I had been avoiding looking through them. I went back to my room, still naked, and set them next to my bed, ensuring I'd see them that night.

"What's this?"

"Some of Dad's things."

"He'd be happy I was here."

"There's no question about that. Now I have to shower before I'm late for work."

"Enjoy washing the smell of me off," she said.

It was becoming harder and harder to get to the shower. Pun intended.

"Fine, you win," I said.

I jumped back on the bed and we made love for a fourth time.

Usually, work would pale in comparison, and while that was still largely true, I had no shortage of excitement there either. My article about the death of Griff Bauer was getting a lot of hits on our website. The story of the four murders had received plenty of attention across Oakland and from the early numbers, Walnut Creek was enthralled as well.

I normally tried to avoid reading the comments on my articles, but I couldn't resist this time. Of the six comments, four said, in one form or another, that Griff Bauer had always been an asshole and he deserved what he got. One comment claimed that it went back to the fifth grade, when he was the school bully. More information that I stored away. Whether it amounted to anything was doubtful, but my mind had become like a sponge when it came to this case. I absorbed all I could.

Although tempted, I decided not to call Cara when I got home. It was too easy to jump back into being boyfriend and girlfriend and that never ended well. I wanted her for sure, in fact, I probably always would. But I tried to walk a fine line that would work. Being together every day had never worked in the past and wasn't going to this time.

Maybe we could set some parameters. Seeing each other only a couple of days a week seemed reasonable. Although I had my doubts about that as well.

I was lying on my bed thinking about Cara when, out of the corner of my eye, I saw the bag of my father's stuff I'd set nearby. I hadn't even taken a peek since my mother gave it to me several days ago. I owed my mother that. My father too.

I took the bag into the living room and scattered the contents on the kitchen table. There were some old pictures of my parents. Judging by their outfits, it looked like the '70s. And with no sighting of me, these pics had to be pre-1980. I started a keeper pile and set them there.

Some ancient Christmas tree lights quickly made their way into the garbage pile. As did a pair of old shoes and argyle socks with holes in them. Some old cords soon joined them.

I rummaged through some loose mail, but nothing seemed important. I was throwing the papers in the garbage pile when one of them caught my eye.

It was a credit card bill, but that's not what gave me pause. There was writing on the side of the bill.

It read: *Mason Anderson. Has had a few bruises throughout the course of the year and now he's missing days with only two weeks left in the school year. Possible he's being abused. He lives at 254 Oakland Ave.*

The message itself was disconcerting enough, and something more grabbed my attention. I went back into my bedroom and grabbed my laptop, bringing up the notes on my current case.

Aubrey Durban and James Neil. 244 Oakland Ave.

I went to Google Earth and typed in the addresses.

The houses stood on the same side of the street with just one house in between them.

I wasn't a big believer in random coincidences, but I prayed this was one.

The ramifications, if they were in fact related, weren't something I wanted to think about.

Especially regarding my father.

10.

"Mr. Adler, Detective Daniels will see you now."

I was back in San Francisco the next morning. My GPS must have looked like a seismograph after a big earthquake. Walnut Creek to Oakland. To San Francisco. Back to Walnut Creek. Rinse. Repeat. Zig-zagging all over.

I followed Detective Jameson Daniels to his office. His name could have been an alcoholic's worst nightmare. In his early thirties and very affable, he'd been fair and generous with his time when my father had been murdered. And willing to meet with me on very short notice after I found my father's note. That meant a lot.

"What can I help you with, Mr. Adler?" he said once we'd sat down.

Having such a memorable—for better or worse—first name, it always surprised me when people called me Mr. Adler.

Jameson Daniels's office wasn't much more than an interrogation room. Each of the detectives had their own cubicle with a computer and desk, but if you wanted to talk to them privately, they'd escort you to one of their "offices." They weren't individual offices and you could tell. The walls were barren and it was just you, the detective, and a table.

Not that I was there for the aesthetics.

"A few days ago was the one-year anniversary of my father's death. I wanted to know if there's been any progress?"

"I'm sorry, but there hasn't been."

"Is the case still open?"

"Theoretically, yes it is. But, and I know this is going to hurt, it's way down the totem pole. We've got new murders every week and those tend to take precedent."

"Was there ever any suspect?"

"Sadly, no. It was a mugging and there were no fibers or anything that we could run. The killer obviously wore gloves."

"Is that common for a mugging in June? Not exactly a cold month," I said.

"It is if you don't want to get caught."

"Excuse me for stepping on your toes, but my guess would be that most muggers aren't planning their crime that far ahead of time."

"I'd say that's generally a fair statement. But that doesn't mean one couldn't put on a pair of gloves right before they commit the crime."

"Seems unlikely to me," I said, more to myself than to Detective Daniels.

"What are you trying to say, Mr. Adler?"

"Was this case always assumed to just be a random mugging?"

"Yes. We talked to you, your mother, and many of your father's fellow teachers. It became obvious he didn't have an enemy in the world. Plus, he had just retired. Why kill him then? We never thought, and still don't, that this was some pre-meditated murder. Plus, he was walking in the Tenderloin."

I bowed my head, imagining the last moments of my father's life. And I still, for the life of me, couldn't figure out why he was in that neighborhood. Or even in San Francisco, for that matter.

"I'm sorry, that came out the wrong way," Detective Daniels said. "My point is, if he'd been mugged in Pacific Heights, we'd be more suspicious. Muggings in the Tenderloin are far from rare."

"And the only witness was that one guy?" I asked.

"Only the one guy came forward. It's possible other people saw it and chose not to. It happens all the time."

"And what did he describe seeing?"

Detective Daniels could have told me we'd been through all this, but he was taking time to go over it again. I appreciated that.

"He saw a guy in a long coat stab your father three or four times, before running through an alley. Looked like a clean-shaven white guy, but that's all he could say for sure."

"Would you say that the majority of people on the streets have facial hair?"

"Yes."

It became obvious I was calling into question whether it was a random mugging.

"Has something come up that makes you think this was pre-meditated?" he asked.

I'd prepared myself for this question. And like with everything else lately, I was going to keep it close to the vest. "No, just throwing things out there.".

"Maybe the guy just got a shave. Or maybe he wasn't living on the street. I think you are taking a few leaps, Mr. Adler. Your father seemed like a great man and there was certainly no one who wanted him dead."

I could tell this wasn't going anywhere.

"Thanks, Detective Daniels. You're probably right. But as his son, I just wanted to follow up and make sure there was nothing new."

"I completely understand."

I turned to go, but swiveled around for one more question. "Were any of those credit cards ever used?"

"As a matter of fact, no, they weren't."

"That seems a little odd doesn't it? You steal someone's wallet, a man who as we told you doesn't carry much cash, and then you don't even try to use his credit cards."

Detective Daniels paused.

"It's a little suspicious, yes."

I decided to leave it at that.

"Thanks for your time, detective."

And I walked out the door.

As I drove back over the Bay Bridge, questions flooded my brain.

Was there really a chance my father had been targeted? Could the note I'd found have anything to do with it? Did this mean my father's death and the case I was working on were related?

It seemed like a giant leap. But the fact that Aubrey Durban and James Neil had been killed two houses down from an address my father wrote about was alarming. To say the least.

And that's where I decided to head next.

I exited off Interstate 80 and took 580 East before getting off at Harrison Street. I followed that to Oakland Avenue, where I turned right and drove a little further until I started to recognize the houses. I approached the home in which Aubrey Durban and James Neil had been killed.

Parking in front of that house, I could explain away. I could say I was doing research on the killings that took place there. Parking in front of 254 would have been suspicious.

I got out of the car and looked upon 244 Oakland Avenue. I shuddered at the pain that Ms. Durban and Mr. Neil must have endured. And merely for being in the wrong place at the wrong time.

Could that have involved the people a few doors down? Tricia Knox had said it had something to do with the neighbors.

I walked backward on Oakland Avenue. To the layman, it might look like I was just trying to get a more panoramic view of 244. And if by chance someone in the neighborhood was watching, that's what I wanted it to look like.

But in reality, I was trying to get far enough back where I could see 254 as well. Maybe I acted overly cautious, but after all that happened, I thought it for the best. When I had backed up enough, I looked to my right, in the direction of 254.

An ugly brown house with zero personality. Trees surrounded the property and you couldn't see much of it. While most houses lay flush on the street itself, this one branched away from Oakland Avenue and you could only see sections of the home. That gave it an ominous feel, no doubt heightened by my uneasiness.

A blue Chevy Silverado sat out front, and in the back I could see a dark-colored van with no windows. A "rape van," as my father used to call them. Hey, it was a different time and surely wouldn't be called that now.

I told myself to snap out of it.

I was jumping to way too many conclusions. I let my imagination get ahead of my rationality.

All my father had written was that potentially Mason Anderson had been abused. Potentially. And I was jumping to rape vans and sinister things going on in the house I now looked at.

I needed to pump the brakes.

Still, my inner rebel wanted to approach the house. But my logical, sound-minded side won out. I decided to find out a little more about Mason Anderson's parents first.

All the same, I'd be back to 254 Oakland Avenue sooner rather than later.

There was no doubt about that.

I called my mother that night.

"Hi, Mom."

"Hey, Quint. It's good to hear from you, honey."

"Went through those things of Dad's. There's some great pictures of you two from before I was born."

"Don't tell me I was wearing bell bottoms…"

"You want the truth?"

"Heaven forbid," she said and I heard her laughing on the other end.

"I think you'll really like them. Dad looks like he's got an afro in one."

"No judging. We were crazy kids back then."

"I wasn't judging, I was entertained."

"Well, I'm glad your father and I could do that."

"There wasn't much else. Some old clothes, some Christmas lights."

"Toss those."

I had to tread lightly with what I said next. "Yeah, I will. Did Dad ever mention a student named Mason Anderson?"

"No, not that I can think of."

"He lived in Oakland. That's kind of odd, isn't it?"

"Not these days. I don't think Oakland has the best educational system, so a lot of students come further east to high schools out here. It's easy to get exemptions, use other relatives' addresses, etc. Happens more than you think."

"Okay, thanks. And he never mentioned a student he was worried about?"

"He was worried about all his students, Quint. Drugs, the internet, spending their lives on their phones. He worried daily."

I decided I'd asked her enough questions. My mother didn't know anything and I saw no reason to include her in the crazy conclusions my mind was jumping to.

"Great, thanks, Mom. I'll bring the pictures by when we have lunch next week."

"Keep a few for yourself as well."

"I will. There's this one with you two on roller skates at a disco."

"There is not!" my mom yelled.

We both laughed.

"Okay, maybe not. But there easily could be."

"I'll see you next week."

"Love you, Mom."

"Love you, Quint."

11.

Mason Anderson didn't return for his senior year at Northgate High School, where my father had taught. He had transferred after his junior year, which, judging by my father's note, he may not even have finished.

I'd driven to Northgate itself and told them I was the son of Arthur Adler and wanted to look at some of their recent yearbooks. They happily obliged after expressing their condolences to me. I'd dealt with two people in the main office and then the librarian. They all had glowing things to say about my father.

I'd occasionally come meet him at work, and he'd usually bring me to the library. I'm sure me being a writer had something to do with it. We'd always sit in the Classics section, looking up at books by Joyce, Hemingway, Tolstoy, and Dostoevsky. This was probably his way of telling me I had that type of book in me. Not just throwaway articles for the *Walnut Creek Times*.

I intentionally sat in the Classics section as I read thorough the yearbooks.

It appeared Mason Anderson was a shy kid. I only found two pictures of him. One yearbook photo and one of him studying with a few classmates. He wasn't smiling in either picture, and the only extracurricular activity he listed was Chess Club.

He looked diminutive and his expression in the photos would best be characterized as quizzical. It was a terrible leap to make, but I didn't think he looked all that intelligent. He looked spaced out, not quite sure of himself. And possibly not all there.

If my father's suspicions were correct, there would certainly be good reasons for that.

I tried to find if they listed birthdays anywhere in the yearbooks, but I couldn't find them. He'd likely be eighteen by now, but I couldn't be sure.

If Mason Anderson had been of legal age, then I'd be well within my rights to approach him and ask a few questions. Asking a minor some unsolicited questions was definitely a gray area. Not that I was ruling it out.

I had to decide if I was willing to drop further into the abyss for this case.

I returned the yearbooks to the librarian and headed to my car. I left the school thinking it was less likely that my father's suspicions were related to his death. After all, Mason Anderson had already transferred from Northgate at the time my father was killed in June. It didn't make any sense.

Still, the coincidence of the address was too much for me to toss the possibility out entirely.

When I arrived back at the *Walnut Creek Times*, I took a couple of minutes in my car to look on Facebook for Mason Anderson. Several Mason Andersons lived across the Bay Area, but I couldn't find the right one.

It's very possible that someone his age didn't have Facebook, relying instead on Instagram or Snapchat. Another possibility was a more sinister one. If someone had a shitty home life, he could be less inclined to have social media for the world to see.

I put away my phone and walked into work.

"Quint!" Crystal said as I made my way past her cubicle space. "Always out of the office on some taciturn mission these days."

"I've got a secret to tell you."

"What's that?"

"I'm a secret agent!"

"Oh yeah," she said, playing along. "What branch?"

"FBI. CIA. ATF. WTF."

She laughed. "Yeah, I don't think WTF is one. Nice try, though."

We'd been co-workers for nine years and I'd always enjoyed Crystal's company. Tom Butler had made the right decision by telling me she was off limits early on, and that allowed us to have a nice professional relationship all these years. It never grew awkward like it would have if we'd gotten together.

"It's the Whiskey, Tobacco, and Firearms division. WTF."

Greg and Trent heard the banter and walked over.

"There's absolutely a WTF division. And do you know how it got its name?"

"No, how's that, Greg?" Crystal asked.

"Because you say 'What the fuck?' the morning of a whiskey hangover."

Trent didn't want to be left out. "It's a sister branch to OMG. Old Fashioneds, Margaritas, and Gin and Tonics!"

"Wouldn't that be OFMGT?" Crystal said.

"Hey, I don't make the rules."

It was nice to share a laugh, even over something so silly. We all worked within thirty feet of each other, but it was usually a very businesslike setting.

"This is a sign," Crystal said. "We need to all get together for a night of drinks. It's been too long since we've all done that. We'll have a bunch of WTFs and OMGs."

We looked at each other and realized everyone loved the idea.

"Brilliant idea, Crystal," Greg said. "Do we invite the aristocracy upstairs?"

"Of course. After we give them a few drinks, they'll start behaving like proletariats," Crystal said.

We shared another hearty laugh at that.

"Hey, the aristocracy can hear you?" Tom Butler's voice came from above.

We looked up to see him gathering Krissy and Jan. They walked down the stairs to join us.

"One big happy family," I said.

"I heard something about a party," Tom said.

Crystal took the lead. "This Friday. In two days. I'll bring some mixers to the office and then we'll all hit a bar for Happy Hour."

Tom looked over at Krissy.

"You know I'm in!" she said.

"Jan?" Trent asked.

"I used to enjoy a good strawberry daiquiri back in the day."

I'd always assumed Jan was the biggest square in the office, and mentioning a strawberry daiquiri only furthered that opinion.

"I'll bring a blender," Crystal said.

"And I'll bring stories about the time Quint had one too many tequila shots at our house," Tom said.

"The aristocracy is turning on us. Don't believe a word he says," I warned.

"And I'll tell the story of when my husband had five too many tequila shots in Mexico," Krissy added.

"Oh, shit. They might never look at me the same again."

"I know I haven't," she went back at him.

Tom turned to us. "She's right. Now she looks at me with even more awe."

"Yeah, but it's 'Ahhhh, shit,'" Crystal said.

"Crystal for the win!" Krissy said.

"I'm glad Krissy and Crystal are on different floors. I'd be screwing up their names daily," Jan said.

"Don't worry, we'd love to be able to correct you for a change," Greg said.

We all enjoyed that funny jab at our editor.

It was the best office moment we'd had in weeks. Everyone was smiling and having a good time, like some non-existent alcohol had already kicked in. Crystal said she'd be in charge and all we had to do was show up on Friday. After a little more ball busting, we slowly returned to our stations, looking forward to the upcoming party.

Before she went upstairs, Krissy took me out of earshot of everyone else.

"You've got another letter," she said.

"I'll follow you upstairs," I said.

"Anything you want to talk about?"

I couldn't blame her. Three letters, obviously from the same person, were a bit suspicious.

"It's nothing, Krissy."

She looked at me skeptically. "Maybe I'll get the truth out of you after a few shots on Friday."

I laughed. "Maybe…"

I walked the stairs with her and she gave me the letter. I tucked it under my arm and put it in my backpack when I made my way back down.

I waited until I got home that night to read it.

I'd like to have seen the look on your face when Paddy Roark confronted you. He's a peach, isn't he? And I told you I'd find out. Think of me as the eye in the sky. It's time you alluded to McCarthy or Roark in one of your articles. Once I see that, I'll send you the information that will change your life. Take care, new friend.

I took the piece of paper, crumbled it up, and threw it at my wall.

Why the hell had I been burdened with the hospital bed next to Griff Bauer? It had created nothing but trouble. And was only getting worse.

And yet, I knew I couldn't turn back. I was fully immersed.

For the two hundred and ninety-seventh time in the last two weeks, I considered my options. I narrowed them down to two. Go to the cops or go all-in on my investigating, even if it put me in harm's way.

"Well, fuck, I'm already in harm's way, so why the fuck not?"

Dropping two F-bombs in a single sentence wasn't like me. Neither was talking aloud to myself.

So I guess you could say my decision had been made.

12.

Paddy Roark and Mason Anderson. One I wanted to talk to and one I hoped to never see again.

The problem was I knew where to find the one I didn't want to see. But not the other.

Well, that's not entirely true. But I couldn't just sit outside of the Andersons' house and "randomly" start up a conversation with their son.

Maybe I'd have to start with his parents.

Through some easy Google searches, I'd found that his mother was named Pam and his father Doug. Two short, nice-sounding names. Hardly ones that jumped out as potential monsters. Then again, which do? Maybe Charlie in the '70s, Ted in the '80s, and Jeffrey in the '90s. And that was merely because one wacko fucked up that name for everybody else.

Names, like books, couldn't be judged by their covers.

I wanted to get more information on the Andersons before I met them. I needed to be prepared ahead of my return to Oakland Avenue.

And I decided to push the envelope further.

"Hi, how can I help you?"

A pleasant-looking woman in a green tracksuit and with silver hair answered the door. She lived in the house between the Andersons and the house where Aubrey Durban and James Neil had been killed.

"Hello, my name is Quint and I'm a reporter for the *Walnut Creek Times*."

On the off chance this got back to the Andersons, I decided not to use my last name. Nothing to tie me to my father. If there was even a possibility his death was related.

Off chances. Possibilities. I was certainly grasping at straws.

"Nice to meet you. I'm Annie Ivers."

"My pleasure, Annie. I'm doing some more research on the murder next door."

"It's just been terrible. The police told us they think the young couple was targeted. As if that's supposed to make us feel safer."

Because she said "young couple" instead of Aubrey and James, I quickly assumed they weren't that close.

"I understand. If it makes you feel any better, I've worked with the police and they don't think the general public is in any danger."

"Thanks, but I'm not sure I'm the general public. I'm the next-door neighbor."

"Your point is taken," I said. "Did you know Aubrey Durban and James Neil well?"

"Not all that well," she said, confirming my suspicions. "They were pretty quiet and kept to themselves. I baked them some cookies when they moved in earlier this year, but saw them only sporadically since."

I saw a little wiggle room into the real reason I was there.

"Is this a pretty tight-knit neighborhood overall?"

"I'd say cordial, but not exactly tight-knit."

"So I'm guessing you don't know your neighbors to the left all that well either."

"The Andersons? Well, yeah, they've lived here many years. So I know them a little better."

I wanted to get information, but had to tread lightly.

"What are they like? I knocked earlier and swear I heard someone in the house, but no one answered."

That was a lie, but a push in the right direction. Especially if she wanted to vent about the neighborhood. Or hopefully, the Andersons specifically.

"They can be a little standoffish, but they are polite people. If someone was home, I'm sure they would have answered the door."

"I was probably just hearing things. It can be creepy being in the neighborhood where people were killed."

"Imagine living here."

"Of course. I'm sorry."

"Is there anything else you want to know? There's not much to tell. I've talked to the police a few times already."

"I'm just trying to get a feel for the deceased and the neighborhood itself. I'm not trying to find the killer," I said.

One more lie to add to the pile.

"Well, like I said, the neighbors are nice enough. After the Andersons, you have the Elliots and on the other side of them are the Craigholms. I could probably name a few more."

"Thanks, Annie, but that's not necessary. I'm only concerned with the neighbors who were close in vicinity to Aubrey and James. Probably just you and the Andersons. Think I may go try them again. Do they have children? In my history, sometimes kids will remember important things several days after the fact."

We were still standing outside of Annie's house. She was very cordial, but obviously didn't want to invite me in. Considering what had happened next door, I couldn't say I blamed her.

"They've got two children. Maddy and Mason. I believe Mason will be a senior in high school. Maddy graduated a couple of years ago. They said she went off to college, but I can't remember which one."

I realized this was becoming too Anderson-centric. I preferred to end the conversation on something else.

"And do you have kids?" I asked.

"Not around here. But you're sweet in assuming they'd still be at home. I've been an empty nester for a long, long time."

"I don't believe that," I said, hoping to earn some brownie points.

"You're a good ass-kisser, Quint."

"That's what my mother always tells me," I said.

"She's a smart lady."

I laughed. I considered giving her my card, but still didn't like the idea of my last name circulating around the neighborhood.

"And you never saw anything suspicious around the time of the murders?"

"I didn't see anything on that Saturday. I'm sorry."

"Okay. Thanks for your time, Annie."

"You're welcome."

She started shutting her front door, slowly. I had a feeling she secretly wanted to keep the conversation going. I couldn't tell if it was because she had more to tell or she was just a bored empty nester.

But it was over. The door shut and I heard a deadbolt lock behind it.

After a murder in the house next to you, safety took precedence over loneliness.

I walked back to the street and meandered around. I wasn't ready to knock on the Andersons' door, but I didn't want to just get in my car and drive away on the off chance Annie was still watching me.

Our conversation played in my mind as I walked Oakland Avenue. I hadn't learned all that much, but my suspicions about the Andersons hadn't exactly gone away either. Annie's "they can be standoffish" reverberated through my brain.

I was still jumping to conclusions, considering being standoffish a precursor to murder or child abuse.

I needed to chill the F out.

13.

I woke up at 7:00 a.m. on Friday, sleeping in a little more than usual. With our little office work party that afternoon and a Happy Hour to follow, I was glad to get some extra rest.

Soon after I woke up, the investigation made its way to the forefront of my brain.

It had become three-pronged. One, the murders themselves. Two, Paddy Roark and Dennis McCarthy. Roark's behavior had done nothing to prove the letters wrong. He acted like someone who would have no problem committing murder. Probably enjoy it. And third, what exactly had my father seen with regards to Mason Anderson? Was it a bruise or something even more sinister? And was this in any way related to the murders that took place two doors down?

I needed a coffee and headed down to the Starbucks below my apartment complex. Got my usual, a half-caf Americano. A few of my favorite baristas worked that morning and they asked me how things were going.

"I'm working on something very, very big.". It was the most honest I'd been in weeks, even though I presented it as a joke.

"Is it about how I make far and away the best Americano?" Sarah, one of the managers on duty, asked me.

"He doesn't write fiction, Sarah. And since he writes non-fiction, you know it would be me," Laurel said. She was wearing a multi-colored sweater and a grin.

"It's about the camaraderie between the two of you," I said.

They were always going back and forth with each other. Laurel and Hardy, if you will. Or Laurel and Sarah, as was the case.

"If you want to do a public interest piece on your local Starbucks, we're up for it," Laurel said.

"We'll break the internet," I said.

"You're damn right you will. The public will love us. Well, love me and tolerate Laurel."

"Yeah, right, Sarah."

And Laurel pushed her.

"It's been a pleasure, girls, but I really do have to get some work done today."

"Bye, Quint."

"Later, Quint."

Sarah handed me my Americano. Quickly turning, I bumped into the person standing behind me and somehow avoided knocking any of my drink on him.

"I'm sorry," I said.

"No problem," the man said. "You didn't get me."

Relieved, I walked over to an open seat. I picked up a paper (not the *Walnut Creek Times*) and read about the local sports teams. It was nice to enjoy something mindless.

After finishing my coffee and putting the cup in the trash, I went back upstairs to get ready for the day. I took the elevator to the fourth floor and looked both ways down the hall as I entered my apartment. I imagined this new tradition wasn't going to cease until my current investigations were over. It had me on edge.

I readied myself for the shower, looking at my body in the mirror. I was in better shape than most forty-year-olds, but there was a small little potbelly taking form. I was on my way to having a dad bod, without possessing the requisite child. Time to start hitting the gym a little harder and my dinner plate a little lighter.

I noticed a scratch on my wrist. I poured some water over it and it became barely noticeable.

It must have happened when I'd turned into the guy downstairs. My own fault for swiveling like a madman with a hot cup of coffee in my hand. After my shower, I put on some jeans and a crisp, short-sleeved white dress shirt. And went to the elevator that took me to the underground parking garage.

I'd started walking the hundred feet from the elevator to my car when a dark SUV pulled up and someone said, "Is that you, Quint?"

"Who the hell are you?" I said.

The back window of the SUV rolled down.

"Someone who would like to talk to you," a man said, although I couldn't see his face yet.

"If you don't tell me who you are right now, I'm going to call the cops."

The man leaned forward so I could see his face.

"My name is Dennis McCarthy. I'd like to talk."

I had balls and I had gumption, but I didn't always have the best instincts. Deciding to get in the SUV certainly proved that. But I was curious. And truth be told, I immediately trusted Dennis McCarthy. I don't know how to explain it. I just did.

I climbed into the back. The SUV had two rows of seats that faced each other. Two huge men sat on the left and right of me. My eyes came to rest on Dennis McCarthy. He was distinguished in the manner that only older people can be. Obviously comfortable in his own skin. Confidence oozed from him. I could tell that in a split second. He wore khaki pants and a pink sweater, which was so at odds with the situation that I almost laughed. His hair was totally gray, but he had a young man's vigor to him. He looked directly at me.

I should have been petrified, worried I could be killed at any moment. A knife to the back of the head, Goodfellas style. Or my windpipe constricted by one of Andre the Giant's cousins.

But I wasn't. I was surprisingly calm.

I expected McCarthy to say something like *"If you tell us the truth, we'll let you live."*

But instead he got straight to the point.

"What made you go to Boyle's Grocery Store?"

I paused.

"If you lie, I'll know."

The SUV went over a familiar bump. We had made it above ground and were leaving the confines of Avalon Walnut Creek.

"I got a letter," I said.

"Go on."

"It said I should investigate Dennis McCarthy for the murder of Griff Bauer."

I didn't really have a card to play. They had found me at my apartment complex. They knew who I was. Lying wasn't going to work. So I hoped that telling the truth might magically turn out to my benefit.

"Go on," Dennis McCarthy said. His voice was measured and melodic.

"I did nothing at first. Then, a second letter came calling me a small timer and saying that Paddy Roark was the henchman for you and he would have done the killing."

I expected a denial or some indignation, but he just sat there with an odd little smile.

"You're doing well. I hope you'll keep telling the truth," he said.

Against all logic, I trusted his melodic voice. I'm sure that sounds crazy, but something about him garnered trust. It wasn't fear.

"Did you receive any more letters?"

The SUV headed away from my apartment complex, driving along Treat Boulevard.

"Yes, one more. It said he'd have liked to seen the expression on my face when Paddy Roark confronted me. Said he always knew everything that was going on. And then he told me if I published something about Paddy Roark or yourself, he'd send me some information that would change my life."

"But you haven't written anything on Roark or I."

That wasn't a question, but a statement. He knew.

"No, I haven't. I can't just use a source I've never met. Especially without any evidence whatsoever."

"There isn't any evidence. Nor will there be." However incongruous with the situation, his voice was truly calming.

"No?" I said.

"You've been, what do they call it? Catfished, I believe. I can assure you that neither Mr. Roark nor I had anything to do with the murder of Griff Bauer. Or any of the other murders in Oakland."

"I believe you."

I was still flanked by the two monsters, but they hadn't said a word. This was basically a two-person conversation despite there being four of us.

"Do I look like someone who leaves bodies all over Oakland?"

"No," I said honestly.

Not that there was ever going to be any other answer.

"You're right. I'm not. I'm a businessman and leaving a trail of dead bodies is not good for business. Or my reputation."

"So where does that leave me?" I asked.

"I'm giving you my word that I had nothing to do with these murders. And pleading with you not to publish the bullshit you've been fed. It would bring a great deal of scrutiny on me, something I've tried to avoid my whole life. And it would be for something that I'm completely innocent of. If the truth matters to you."

Despite my recent actions, the truth still mattered to me.

"You've got nothing to fear from me," I said. "I'm not going to publish unsubstantiated secret letters from God knows who."

I noticed one of the two behemoths move slightly as I'd said *God knows who*. I didn't think it was a coincidence.

"Do you have a suspicion as to who sent me the letters?" I asked.

"I suspect," Dennis McCarthy said deliberately, "you wouldn't live long if you started investigating him."

His warning was tinged with fear. It was obvious he meant what he said.

This had become surreal. I sat across from an infamous legend of San Francisco, the biggest bookie the city had ever known. And we were amicable.

But then I remembered Vern Coughlin. This older man in his pink sweater wasn't someone to be taken lightly. He, in all likelihood, had ordered the murder of a childhood friend merely for writing an article about him. He'd have no problem doing the same to another writer. Me.

We'd built up a nice little camaraderie, but I'd be silly to trust a word he said.

I stared at him, this time without reverence, but with revulsion.

Dennis McCarthy noticed it and his expression changed. It's like he'd caught me with my hand in the cookie jar.

There was a five-second pause where no one said a word. For the first time, I became nervous.

"Let's play a game," he said. "I consider myself a master of the human psyche. And I think I can guess what you're thinking at this very moment."

"I'll play along," I said.

"Your eyes gave you away. You'd been receptive to my wishes and had an expression that showed your trust in me. But then your face, and especially your eyes, took on a more doubtful and suspicious look. And a bit scared, if I dare say so. And so I start to wonder why the switch happened. I'm going to assume you researched me when you got these phony letters. And any inquiry into myself would surely have led you to the infamous article by Vern Coughlin. And his subsequent death. So, in that moment, when your eyes betrayed you, I'm guessing you were thinking about the death of Vern Coughlin. And assuming I had him killed."

I was mesmerized, but nothing came out of my mouth.

"Well?" he asked.

There was really no point in lying. "Very impressive, Mr. McCarthy. You're exactly right."

"Thanks for your honesty. I take great pride in my insightfulness. It's paid great dividends over the years."

"Can I be blunt?" I asked.

"Please do," he said.

"Vern Coughlin was a reporter. As am I. How am I supposed to trust you?"

"I'm going to let you in on a little secret, Quint. I didn't kill Vern Coughlin. I was friends with Vern since we were kids. Did I like the article? Obviously not. He betrayed my trust and it created all new headaches for me. But I didn't kill him."

I believed him.

And yet, I couldn't just go gently into that good night. It wasn't my style. I had to ask the question that was begging to be asked.

"So somebody killed Vern Coughlin in order to bring heat on you?" I asked.

I'd only mentioned Coughlin, but it was obvious I was also referencing the letters I'd received. Because they'd also bring heat on Dennis McCarthy.

He leaned forward. "It's a logical leap you are making. But I assure you, if you enjoy your life, don't follow this path. The man I'm assuming sent you these letters is a former employee of mine. And he enjoyed the shadier aspects of the job. He's a monster."

"Can I show you something?" I asked.

"Please do," Dennis McCarthy said.

I extended my right wrist, palm up, revealing a series of tiny little scars.

"When I was seven years old, I tried to make pancakes for my parents one day. I put the batter in the pan, but the heat was way too high, so the oil and butter started splattering everywhere. My mother grabbed me and said to stay away from the pan until the heat subsided. She left the kitchen. I looked at the pan, knowing the pancakes were going to burn if I didn't flip them. So I walked back over to the stove and started to flip the pancakes, getting burned by the hot oil in the process."

Dennis McCarthy smiled for the first time.

"And the lesson is you're not very good at leaving well enough alone?"

"I served my parents pancakes that morning," I said.

He smiled again.

"And scarred yourself for life," he said.

My story had been trumped. He was right, making the pancakes hadn't really been worth it.

"It's a nice little story, Quint. It really is. However, perseverance and stubbornness will only get you killed in this case. This isn't serving pancakes."

"Just one hint on who sent me these letters," I said. "No one will ever know where I got the information and I'll never come to you again. Please, this has become personal to me."

I saw Dennis McCarthy pondering. He hit the console on the SUV.

"Pull over," he said.

The SUV pulled over and the behemoth to my right opened the door.

"I'm a very deliberate man," Dennis McCarthy said. "I do my research and don't act quickly or blindly."

I didn't interrupt.

"So when you appeared at Boyle's Grocery Store, I learned all I could about you."

He paused, so I said, "I'm listening."

I knew he was building up to something.

"And I found out that you were named after Quint, Robert Shaw's character in *Jaws*."

"That's right," I said.

"You want your hint?" Dennis McCarthy asked.

"Yes."

"Just know that it could easily lead to your death."

"I'm willing to take that chance," I said.

"Okay, here goes. You will be hunting the same thing as your namesake."

I was lost.

"Hunting a shark?" I asked.

"That is all, Mr. Adler. Goodbye."

Calling me by my last name had made it clear the conversation was over.

One of the men took my shoulders and pushed me outside of the SUV. I almost lost my footing, but kept my balance and stayed on my two feet.

When I looked back, the SUV was already moving down the road.

14.

I remained in a sort of trance for the next several hours. After being shoved out of the SUV, I found myself surprisingly close to my apartment, so I just walked home. I was afraid to venture back out.

The one productive thing I did was to call Tom Butler and tell him I'd be in a little late. I worried I'd blurt out what happened and later regret it. I needed time to decide my next course of action.

As had become par for the course, I could go to the cops or keep it to myself. And as usual, if I went to the cops, it would bring me a whole new set of problems. Mainly, why hadn't I told them I'd received letters purporting to know who committed the murders?

No explanation would suffice. I decided once and for all to stop thinking about going to the police. I was too deeply immersed in the investigation. I should no longer consider it an option.

Tired of thinking about the case, I went to my room and took a much-needed nap.

Finally, at 3:00 p.m., I headed into work. I had put off the office party long enough. I wasn't sure if I needed a cocktail more than ever or whether drinking would be a terrible idea.

Both were probably true.

Upon entering, I was greeted with streamers throughout the *Walnut Creek Times*. Some went all the way from the top floor down to the bottom. Crystal had really gone all out. In the center of the downstairs office, a huge table held a few liquor bottles along with several mixers. Next to them stood a stack of red Solo cups and a pitcher full of what I guessed was strawberry daiquiri mix.

Krissy saw me first.

"Shot of tequila, Quint?"

"Maybe later, Krissy. Not sure I want to be that bold to start."

"Quint!!" Crystal had seen me enter from across the room. She walked over, already having a slight gaze in her eyes. "You're late! We started at one."

"Sorry, Crystal. But I'm here now!"

"What's your pick of poison?"

I realized turning down a drink wouldn't sit well with Crystal. "I'll take a Jack and Coke if you've got it."

"I'll be right back."

Jan, Tom, Greg, and Trent waved in my direction from the corner where they talked together. I was left talking to Krissy, who'd become a little suspicious of me and my letters.

"Nothing from your secret admirer today," she said. "What's with all the letters, though?"

I'd have to deal with this down the road, but not yet. I decided to make fun of the situation.

"Can you blame them? What's not to love about this face?" I asked, grabbing my cheekbones tight to make myself intentionally ugly.

"Where do I start?" she asked.

I laughed.

Crystal came back and handed me a Jack and Coke. "Did you hear the good news, Quint?"

"I don't think so."

"We're all inviting our significant others to Happy Hour. And since the rumor is that you're hanging out with Cara again, I suggest you send her a text. We're starting at the Stadium Pub."

I was trying to turn my brain off. Maybe drinking with co-workers and Cara would be exactly what I needed.

"Screw it, why not?" I said. "She'll be glad to see all you guys. It's been too long."

"That's the Quint we like!" she said.

The other four walked over.

"We're inviting our significant others, Quint," Trent said.

"Give Cara a call," Tom said.

"I'm starting to wonder if this is all a ploy to get Cara out," I said.

"Can you blame us?" It was Greg's turn to chime in. "You definitely outkicked your coverage with her."

"That was funny the first three thousand, four hundred and ninety-one times you said it," I said, but I was smiling.

"Cara! Cara! Cara!" my six co-workers started chanting.

"You guys are all drunk! I definitely need to catch up. Pour me that shot of tequila!"

As they all celebrated, Crystal went off to pour me a shot. She was definitely the ringleader of this shindig.

She brought back my tequila. I raised it to everyone, who lifted their Solo-cup concoctions in return.

"This is a toast to Tom and Krissy. They have been great bosses and owners over the last nine years. I think it would be hard to find a company in this country with more loyalty and less of a turnover rate. And for that, I'm grateful. We are generally a businesslike group, but it's only because we take our job seriously. And it's fun to see everyone letting loose today. So I guess, while I started this toast as one to our owners, I guess it's for all of us. Cheers to my co-workers!" I said.

We all clinked our cups and I inhaled a way-too-big shot of Jose Cuervo.

"Ouch!" I yelled.

"That will put hair on your chest," Trent said.

"One more of those and I'll be Alec Baldwin."

"Or Robin Williams," Jan chimed in.

"Good one!" Tom said.

The fun times continued for another hour. And then Tom told us he was locking the doors.

"Toss your Solo cups in the garbage. We're heading to the Stadium Pub in ten minutes."

I had texted Cara earlier and now I sent her a follow-up text, telling her we'd be at the bar soon.

The Stadium Pub was a Walnut Creek staple, and I'm not sure if that's a good thing or a bad thing. It's a dive. Not that there's anything wrong with that. It was located on Lincoln Drive about two blocks from our office. It had a green sign out front with three doors from which you could pick to enter. It was two too many.

The front of the bar was all tables and chairs, with the bar on the back left. If "cluttered" can be a décor choice, then that's what the Stadium Pub was. Tables almost touched and there was no rhyme or reason as to where the seats went. It was chaos. And not the controlled kind.

But I guess that's what gave it its charm.

We took over two tables in the back right corner. Jan's husband, Greg's wife, and Trent's girlfriend all waited there. Cara arrived a few minutes later.

To much fanfare.

"We've missed you, Cara!"

"You look as beautiful as ever!"

"What are you doing with that Quint guy?"

I gave her a kiss on the cheek once she made her way to me. A kiss on the lips would have invited too many questions as to whether we were officially back together.

To be honest, we didn't even know where we stood. And it was kind of a nice position to be in. No responsibilities, just taking it day by day.

"Cara, what can I get you to drink?" Tom asked.

"I'll just take a beer to start."

"That's not going to work. This is a cocktail party."

Cara grinned. "In that case, Tom, I'll take a rum and Coke."

"Here, I'll go to the bar and order that for you."

"I'll join you."

Tom had told me many times over the years that Cara was a special one. I think he took this occasion as a challenge to get us back together in full.

As they walked away, I heard Tom say, "I was busting Quint's balls about all the tequila he drank at my house that one New Year's Eve."

"Oh, I remember," Cara said. "I had to help him into bed that night. From the bathroom, if you get my drift."

"I can hear you guys," I said.

And everyone got a good laugh.

I made my way to the other table and started up conversations with my co-workers' loved ones. I only saw them a few times a year, but over nine years you get to know them a little bit.

It was nice to see them all again. And as someone who didn't currently want to talk about work, I enjoyed the small talk about families and kids and school.

All the things that I didn't have. Not that I was complaining.

"When are you going to have kids?" Greg's wife Ava asked me. "You're not a spring chicken anymore, Quint."

"Luckily, this guy is a rooster. And only the chick has to be young. Wait, that didn't sound right," I said.

Ava laughed. "I get your point. And you're right, Cara is still young."

As if on cue, Cara walked over and put her arms around my shoulders. "Somebody just turned forty and is a little sensitive about it," she said.

"I didn't know," Ava said. "Happy Birthday! What did you do?"

"I got into a fight with some glass and spent most of the night in the hospital."

"Well, so many birthdays blend together; I'm sure this one will stand out."

"You can still see the remnants of the stitches."

"Thank you, Cara!" I said.

"Oh yeah, there they are. Makes you look tough."

"Tougher," I said and Ava giggled once again. She had a bubbly personality and was quick to laugh. Greg had hit the jackpot.

Jan's husband was equally nice, just more reserved. He took after his wife. But her shyness didn't stop her from throwing back two or three strawberry daiquiris.

It was worth it just to see the bartender's face.

"I think we've got a blender somewhere back there," he said.

"Fire it up!" Trent yelled. "I might be getting a piña colada."

We tipped well, so the waitress and bartenders loved us, but I'd admit to us being a bit high maintenance.

By time 7:00 p.m. rolled around, people started to lose steam. Jan and her husband were the first to go. If I'd had to guess, it was the most Jan had drunk in years. But she composed herself pretty well, even if her bright, rosy cheeks gave her level of inebriation away.

Greg was a tank. He had a shot every half hour and seemed sober as a judge. But Ava was starting to feel hers, and they were the next couple to leave.

Trent and his girlfriend Tanya, who had been given the nickname "The Terrible T's" at some point in the night, were next to go. Tanya and Cara spent a long time talking and Cara had set up a double date between we two couples.

I was having too good a time to ask her if we were a couple again.

And finally, we were left with Tom, Krissy, Cara, and me.

As I'd expected.

They weren't going to let a rare night out with Cara end early.

We moved on to another bar, this one aptly named The Rooftop, with a nice view of downtown Walnut Creek. It had already been a long day and we could see the finish line, so we left the hard alcohol at the Stadium Pub, choosing wine at The Rooftop.

"I'll get a bottle for the four of us," Tom said. "And then we'll call it a night."

We all nodded in agreement.

Tom ordered a bottle. I was no wine expert, but I assumed it was expensive.

"This is good stuff. Thanks, Tom," Cara said.

"We've missed you, Cara."

"I know. I've missed you guys too."

"Can we adopt her, Quint?" Krissy asked. "So she can still be there for us even when you guys aren't all hunky-dory?"

"Please do," I said. "She's not all wine and roses." I smiled and raised my glass.

"Quint's not all roses either," Cara said. "Usually, he's more like the thorn."

It was good-natured ribbing. The four of us really did get along well together, despite Cara and me being much younger.

The great conversation continued for the next half hour until it became obvious the night was coming to a close. In the meantime, Cara had set up another double date for us.

We walked Tom and Krissy to their Uber and said goodbye with plans for dinner soon.

"Should we get an Uber?" Cara asked.

"No, let's walk," I said. "It's only a mile. Let's enjoy this fresh air."

Cara took my hand in hers and we turned toward my apartment complex. A place where I'd met Dennis McCarthy that morning.

I could deal with that later. In the moment, I was just happy to be back with Cara, the woman I'd always loved even when we were broken up.

"Let's make it last this time," she said.

I squeezed her hand tighter. And kissed her.

It was my way of saying I agreed.

We walked together in the warm June air. Despite all the shit going on around me, in that moment, everything was perfect.

15.

I was awakened the next morning by a call from Ray Kintner.

Cara was still asleep next to me and I didn't want to pick up my cell phone, but it was the police. I had to.

"Hello?" I said.

"Mr. Adler, this is Detective Kintner. Could you come down to the station?"

I was surprised he'd used both of our last names. It sounded more official than usual.

"I'm just waking up. Can I head there this afternoon?"

"Actually, we'd prefer if you came over right now."

"Okay. I'll be there within the hour."

I expected a thanks, but I looked down and he'd hung up.

"You have to go somewhere?" Cara asked.

"Yeah."

"Want to meet up tonight?" she said.

"Yeah, I should be free. Can you let yourself out? I'm going to take a quick shower and get out of here."

"Sure."

There would be no morning sex this time. I showered, threw on some jeans and an old-school Pink Floyd t-shirt, and headed to the Oakland Police Department.

The police department was quiet when I found a parking spot in front and walked in. Only two police officers manned the front entrance, when I'd seen as many as eight in the past.

I left my wallet, keys, and cell phone on the little tray and walked through the metal detector. Then I took the elevator up to Ray Kintner's office. Ray stood only twenty feet from the elevator and looked up right as I got off, apparently waiting for me. He didn't smile or offer any sort of introduction.

Something was off.

"Follow me this way, Mr. Adler."

I did.

He led me in the direction of the interrogation rooms. He opened the door to one and I walked in.

"What's going on?" I asked.

"I'll be back in just a minute," he said.

It was hardly an answer.

I sat on the cold metal chair waiting for him to return. Maybe Ray acted weird because he felt we had become too close. Or maybe he had big news to tell me and was just following protocol. Regardless, he was not being the cordial, helpful detective I had come to know.

Five minutes later, he returned with the young, buff Detective Marks whom I had met a week previously.

They sat in the two chairs facing me. This was becoming old hat.

"Mr. Adler, we are just going to get straight to the point."

"Okay," I said.

"Were you at Griff Bauer's house the day he died?"

The wind went out of me in one fell swoop. I tried to catch my breath, but I found it a struggle to do so. I concentrated as hard as I could and was finally able to take a deep breath.

"Mr. Adler, are you alright?" Detective Marks said.

"I'm fine," I said, trying to gather my thoughts.

"Then answer the question." Ray Kintner was no longer my friend, that much was obvious. He eyed me suspiciously.

I had no idea what to do. I could keep lying, but they obviously knew something. I didn't think I'd be able to lie myself out of this one.

"Mr. Adler, answer the damn question!" Detective Marks said.

I bowed my head. I didn't have many options. It was time to come clean.

"I was there," I said.

They looked at each other and something passed between them. I didn't like where this was going.

"Why?" Detective Kintner asked.

That's how I saw him now. He was no longer Ray, the one I'd become friends with. I knew he was friends with Tom Butler, but bringing him up couldn't help me now. He looked like he was out for blood.

"The night before was my fortieth birthday and I was in Summit Hospital in Oakland. Griff Bauer was in the same hospital room as I."

"And?"

"And someone came in and told him they needed to get out of the hospital. I was suspicious, so I took a picture of his…"

I paused. Was I saying too much? If this information got out, I'd be fired from my job. And probably charged with hindering an investigation. Or something like that. Maybe it was just better to shut up. And lawyer up.

"A picture of what, Quint?" Detective Kintner said, but I didn't buy his friendly act of using my first name.

"It's all a little hazy now that I think of it," I said. "I might have gotten a concussion when I hit the glass that sent me to the hospital."

They rightfully looked at me with suspicion.

"We heard you got in an argument with him at the hospital," Detective Marks said.

And that's when I knew this was really spiraling out of control.

"What? I didn't say one word to the guy. You're not suggesting I had anything to do with this, are you?"

"You're being pretty evasive, Quint."

"Can I talk to you as a friend really quick, Ray?" By doing the same thing, I hoped to reestablish our previous friendship on the fly.

"Sure," he said.

"I'm just being evasive because I have to worry about my job. I might have done some things that would put it in jeopardy. And I know you're friends with Tom."

I couldn't judge his reaction. It looked like he wanted to believe me, but a lot of doubt lurked in his eyes.

"Depending what happens here, this doesn't have to get back to him," he said, though I didn't believe him.

Still, I had very few options.

"I took a picture of Griff Bauer's address on his hospital card. That's how I knew where to go the next morning."

"What were you hoping to find?" the younger detective chimed back in.

"I don't know. It was just suspicious that someone whisked him out of the hospital like that. So I went to his house as an investigative journalist, I guess. Not sure what I was going to find."

"So you didn't get into a fight with him?"

"No!" I said emphatically. "I didn't say jack shit to him. In fact, I never even saw his face. I was on the other side of the hospital room with a partition between us."

"That's not the information we've received," he said.

"Well, your information is wrong. I didn't say one word to the guy."

"And yet you went to his house the next morning? The day he died."

"He was dead when I got there," I blurted out.

I immediately knew I'd made a mistake.

"You saw his dead body and didn't tell the police?" Detective Marks said.

I was bewildered. Did they think I was a suspect? Who the hell told them that I got in a fight with Griff Bauer?

I'd seen enough suspects hang themselves by talking too much. But I had the truth on my side. That should matter. You'd think.

"Ray, as a friend, I want to ask you something. Should I ask for an attorney?" I said.

"That would probably be your best option," he said.

The only public defender in the building at the time found his way down to Interrogation Room #2 and walked in. Probably in his fifties, he had thinning hair over a much-too-tan noggin.

"Bob Devane, public defender," he said and extended his hand with a fake machismo that rubbed me the wrong way.

"Quint Adler," I said.

"Detective Kintner said you've got yourself in a world of shit. He sent me down here."

"I think they might suspect me of something I didn't do."

"Talk to me, Goose."

I instantly hated Bob Devane. Using a *Top Gun* reference when my life was potentially on the line was tacky and uncalled for. No wonder he was just a public defender.

But I talked to him. I didn't have much choice. I knew another attorney, a friend of my father's, but that would get back to my mother. I still wanted to keep this on the down low if at all possible.

I told Devane about hitting the glass, about being in the room with Griff Bauer, and about making the big mistake of going to his house the next morning and seeing his dead body. I told him almost everything. But I left out the letters and having met with Dennis McCarthy. I might have had attorney/client privilege with Bob Devane, but he was never going to be my long-term lawyer. I didn't feel a need to tell him more than necessary.

I finished by telling him about my job and how it was a big consideration for me.

"There's a lot going on here," he said.

"Yeah, I know."

"Let me talk to the detectives and see if I can get a sense of what they're after. If they just want to know what you were doing there, we can make this go away rather easily. If they suspect you of something, this becomes a lot more serious."

It all scared me, there was no doubt.

Twenty minutes later, Detective Kintner walked back into the interrogation room. Bob Devane was there, but I only planned on asking him something if absolutely necessary. I hoped to look innocent. Which I was.

"You don't really think I had anything to do with Griff Bauer's death?" I asked Kintner.

"You've lied quite a bit."

"I left things out. There's a difference."

"Not from where I sit."

"This is one big nightmare," I said.

"I'm going to ask you one last question, Quint. It's an important one. Be sure you answer it honestly."

"I will," I said.

"You told us he was dead when you got there."

"That's right."

"My question is this. Did you ever step foot in the house?"

This was going to be my saving grace.

Devane whispered in my ear, "Did you?"

"No," I whispered back.

"I'd answer him," he said.

Ladies and gentleman, Bob Devane.

"I never went in the house!" I said emphatically. "I saw the man was dead by peering through the splintered door. And I walked around the outside. But I never stepped foot inside."

"Okay, Quint. Would you mind leaving a fingerprint and DNA sample so we can verify that?"

"Of course."

I was starting to feel better about myself for the first time all morning.

"I'll send the specialist in and then we are prepared to let you go. I'll be in touch in the next few days."

"Thanks, Ray. I promise you I had nothing to do with his death."

It was subtle, but we were going back and forth using each other's first or last names, depending on the situation.

"I hope you're right, Quint. Would you like me to contact you through Mr. Devane?"

I was done with Bob Devane. "No, you can contact me directly."

Mr. Devane said nothing. It was his best moment yet.

"Alright, I'll be in touch. Wait here until they come back for your fingerprints and DNA."

He walked out of the interrogation room and I waited.

Thirty minutes later, I was finally able to leave the Oakland Police Department. Luckily, since it was Saturday, I didn't need to go in to work. That would have been too much.

I drove back to my apartment, where I was happy to see that Cara had gone. I didn't want to lie to her, or even worse, have to be honest about what happened.

I wasn't ready to talk to my mother either. I just prayed this would all go away.

It was going to be tricky. Even when the police realized that I never went into the house, there was still the fact that I had withheld information.

Was that something they could keep to themselves? Would they have to tell Tom and Krissy Butler?

I still held out hope I could retain my job.

The day went on and I didn't do much. Cara texted me and I told her I was just too tired from the night before. There would be no hanging out.

Tom sent me a text saying how much fun he'd had and that we should do an employee Happy Hour once a month.

If I'm still employed in a month, was what I thought.

Good idea. I had a great time too, was what I texted.

Before I knew it, the sun went down and I shut my blinds. I liked to keep them open while the sun set as it often supplied a beautiful view from my apartment.

This day was no different. It was gorgeous.

I decided to watch a movie before bed, somehow spending thirty minutes going through Netflix and Amazon Prime before deciding on one I'd seen ten times. *L.A. Confidential.*

The beginning credits were going when I heard a knock.

I walked toward the door, not sure who to expect. After these past few days it could have been anyone.

Looking through the peephole, I saw Detective Kintner.

He knocked again, louder this time.

I opened the door. Detectives Kintner stood in the hall with Marks and two others officers I didn't recognize. I knew something was wrong.

"I could have come to the station," I said.

"Quint Adler, you are under arrest for the murder of Griffin Bauer."

My legs buckled beneath me and I fell to the ground.

PART II: THE ACCUSED

16.

I was handcuffed in my apartment and led to the hallway. I asked them to lock the door behind them. It's weird what springs to mind when your future is flashing before your eyes. But in the moment, that mattered to me.

A woman on the lobby floor saw me escorted out of the elevator. I hoped she either didn't know who I was or didn't like to gossip. Word could spread in our complex fast. Only a handful of people living at Avalon Walnut Creek would fit my description.

Did you hear that Quint got arrested? Four armed policemen with him. Escorted out in handcuffs. I don't want to be living in the same complex as some felon. I'm going to talk to management.

This was another odd thing to worry about, considering the State of California aimed to be my new landlord.

I sat in the back of a squad car for the drive back to the Oakland Police Department, where I was fingerprinted (again) and processed. I was put in a holding cell and told I'd likely be transferred to Santa Rita Jail in the morning, thirty minutes from downtown Oakland.

I was in a complete haze, but tried to pick up on the most important things I was being told. An officer said I'd be seen by a judge early on Monday morning, when my bail would be set. That one registered.

I'd be spending the weekend in jail. When you're being charged with murder, a weekend shouldn't concern you, but it definitely hit home for me. I wanted to break down, but couldn't resort to being weak. I had to stay strong.

Mostly, I wanted to rewind a few weeks and change my terrible decisions. None of them had included murder, but they had all brought me to this point.

They gave me my one phone call, and though I dreaded making it, I had to call my mother. It would kill her to hear it from a secondhand source. Not that hearing it from me was much better.

It was almost 11:00 p.m. at this point and I just hoped she was still awake.

I heard the recorded message say the call was coming from Quint Adler from a correctional facility. I was gutted for my mother. How could I put her through this phone call? Truth was, I didn't have much choice.

"Hello? Quint? Correctional facility, what does that mean?"

There was a slight pause before I was allowed to talk from my end.

"Hi, Mom, it's me. First off, I have to let you know I didn't do what they are accusing me of."

I had to get that out of the way first.

"What are they saying you did?" she asked, obviously scared.

"They're charging me with murder," I said.

"What? How? That's not possible."

And then I heard her start crying on the other end.

"Mom, I know this is tough to hear, but try to stay with me. Are you there?"

More sobbing. Finally, she came back on the line.

"I'm here. How could anyone suspect you of murder?"

"It's all a huge misunderstanding," I said. "I'll tell you everything once I see you. But for now, I need a favor."

"Of course. What is it?"

"I need you to call Dad's old friend Gary Rogers. The lawyer. Do you have his number?"

"Yeah, I've got it here somewhere."

My mother wasn't the best with her cell phone and probably had it in some old Rolodex or address book.

"Call him right when we hang up. Tell him that I've been arrested on a murder charge, but that I'm innocent. I'm currently at the Oakland Police Department, but they might transfer me to Santa Rita Jail. I'll explain everything to him when he gets here. And he can relay it to you."

"I'll call him immediately. Is there anything else while I have you on the line?"

"I just want to reiterate that I'm innocent, Mom. I promise you."

"I believe you, son."

"Thanks. Now please call Gary."

Gary Rogers had been one of my father's oldest and dearest friends. They met in grade school and remained close through childhood, high school, and college. At that point, most people thought my father was going to become the lawyer, but while Gary went off to law school, my father went to get his teaching credential.

They had both returned to Seattle after college, but Gary decided to come to California. He attended Stanford Law School, met his future wife, passed the bar in California and chose to stay. My father didn't make it to California till more than thirty-five years after Gary, but they remained great friends in the meantime.

My father was the best man at Gary's wedding. He hoped to respond in kind, but with my father having an older brother, Gary was second in line when my parents married. The two couples went on many trips over the years, and Gary's wife Laurie got along swimmingly with my mother. With the names of Linda and Laurie it was almost inevitable.

Once my parents moved to California, Gary and my father just became tighter, going on many fishing and camping excursions over the years. The Rodgers had two children around my age, so the kids often accompanied the parents.

When my father passed away, Gary spoke at his funeral, bringing down the house with stories from their childhood. Anyone who saw him speak that day knew he belonged in a courtroom.

He revered my father and I knew he'd do anything for Arthur Adler's only child. It didn't hurt that he was a very well-regarded lawyer in the Bay Area. I knew I'd be in good hands.

Less than an hour after I got off the phone with my mother, a bailiff came by my cell and took me to a meeting area. It held a long row of seats, sitting across from other seats, with a long glass partition in between. Gary Rogers sat on the other side, replete with a three-piece suit that must have cost more than a month's worth of my clothing.

My father had died at seventy, and considering they grew up together, I knew Gary was around seventy himself. He didn't look it. He was in better shape than most men thirty years younger. His hair had become almost completely gray, but that just made him appear distinguished. Something that could only help in a courtroom.

Although you couldn't tell it by him sitting down, Gary was 6'3" and cut an imposing figure. I hoped that would help in front of a jury as well.

I grabbed a phone on my end and he grabbed one on his.

"How are you, Quint?"

"I've been better," I said. "But thanks so much for coming."

"You don't look the worse for wear," he said, and I reflexively looked down at my orange jumpsuit.

"If only you could look inside my brain."

"I'll be getting there shortly."

And he did. Gary spent the next fifteen minutes picking my brain about all that happened. He had a slight little smirk when I mentioned Bob Devane. I was happy to see he held him in the same low regard as I did.

Besides that, I didn't get many reactions from him. I had hoped he'd nod his head or give me a knowing look when I told him I was innocent. But that didn't happen.

"Not guilty," he corrected. "We don't need you to be innocent. We just have to prevent them from proving you're guilty."

"But I'm innocent."

"That's fine. And you can tell your mother and friends that, but in a court of law, you are not guilty."

I continued with my story and finished by describing being arrested in my apartment. It was then Gary Rogers's turn to speak.

"First the bad news," he said. "You don't have an alibi, do you?"

"No. Not from the time Cara dropped me off on Saturday night till Monday morning at work."

"No one in your apartment complex?"

"If so, they just saw me in passing. Not something they'd remember a few weeks later."

"It's still something we'll look into."

"Okay," I said.

"And it appears they have your DNA at the crime scene. In the house."

That couldn't be.

"No chance. I never set foot in that house."

"That may be true, but dollars to donuts they've found your DNA there. The last thing they asked you this morning was whether you were in the house. You say no and then they come back and arrest you that night. To me, that screams of them finding your DNA."

My mind was trying to process everything. "How is that even possible? Did the cops make a mistake?"

"I don't know, Quint."

"Something is going on here."

"Maybe. But if I'm being honest, it's not usually some outlandish conspiracy that gets people arrested."

"I'm telling you I never set foot in that house."

"Is there anyone who would want to frame you?"

"No," I said. "I'm a small-town newspaper reporter. What enemies have I made?"

My question was rhetorical, but Gary Rogers didn't take it that way.

"That's what I'm asking," he said.

"None. No enemies," I said. "But what about the mysterious notes?"

"Why would they try to frame you? You just said you have no enemies."

"I don't know."

"There's also a problem with bringing up the notes in front of the judge."

"Why's that?" I asked.

"It will then be public record, and assuming your employers are keeping track of your case, which I'm sure they will be, you'll undoubtedly be fired. Receiving notes about a murder case and not reporting them would lead your employers with no option."

"But we can't just not mention it," I said. "I care more about my freedom than my job."

"Remember, Quint, Monday is just the arraignment and bail hearing. It's not the trial. If it ever gets that far, then obviously we'll introduce every other potential suspect to the jury. But there is no reason to give information out too early. Even if I told the judge you'd received these mysterious letters, he's not going to throw out the murder charge. That I can promise you."

"The same with meeting Dennis McCarthy?"

"I hate to say it, Quint, but that does nothing, either."

"This is fucked!" I said.

It was the first real emotion I had shown.

"It's only going to get worse," Gary said.

I shook my head. "An innocent man charged with murder. Thought this only happened on T.V."

"It happens more than you think."

"You believe I'm innocent, don't you, Gary?"

"I do, Quint. But as I said earlier, to me you are not guilty. At a later point, we'll see the motive they're going to present, but a fight in a hospital room seems pretty weak to me. If they do, like I'm assuming, have your DNA in his house, that's going to be more problematic."

"I told you I never went into that house."

"It's not me you have to convince, Quint."

"I'm sorry, this is all too much," I said.

I bowed my head and suddenly realized something else.

"There's one thing I forgot to tell you. It's most likely unrelated to what's going on, but it involves my father."

Gary Rogers leaned forward. I told him of my father's note about Mason Anderson and everything I'd learned about their family, which admittedly wasn't much.

He listened to it all and looked at me in a very serious manner. "I can't tell whether you've got yourself mixed up in something deeply sinister or you've lost your mind and none of these things are connected."

"I can assure that I haven't lost my mind," I said. "Must be that other option you mentioned."

We shared wry smiles.

"Let's hope not," he said. "But just to be safe, we will be mentioning absolutely nothing about your father on Monday, either. There isn't anything connecting his death to the murder of Griff Bauer. And there's no reason to give this case more publicity than it will already have. We'll try to do the opposite."

"Okay," I said.

"There's nothing more I can do for now, Quint. We'll find out your bail amount on Monday. You've been a model citizen, but for a murder charge, I doubt they will go much less than $500,000. Which would mean paying $50,000 cash to a bail bondsman or putting up a million dollars in property, which always has to be double."

"I can't have my mother putting up her house," I said.

"Then you might be staying here awhile."

"Fuck!" I yelled.

"Do you have $50,000?"

"That's my entire life savings. And I'm including checking account, stocks, everything."

"I'll see what I can do come Monday."

I tried to calm down. "I'm sorry about the profanity."

"You don't have to apologize, Quint. You're in a terrible spot."

"What about your fee?" I finally got around to asking.

"You think I'm going to charge my best friend's son? Your pops would kick my ass," he said, looking toward the heavens as he did.

"Thanks for everything, Gary."

"See you Monday in court."

He knocked on the impenetrable glass that divided us, hoping to show some kinship with me. Once he was gone, a guard escorted me back to my cold, dark cell.

I somehow managed to fall asleep, but was woken in the early morning hours by a loud banging on my cell door.

"Let's go, Adler. You're being transferred."

I was escorted from my cell to a waiting bus and driven the thirty miles from the Oakland Police Department to the Santa Rita County Jail. I'd never felt more discouraged or humiliated in my entire life. It was the sum of a million terrible feelings all bottled into one.

I looked out at the cars on the freeway. The sun was rising and I imagined the commuters heading to work after just having left a loved one.

Not me. I was being transferred from one jail to another. With no wife or kids to come and see me. Just a heartsick mother somewhere out there.

What the hell had happened?

17.

Mercifully, Sunday managed to go fairly quickly. It's not a day I'd want to live over and over Groundhog Day-style, I can assure that, but it wasn't quite as bad as I expected.

Likely because I spent the entire time inside my own head. I tried not to think about where my worldly body was. Instead, I focused on all the things I had in my favor.

My situation was untenable, but my defense wouldn't be.

After all, I had innocence on my side.

Monday morning. I had to take a bus from Santa Rita Jail to the courthouse in Oakland. The two bus rides I'd taken were more demeaning than being in jail. They felt like a public flogging without the whip.

Upon arriving, I was led to a holding cell and given some alone time with Gary Rogers. I told him several of the things I'd remembered from the day before.

"I appreciate them all, Quint. But again, none of them matter today. The judge isn't going to drop the case. He or she will be loyal to the DA and the police. This is information we'll use if and when we go to trial."

I understood what he was saying, but it was terribly frustrating. I wanted to have the trial that day, so I could tell my side.

Gary left the holding cell with promises to see me soon.

Twenty minutes later, my handcuffs were removed and I was escorted to a courtroom. I'd worked a few trials over the years and the courtrooms were always smaller than you expect. The movies make courtrooms look like a rollicking good time, but that's rarely the case.

I looked around and saw a few reporters in the back. So much for going unseen.

Approximately fifteen defendants were there. And sadly, I assumed my case was the most infamous one.

Most turned out to be breaking and entering or DUIs. There was one carjacking. I started to get the feeling they were holding the most extreme charges for last. Mine.

I was proven correct, being the last defendant called. I stepped forward, flanked by Gary Rogers.

The judge, the Honorable Howard Easton, was a black man in his sixties, with bright red glasses which seemed out of place considering the seriousness of his job. My impression of him from watching the earlier defendants was that he was tough, but fair. Not that it would really matter. It was unlikely he'd be my trial judge if it ever went that far.

"Quint Adler, you are being charged with the murder of Griffin Bauer under section 187 of the California Penal Code. Mr. Brent Segal from the District Attorney's office will be representing the state. Mr. Segal."

Brent Segal was young, maybe thirty-five. He was handsome and sharply dressed. I'm sure juries loved him. Detective Kintner and Detective Marks sat behind him. I looked in their direction and they looked back at me. But no expressions were exchanged.

"Thank you, your honor. Mr. Adler is a reporter for the *Walnut Creek Times* and he was following the murder of Griff Bauer early on. He was at the crime scene within hours of the murder and continued to show up at another crime scene that the Oakland Police Department thought might be related. Detective Ray Kintner, a decorated member of the OPD, became a little suspicious. It seemed that Mr. Adler was a step ahead of the police. He even met with Tricia Knox before the police and she ended up dead less than a day later. Still, they had no proof he was involved. The OPD was recently notified that Mr. Adler got into a verbal argument with the deceased Mr. Bauer in Summit Hospital the night before his death. They brought this up to Mr. Adler, who denied it, although he did admit to being at the crime scene before the police and seeing the lifeless body of Mr. Bauer. He had not notified them of this before. Finally, they asked him if he was ever inside the house where Mr. Bauer was killed. He said no. Going back to the crime scene that afternoon, they found Mr. Adler's DNA at the crime scene, as well as fingerprints on something belonging to him. Detective Kintner and his partner, Detective Marks, felt this information along with the continued lies were enough to charge him with murder. They arrested him Saturday night."

The courtroom fell silent as they lay out their case against me. When he mentioned Tricia Knox, it astonished me. Where they going to try and pin that murder on me too? The way things were headed, it wouldn't have surprised me.

Brent Segal was professional, but you could tell he had a killer instinct. He talked as if I should unquestionably be locked up with the key thrown away forever.

"Is there anything you'd like to say, Mr. Rodgers?" Judge Easton asked.

Gary Rodgers took an unnecessary step forward. He had on a bright red tie that matched the color of the judge's glasses.

"This case is thinner than the fishing line I use to catch bluegills."

A few muffled laughs came from around the courtroom. Gary Rodgers commanded the room. Of that, there was no debate. And he wasn't done.

"And I think fishing is a fair analogy, considering that's what Detectives Kintner and Marks are doing, along with DA Segal. They know there isn't enough to charge my client with murder, but they figured they'd arrest him and see what happened. See if they'd get a bite, if you follow my analogy."

"It would be hard not to, Mr. Rodgers. But as you well know, you are not arguing your case today."

"No, I'm not. But I am arguing for minimal bail. Mr. Adler is a respected member of his community and has never been in trouble with the law. Not even a parking ticket, your honor."

"This is a murder charge. I'm not sure what you mean by minimal. But considering your client's lily-white past, I will not make his bail egregious. It will be set at $500,000. If you want to bail him, you can talk with the clerk."

"I think we have a different definition of egregious, your honor. But yes, we plan on bailing Mr. Adler," Gary Rodgers said.

That was news to me. It delighted me, obviously, but I hoped Rodgers hadn't gone to my mother behind my back. I wouldn't have allowed her to put up her house as collateral.

"We will reconvene in three weeks for the preliminary hearing," Judge Easton said.

This was no time to celebrate, but all things considered, things had gone as well as I could have hoped.

Brent Segal and the two detectives left the courtroom.

"Now let's get you out of here," Gary said.

"How? You didn't talk my mother into putting up her home, did you?"

"Nope. I put up my own," he said.

"You're kidding! You shouldn't have done that."

"I know," he said. "But I felt your father looking down at me and pushing me in that direction. Funny for a guy who doesn't believe in the afterlife."

I was floored. "How can I ever repay you?"

"We'll deal with that down the line. For now, let's get you out of this hell hole," he said.

A bailiff led me away, but it looked like my time in jail was coming to a close. For the time being, at least.

I was bailed a few hours later. It's a long process, and part of me wondered if there was going to be some glitch and I'd have to remain in jail. Luckily that didn't prove to be the case, and at 12:21 p.m. on Monday afternoon, I was released back into the general population.

Bad choice of words. The general population that didn't have bars surrounding them.

They gave me back the clothes I was wearing on Saturday night. In them, I walked out the front gate of the Oakland Courthouse. My phone hadn't been returned, but I had a lot of people I needed to call. Cara would be at the top of my list.

Gary Rodgers stood outside with my mother, who broke down in tears as soon as she saw me. I approached and gave her a huge hug. She kept sobbing to the point where I became concerned.

"It's going to be okay, Mom. I'm innocent. Just let it play out."

Gary mouthed the words *"Not guilty"* to me.

More tears from my mother.

"I've got the best lawyer around," I said and smiled at Gary.

It was nice to be able to smile. There likely wouldn't be an abundance of opportunities in the near future.

Finally, my mother stopped crying and hugged me tighter.

"I wanted to be here earlier and see you in court, but Cara called and we talked for a long time."

"I was just going to call her. How did she know?"

"Apparently an Oakland blogger said a suspect for the Bauer murder was arrested on Saturday night." My mom sighed. "They used your name."

My smile vanished. If Cara had found about it, surely at least one of my co-workers had, which meant Tom and Krissy would know.

"A blogger is the least of your concerns," Gary Rodgers said. "I saw KRON and KTVU with cameras outside."

Those were two of the most famous Bay Area news stations.

"Yeah, I saw them too," I said.

Gary Rodgers took a cell phone out of his pocket and handed it to me.

"Your phone is state's evidence now. Here's a cheap backup. I've texted you my number."

"Thank you, Gary."

"Only keep in touch with those people closest to you. You never know what might get back to the DA."

"My mother, you, and Cara. That's about all I can think of," I said.

"Don't tell Cara too much about the case. For that matter, try not to talk to anyone about the case."

"You have nothing to worry about with her, Gary. She's a fabulous young woman," my mother said.

"Then what's she doing with an old man like Quint?" Gary deadpanned.

My mother's puffy eyes were at odds with her newfound laughter.

"Hey, forty seems young to me," she said.

"Touché," Gary responded.

We stood there for a second and no one said anything.

"Come with me, Quint," my mother said. "I'm driving you home."

"Go catch up on your sleep. And come by my office tomorrow morning and we'll talk," Gary said.

I shook his hand vehemently. "Thanks for everything."

"You're welcome."

"Thanks for getting my baby out," my mother said.

And they hugged. It was a mutual admiration society, but for all the wrong reasons.

Gary started walking one way and my mother and I went another. As we approached her car, I used my new phone to log in to email, where I could check the text messages from my old phone.

There were over twenty emails of texts, but one caught my attention immediately. It was from Tom Butler.

I wish there was another way, Quint. I really do.

That was all that fit on the subject line, but the rest wasn't really necessary.

I knew I'd been fired.

18.

"Why are these police detectives such assholes?"

It wasn't like my mother to use profanity, but clearly, this was a special case. I had ignored Gary Rodgers's orders and spent most of the drive telling her all that had happened. I assumed he didn't mean blood relatives.

Luckily, my mother didn't focus on my ample missteps, instead focusing on the crime I didn't commit. Namely, murder.

"I think they jumped the gun," I said. "This case, and the other murders, are getting a lot of attention and they wanted to make an arrest. After what they'd seen as my lie about not being in the house, they jumped on it. A bit too early, obviously, since they arrested the wrong guy."

We were pulling up to my complex when she finally asked, "What about your job?"

"I've got a feeling it will be mutually beneficial if we take a break from each other."

"What do you mean?"

"Mom, they can hardly have their lead reporter be a suspect in the murders he's covering."

"But you're innocent."

"I am, but not in the eyes of the public. Yet."

"They'll find the truth out soon," my mother said.

"They will. In the meantime, don't watch too much news or go checking the internet. That's a rabbit hole you don't want to go down. I don't want you to see that stuff."

"No guarantees, but I'll try to avoid it," she said.

"That's all I can ask," I said. "You can drop me off right up here."

She did and gave me another huge hug. "Call me later today."

"I will," I said. "I've got a lot to deal with. And some sleep I need to catch up on."

"Of course. When you have time."

"I always have time for you, Mom."

I hugged her and walked into Avalon Walnut Creek, the place I'd been taken out of in handcuffs only two days previously.

Cara was beautiful, sweet, smart, sexy, and all the other superlatives you could throw at her, but she could also be a bulldog when she wanted. As she was in this case, telling me she was coming over. Not asking. Telling.

This had come literally seconds after I'd texted her my new number. And before I'd had a chance to take a nap.

Truth was, I looked forward to seeing her. Especially after being surrounded by inmates and prison guards for the last few days. I could use a woman's touch. In the figurative sense. Not that I couldn't use it in the literal sense, that just wasn't front and center in my mind.

I'd scrolled through all of my remaining emails and knew I'd have to address them at some point. The only one I texted back was Tom Butler.

I said: *I was just released, Tom. This is my new phone. I promise you with all my heart that I'm innocent of these charges. But I do understand why you can't have me working right now. Can we meet up and talk tomorrow?*

Less than a minute later, I received a follow-up text: *Sure, let's do that. But not at the Times or in public. I'm sure you understand why.*

Is that what I'd become? A social leper you couldn't be seen out with?

The weeks (or months) before the trial were going to be a lot more difficult than I'd prepared myself for.

I went against my own advice, googled myself, and instantly knew it was a mistake. Several articles said I'd been arraigned on the murder of Griffin Bauer. These included local outlets like KRON and KTVU, which ensured that I'd been on the T.V. news as well.

A loud knock at the door instantly sent me back to Saturday night when the cops came to arrest me. But then I heard that sweet, soft voice.

"It's me."

I opened the door to find Cara, in jean shorts and a lightweight white hoodie. We kissed for one second and hugged for ten.

I locked the door behind her and we made our way to the couch.

"How are you holding up?"

"I'm alright. More worried about my mother."

I told her about googling myself.

"You may not want to hear this, but I watched the news at noon today and they led with your arraignment."

"Great," I said sarcastically. "Lucky, she was already at the courthouse by then. I might text her and tell her not to watch the local evening news."

"I love your mother, Quint, but that's not what you should be worried about. They are charging you with murder! That should be your concern."

"I feel like a recorded message, but I didn't do this, Cara. You of all people know I'm not capable of something like this."

"Of course not. But the important thing is why the police think you did."

I respected Gary Rodgers and my life was in his hands, but I had to tell Cara about the case. I trusted her with all my being. Cara and my mother. That was it. Any friendships I had at the *Walnut Creek Times* had gone out the window.

I ran through most everything that had happened, leaving out the part about my father and my "meeting" with Dennis McCarthy. Those didn't seem pertinent to the Bauer murder. At least, not to why they charged me.

"That's a lot of information," Cara said. "If Rodgers is right and they have DNA from the house, how did it get there? And if you're assuming it was planted there after the fact, there wouldn't be any on the murder weapon, right?"

"Yeah, but that could be explained away. That I wiped down the hammer immediately after, but didn't have the time to get rid of all of my DNA."

"To me, saying this all started over a fight in the hospital sounds ridiculous. I saw you that night. You weren't agitated."

"Thanks. Now that I think of it, you may well be called as a witness."

"I'll say the defendant is handsome. And sexy."

I laughed. "Guess I've got nothing to worry about," I said.

She gave me a huge hug. "You're going to be okay."

"That's what I keep telling myself. But they wouldn't charge me if they thought they couldn't win."

"What else could they have? Did someone see you near his house?"

"Sadly, that's very possible."

"You're not going to like this, Quint. I'm obviously trying to spin a positive light on this, but maybe their case isn't as poor as you think. There's an argument at a hospital. One of the two arguers ends up dead. And the other guy was seen in the vicinity of the murder victim's house. And his DNA was found there. Plus, he repeatedly lied to the cops."

She was right.

"You're scaring me. But that's all predicated on there being an argument at the hospital. There wasn't."

"That means someone called the cops and lied. That makes it even scarier. If they lied about that, what else could they lie about?"

"I don't want to talk about this anymore," I said, getting more petrified by the moment. Was I really going to spend the rest of my life in jail for a crime I didn't commit?

"Okay," Cara said. "I just want you to know I'm here for you."

"Thanks," I said. "And I appreciate you coming by, but I think I need to be alone right now. I've slept terribly the last few days and just want to take a five-hour nap."

I thought she'd protest, but she knew this was important to me.

"I'll get out of here. Just know I'm a call away."

"I appreciate it, Cara. We'll see each other soon."

She left a few minutes later, but I couldn't shake her idea that someone out there might be lying about me.

How do you deny what you don't see coming?

When I woke up after a four-hour nap, the sun had already gone down. My own version of jet-lagged, I wasn't going to be falling asleep at a reasonable hour. So I did the unthinkable, something my lawyer would surely chastise me for. I decided to get back out there and continue my investigation.

I would swing by the house where Bauer was murdered. And stake out the Andersons' home. And do whatever the fuck else I could to exonerate myself. Cara had scared me about the strength of the DA's case. I convinced myself that I had to find my own evidence.

The irony that that's what got me in trouble in the first place was not lost on me.

On my way to Oakland, I found myself daydreaming.

I'd knock on the door of Clarence, the older black man I'd befriended, asking him if he'd seen anyone enter Griff Bauer's house in recent days. He'd tell me he saw a man, grew suspicious, and took a picture of him entering said house. I'd take Clarence's photo to the police, who would realize I'd been framed.

And the charges would be dropped.

But I knew this scenario wasn't going to happen. I'd been on the news, charged with murder. Asking questions around town would just get the police called, and I'd land back in jail. And they wouldn't give me bail this time around.

So I wouldn't be talking to Clarence.

In fact, I decided not to stop at Griff Bauer's house at all. There was nothing to be done there.

The Andersons' house was different. At least people lived there and maybe, just maybe, I'd see something.

But if I was truly trying to find evidence that exonerated me, what was I doing at the Andersons? Absolutely zero proof existed that my dad's suspicions had anything to do with the murders a few doors down. Or the murder of Griff Bauer.

This was all a wild goose chase.

I parked outside of the Andersons' house. I saw some movement inside, but no one came outside. After almost two hours, I got bored and drove back home.

A complete and total waste of time.

19.

"I've outlined a bit of a defense," Gary Rodgers said as I sat in his office.

He worked in the heart of San Francisco, on Market Street in a huge high-rise known as One Front Street. His office was home to three or four other lawyers, but it became readily apparent that Gary ran the show. His face occupied the majority of pictures on the walls.

I had been greeted by an older-than-expected secretary, who walked me through a legal library which must have had hundreds of books. Smart to place the library on the way back to Gary's office. Helped suggest they'd be prepared.

Gary was hanging up the phone right as I walked in, and in between thanking the secretary, he greeted me with the line about our defense.

"Before we get into it, is there any way I can meet with the two main detectives working the case?"

"I'd highly recommend against it, Quint."

"I understand. But is it possible?"

"It's more than possible. The two detectives would love to meet with you. But they'd be meeting you with a different goal in mind. They'd be looking to cross you up, to find something to use at trial. And considering you have already lied to them, it would be pretty easy to trip you up."

"I didn't lie about being inside of the house."

"I know. But you hadn't told them you went to the house on the morning he was killed. Amongst other half-truths. You start talking to them and remind them you were there that morning, then they go knocking on doors and find someone to testify, putting you at the crime scene around the time of the murder. Look, they are likely doing that anyway—it's their job, after all—but my point is, the more you talk to them, the more rope you will give them with which to hang you."

"I just wanted to explain my actions to Detective Kintner and tell him I didn't do this thing. We'd become friendly and I think he'd listen."

"He's no longer your friend, Quint. Right now, he's out there gathering evidence to put you away for life. You need to stop thinking of him as a friend."

I bowed my head, knowing I acted like a naive child. "You're right. It's just tough to sit here, doing nothing."

"Unfortunately, it's not till the trial that you'll get your chance to tell your side of the story. Which we should discuss now."

We spent the next hour talking about my defense, potential character witnesses, and things in my favor the police were not aware of.

Gary asked all the right questions and explained the legal ramifications thoroughly. I was blessed to have him on my side.

We finished, but as I turned to go, he called me back.

"You're not doing any investigating about your father, are you?"

"No," I lied.

"If the detectives see you by any of these crime scenes, they'll arrest you again. And I won't bail you out this time."

"Understood."

"Alright, Quint, thanks for stopping in. Let's talk later this week."

"I have one last question," I said. "When do we start getting discovery so we can see the case against me?"

"It doesn't always come in at once. We'll start receiving it once a trial date is set. Which should happen at the preliminary hearing in a few weeks. I'd suggest delaying the trial as long as we can, especially since you're out on bail, but we can talk about that as it gets closer."

"Got it. Thanks again for everything, Gary. I'll see you later this week."

Next on my list of things to do was to see Tom Butler. Ironically, the man I'd just brought up as a potential character witness was about to officially fire me.

Tom had invited me to come by his house. Considering the charges against me, I appreciated the offer. It must not have been easy.

Krissy and Tom lived on the top of a cul de sac in the hills of Walnut Creek, looking upon the downtown area. It was a beautiful home in one of the most desirable sections of the city. I'd been there many times over the years, but never, of course, under circumstances like these.

I parked by their mailbox and walked up the slight hill to their house. I'd been unsure if Krissy was going to be there as well, but they both stood there waiting as I approached.

"Hi, Krissy. Hi, Tom. I'm so sorry."

I shook Tom's hand and Krissy gave me a hug.

"Let's talk inside," Tom said.

We sat around their dining room table. I turned down anything to eat, but accepted a cup of coffee. They each had a mug in front of them as well.

"Before I give you the disappointed dad speech, why don't you tell me what you were thinking, Quint?"

While I'd told my mother and Cara most everything (leaving Dennis McCarthy and my father's unlikely connection out), I had to tread lighter with the Butlers. Tom and Detective Kintner were friends and I couldn't afford to say something that would incriminate me. So I decided to talk in generalities if possible.

"First off, guys, thanks for having me in your house. I know the charges against me sound terrible, but I'm innocent. I promise."

I kept saying innocent, even though I knew "*Not guilty*" was all that would matter if we went to trial.

"We believe you," Krissy said. Tom nodded in agreement.

"When I was in the hospital on my fortieth, I heard a scary conversation from the other hospital bed in the room. I could tell these guys were up to no good. So I took a picture of the man's address, with the idea of doing some investigating. You may not believe me, but this all started because I thought maybe I'd had a big case thrown in my lap. The address led me to the house the next morning, where I saw the dead body. I should have told the cops immediately, there's no question about it. But my own greed about potentially writing a signature article got the best of me."

I realized that I was probably already giving away too much information. I had to tone it back.

"And this one mistake led to more, because I didn't want to admit my initial error. But I promise you with all my heart, I didn't kill the guy. I just thought I'd stumbled on a big article for our paper and I went with it. I was wrong and went too far investigating it, but that's the only thing I'm guilty of."

"I believe you, Quint, but why do the cops think you did it?" Tom asked.

"I think I'm being framed."

"By who?"

I'd done enough talking, but I could safely answer that question.

"I have no idea," I said.

"As we've said, Tom and I believe you, Quint," Krissy said. "But you can understand why we can't have you working at the *Times* right now."

"Of course," I said. "But am I being fired?"

They looked at each other. Tom took the lead.

"Even if everything you told us is true, you still broke some serious journalistic codes. We take those very seriously, Quint. Because of that, we have to terminate your employment at the *Walnut Creek Times*."

They'd been so polite and told me they'd believed me. But their hands were tied and I couldn't blame them.

"I expected it," I said.

"It gets worse, Quint. We are going to have to cover your case and your trial. You worked for us for nine years, after all. We can't just pretend you didn't."

"It should make great theater. Having Greg or Crystal or Trent write about their ex-co-worker, the murder suspect."

"We don't have a choice. We'd be accused of journalistic dishonesty if we didn't cover it."

I lowered my head till it softly hit the table.

"I'm so sorry I put you in this spot. I have no doubt this is hard on you guys as well."

"We treat our employees like family, Quint. Especially you."

"You've always been more than fair."

"How's Cara taking this?" Krissy asked.

"She'll be fine. It's my mother I worry about."

They both sighed.

"We're so sorry, Quint," Krissy said.

"Yeah, me too. Imagine being an innocent man and worrying they'll send you away for life. Now I'm unemployed and my friends are dropping like flies."

"Put yourself in our shoes, Quint."

"I'm not blaming you two." I stood up. "I should go," I said.

They walked me to the door.

"Quint, when this is all over and you want to write a tell-all book, I know some publishers."

"Thanks, Tom," I said. "The way things are going I'll be writing it from jail."

"It may not feel like it right now, but we are on your side."

"I know you are. Tell everyone at work that I said I'm innocent."

"We will," Krissy said. "Take care of yourself."

I waved goodbye and started walking back down the hill to my waiting car. It was getting lonely on Team Quint.

20.

Although innocent of murder, I'd certainly been guilty of making bad decisions. And they continued. I parked outside of the Andersons' home the next two nights, hoping I'd see something that would be a game changer.

I didn't.

I shouldn't have been surprised. When people get off work and head home, they usually stay in for the night.

But staking the house out during the day would be incredibly risky. If someone saw me, grew suspicious, and the cops were called, I could kiss my freedom goodbye.

But I also couldn't just sit around, doing nothing. That wasn't my style.

So on Saturday, after my first non-working workweek in a long time, I drove back to the Andersons' early in the morning, determined to find something out. To my shock, about thirty minutes in, the dark "rape van" pulled out from the back of their house.

As the vehicle pulled out onto the street, I saw an older man behind the wheel. I had to assume it was Doug Anderson. No one in the passenger seat.

I'd followed the van for about ten minutes when it took an exit off of Interstate 80 and headed toward Golden Gate Fields, the local horse track.

I'd been several times over the years. It was a slowly decaying track, but still a lot of fun. The three strata of Golden Gate Fields were almost a microcosm of living in America. On the top level, the Turf Club, the fat cats, rich people who had done well in life, were catered too, waited on, and served good food and stiff drinks.

The middle level wasn't bad. A few miscreants, but the majority of people were decent, law-abiding people. The clothes weren't as nice as the Turf Club, but nothing to scoff at either.

The lowest level, which put you trackside, was full of degenerates and reprobates. Shirts were torn, cigarettes dangled, and betting two dollars on a race was on the high side.

I wouldn't want Cara walking by herself on the bottom level of Golden Gate Fields, let's put it that way.

Mr. Anderson drove his car up the hill that led to the racetrack. I followed from a distance. He passed by the bottom level, as I knew he would. He parked at the middle level, and I drove past him and parked as well. I got out of my car and watched as he entered the middle level but bypassed that as well, taking an elevator toward the Turf Club. I couldn't just follow him into the elevator, so I took the stairs up to the top after waiting a few minutes.

I pulled my hat down tighter around my head, hoping no one would identify me. I paid the exorbitant fee ($16) to get into the Turf Club and looked around for Mr. Anderson. I saw a buffet, a few bars, and huge windows that looked out over the Bay and Golden Gate Bridges. Hard to imagine that only a few hundred feet below, the troublemakers roamed trackside. It was like a different world

I found him. Mr. Anderson sat near the glass above the racetrack, overlooking the finish line. It had to be the most expensive table at the Turf Club.

It was hard for me to see the man he spoke too, because I couldn't risk getting too close. He wore a nice suit, that much was for sure. He appeared to be in his mid-fifties, and had a panache to him that I could sense even from far away.

I took out my phone and pretending to take a picture of the racetrack, instead snapping five quick pictures of the two of them. The gorgeous view looking down on the track was likely photographed many times every day. So I didn't think I was bringing attention to myself. I looked at my phone, and while the picture wasn't perfect, if you focused in on the other man, you could definitely see his face. I didn't recognize it.

I almost wanted to bet a race just to try and get even from the ridiculous entry fee, but I decided to leave well enough alone. I left the Turf Club and walked back to my car. And waited. It wasn't long until I saw Mr. Anderson approaching his. Less than fifteen minutes.

It made me even more suspicious. He'd gone to Golden Gate Fields and barely stayed long enough for one race. He wasn't going to the racetrack. He was meeting someone who just happened to be at the racetrack.

He drove his windowless van back onto Interstate 80 and I once more followed at a safe distance.

He turned off at the first exit, an industrial area that was really run down. He took a left, then a right, and pulled up to what looked like an abandoned warehouse. I couldn't pull in without being seen, so I remained on the street.

Mr. Anderson got out of his car and walked to a similar windowless van a few feet away, jumping into the passenger seat. I realized this meeting would take place out of my point of view.

However, I could still get some information out of it. I grabbed my phone and, zooming the picture to three times its usual size, took a photo of the other vehicle's license plate. I then took one of Mr. Anderson's for good measure.

Less than a minute later, Mr. Anderson left the truck and walked back toward his. He held two brick-size packages in his hand. Realistically, they could be anything, but if we were still at the track, and there were horses named Drug Bricks or Cash Bricks, I'd bet on both.

He was about to reverse in my direction, and he might start recognizing my car. I'd gained some hopefully valuable information without being spotted. I'd take the win.

I drove away from the abandoned warehouse and got back on the freeway, heading home to Walnut Creek.

At home. I turned on some quiet jazz music and started doing some thinking.

I'd become friendly with Tina Vetters, a thirtyish woman who worked at the DMV, and she helped me out from time to time when I needed to verify a license plate number. She would have been a perfect ally right now, but this was entirely different and I knew it.

No one would be willing to help out a suspected murderer, unless they wanted to land themselves in jail as well. I couldn't put anyone in that spot. So I didn't call Tina Vetters.

Finding out who the car was registered to would have to wait.

How about the man that Anderson met with? Could I ask Gary Rodgers if he recognized him? He'd probably chastise me to no end, but he was my attorney and I did have attorney/client privilege with him. That was a possibility. I could always go back to the track and ask someone on the staff, but that didn't seem all that bright. I'd be found out in no time.

I'd paid almost no mind to Dennis McCarthy's suggestion that I'd be chasing after my namesake. When I googled "Shark San Francisco" or

"Shark Bay Area" the only results I got were links to shark attacks or stories about the San Jose Sharks, the Bay Area's hockey team.

I had certainly put the man who had sent me letters on the back burner, but was that a mistake?

I started running through all that had happened. A man (it could have been a woman, but I doubted it) starts sending me letters. I'd assumed it's because I worked at the *Walnut Creek Times.* The goal was to get a reporter to investigate the man's enemies. Possibly write something negative about them. So me being a reporter would be more important than me being Quint Adler.

But what if he had targeted me intentionally? What if it wasn't just any reporter, but me that he was after? Is there any way he could have known that I'd been in the same room as Griff Bauer the night before his murder? Or that I'd been at his house the morning of his murder?

I thought back to that morning and one suspicious thing had happened. That car that stayed at the stop sign a few seconds too long before quickly driving off.

A pit rose in my stomach, but I continued brainstorming.

Even if that had been him, and this was a huge hypothetical, how would he know that I was a reporter? Or that I'd been twenty feet from Griff Bauer the night before?

I had no answers. The only thing I knew was that someone lied to the police and said I'd had an argument with Bauer at the hospital. But who? The anonymous secret admirer seemed as good a candidate as any.

Still, and I was now out in far left field, if all he wanted was for me to publish articles that would hurt Dennis McCarthy, why would he then make up a story about me fighting with Griff Bauer? Revenge for not publishing what he wanted? That sounded like a huge stretch.

My head hurt and I hadn't come to any conclusions. In fact, I'd just brought more questions into the equation.

I googled "Dennis McCarthy rival", "Dennis McCarthy fight", and "Dennis McCarthy Shark." Nothing of substance came up except the article by Vern Coughlin.

Could this all be something that Dennis McCarthy set up? That seemed highly unlikely as well. I didn't think he was anything but a fringe player in whatever the hell was going on.

And what the hell was going on?

All I knew was that I wouldn't figure it out lying on my bed.

My brain was officially on empty. The clock had barely ticked past noon, but I decided I needed a nap. Like everything else in my life, my sleeping patterns were fucked up too.

21.

"I'm talking to a dead man," Paddy Roark said to me.

I'd gone into full on fuck-it mode that morning and taken BART into San Francisco and an Uber to Boyle's Grocery Store. I found Roark and showed him the picture of the two men at Golden Gate Fields. He hadn't recognized Doug Anderson, but he'd done an obvious double take when I asked about the other man.

"I just want his name," I said. "And then you'll never hear from me again. You owe me that after basically kidnapping me."

"We did no such thing. If anything happened, someone just asked you to join him in a car. We have several witnesses."

"I didn't go to the police. I could have."

"And we appreciate that."

"Then tell me his name."

"You'd be dead in a week."

"If not, I might rot to death in prison. Believe me, I'll take my chances."

He took me by the arm and pulled me to the deep recesses of Boyle's. We passed by two flapping doors and he led me into a small office.

If I was ever going to get whacked, this was the time. And yet, oddly, I knew I could trust Paddy Roark.

"Sit down," he said.

It was an order, not an invitation. I sat.

He shut the door behind him and talked to someone on the phone just outside of the office. I couldn't distinguish a word, which I'm sure was his intention. My guess was that he was getting confirmation from the boss to talk to me. He reappeared two minutes later.

"If you ever mention a word of this to anyone, I will deny it."

"I'm not after you guys," I said.

Roark looked me up and down. "He's a former co-worker of ours. He was a complete and total maniac and we had to let him go. His name is Charles Zane."

"And people call him the Shark?"

"A very select few. Would you like to know how he got the name?"

I shifted in my chair. "Sure."

"One of his subordinates gave him the nickname and it got back to Zane. He asked his subordinate why and the man said it's because Zane prefers not be seen and only surfaces when he comes up to kill."

"Sharks kill below the surface all the time," I said.

"Not humans," Roark said.

"True," I said.

"Zane wasn't enamored with the nickname, so he and a few of his men took the subordinate far out in the ocean on one of Zane's boats. They threw chum in the water and waited until some sharks appeared. They then slowly started cutting off pieces of the man's body and throwing them in the water for the sharks to feast on. First, a toe. Then, an ear. Then a piece of flesh from his abdomen. All the time, throwing out fish too to keep the sharks interested. They did this for an hour, all while the subordinate remained alive, seeing his former body parts being eaten by sharks. When he'd been reduced to a man with four total toes, zero ears, no nose, and half a torso, they cut off his penis and fed that to the sharks. After they let him see that, they tossed him overboard and let the sharks do the rest. This is the type of man you are dealing with."

What scared me most of all, out of several things, was that the tough man in front of me—and there's no doubt that Paddy Roark was just that—was petrified of the man he described. You could see it in his eyes.

"You still have the chance to do nothing," Roark said. "That's what I'd advise. You've got a lot of balls, I'll give you that, but you have no chance against Charles Zane."

I walked out of the grocery store a few minutes later, trying not to imagine the scene Roark had described.

But there was no avoiding it. The imagery now rented space in my head forever.

Since I was already in San Francisco, I dropped by Gary Rodgers's law firm unannounced. I wasn't sure if he'd be there, but I chanced it anyway. And sure enough, he answered the door within seconds of me ringing it.

"Quint!" he exclaimed.

"Hi, Gary."

"I hope you didn't come all the way to San Francisco to see me. I'm not usually here on the weekends"

"I was out in the city and decided to pop in," I said, leaving it at that.

"It's good to see you, but there's nothing new. We're still a week away from our initial hearing and we'll know more then. But until that day, we just sit tight."

I nodded, but he seemed to be looking right through me.

"We are sitting tight, aren't we, Quint?" he said.

"Of course," I lied.

Would the lying ever end?

Of course I was tired of it, but I felt each little lie could be rationalized in its own way.

He eyed me suspiciously. "Because as I already I told you, bailing you out a second time is not an option."

"I understand, Gary. You've gone above and beyond for me. I appreciate it more than you know."

"Alright, if there's something you want to tell me, now is the time."

I pondered it. I really didn't have any friends I could talk to. I certainly wasn't going to tell my mother or Cara what I'd learned about Charles Zane. It would consume my mother and I didn't want to involve Cara.

But should I tell my attorney? He saw me contemplating it, which already partly gave me away.

"Quint…" he said, basically leading the witness.

I decided not to bring up Charles Zane. Not yet. But there was one thing I could ask.

"If I think a car has been tailing me and I took a picture of the license plate, how would I find out who it belonged to?"

He eyed me suspiciously a second time.

"I've made myself a few connections over the years," he said and his meaning was clear. "But obviously I can't do anything that aids or abets a client. So I'd need to know exactly how and why you got the license plate."

I needed to stall. "Let's talk about that on our next visit. The information is on my laptop anyway."

I'm not sure he believed me, but he was probably just fine dropping the subject as well.

"Again, our first court appearance is only a week away," he said. "There's really not a whole lot we can do before then.

"Alright. I'll keep laying low in the meantime."

And he eyed me suspiciously for a final time.

22.

I spent the next few days trying to investigate Charles Zane.

From behind my laptop.

Paddy Roark's story of severed body parts had me thinking that researching Zane was better done in the safety of my apartment. I valued my penis. And my nose. And my ears.

After feeding one of his subordinates to the sharks, he'd have no problem doing the same to a man named Quint. Probably enjoy the irony.

So I resisted my usual urge to get in the mix and became an armchair quarterback instead.

Unfortunately, there wasn't much to learn online. He truly did swim below the surface, I found nothing concrete. No bio. No address. No high school or college he attended. It's like he had been permanently scrubbed from the internet.

After realizing my online search for Zane had reached a dead end, I decided to spend my time more fruitfully. Using my bedroom wall, I built my own little storyboard listing the four murders, the addresses, the dates, the victims, and how I thought they might be related. It was a good four feet wide and three feet long. I drew a makeshift map of Oakland and put tacks at the location of each murder. I got a little choked up when I inserted one for Tricia Knox.

If I wasn't looking at life in prison, I probably would have enjoyed the work. It was my own little murder mystery. Sadly, the authorities thought I was involved. That made it just a tad less enjoyable. And by a tad, I meant a Grand Canyon-sized gap.

I started going through the evidence again.

I saw Doug Anderson talking to Charles Zane. Dennis McCarthy told me that Charles Zane was the one sending me the letters. A couple who lived two doors down from Anderson were killed. My father thought the Andersons' son might have been abused. I didn't know how it all fit, but there was something there. I felt more confident of that than ever.

I just hoped it was somehow all related to the murder of Griff Bauer. After all, I could have found out all I wanted on Anderson and Zane, but if it didn't lead to evidence exonerating me of Bauer's murder, it was all for naught.

As I looked at my wall for the tenth time that morning, I came to the realization that I couldn't just sit researching through the internet. My life was on the line. I had to get back in the game.

Not that I'd been sitting on the sideline for long…

23.

"Give me ten dollars on the four horse to win," I said.

At Golden Gate Fields, I was trying to blend in with the upper classes at the Turf Club. For the third day in a row. And the first one on which I'd seen Charles Zane. So I pretended I was actually there to bet the ponies, which led me to bet $10 on a horse named Promises Kept.

The many hours on the internet researching Charles Zane may not have amounted to much, but I did know one thing about him. He went to the horse track. And when I saw him talking to Doug Anderson, it was pretty obvious that Zane wasn't just there for the day. His table was in a prime location and I assumed he owned it.

I was pleasantly surprised to see a man who cuts off parts of people's bodies and feeds them to sharks. It was an odd reaction.

I got a better look at him this time. Although not as old, he had a similarly distinguished look to Dennis McCarthy. Only not as regal. His grittiness distinguished him. He looked like a tough guy. Someone you didn't fuck with. Which, if all I'd heard about him was true, was certainly the case.

Zane wore a form-fitting light blue suit with a fancy yellow tie. He stood shorter than I'd remembered, probably not more than 5'9". Somehow that made him more threatening. If a criminal rose high despite a diminutive stature, you could be sure he was tough as hell.

I didn't know if he knew me from Adam, but I certainly didn't want to find out. So I kept my distance and only looked in his direction a few seconds at a time. Like I'd done when Anderson was there, if a race was going on, I brought out my cell phone and took pictures of the horses on the track, being sure to get Zane and his friends in the foreground. On this day, two other men sat with him. Both were white, in their fifties or sixties, and rich. You could just tell. It oozed from them.

"I like Promises Kept also," the ticket seller said. "And 6-1 odds is juicy."

Her observation proved correct. Promises Kept won by two lengths at 6-1. Not that I saw the end of the race. I was too busy taking pictures of Charles Zane and his ultra-wealthy friends as the horses crossed the finish line.

But I'd take the win. The $60 paid for my entry into the Turf Club for the last few days with a little left over. For a man who was unemployed, every dollar counted. A job would have to wait until I was found innocent or the case was tossed out. I tried not to think about the third option.

Obviously, no company on earth would employ a man facing a murder charge and an impending trial. Not that I wanted to work anyway. Clearing my name was much higher on my list of things to do. I had enough money to last me while this whole terrible thing played out.

After Promises Kept won the seventh race, only two remained on the card. I decided to stay and see where the final races took Zane.

When they ended an hour later, Zane hugged his friends, all of them smiling. It appeared they had won. Probably a lot more than my measly $60. They started walking in my direction and I turned around so they wouldn't see me. When they approached the betting window, though, I couldn't stop myself. I walked closer.

"Nice win," the ticket seller said. "Seven thousand three hundred and twelve dollars."

Slightly more than my sixty bucks.

I heard her counting, "One thousand. Two thousand. Three thousand."

I decided what I had to do.

I went outside and got my car. I drove within thirty feet of where they valeted cars and waited for Charles Zane to show up. He didn't strike me as someone who self-parked.

Less than ten minutes later, he appeared, flanked by his two wealthy cohorts. The head valet gave them a nod and three of the drivers set off running in the direction of wherever they parked the cars. It was fascinating to see. The rich didn't even need a ticket to redeem their car. A look in the valet's direction was enough to ensure your car would be there shortly.

Which they were. Three beautiful cars arrived in unison: a convertible Benz, a Rolls Royce, and a mere Tesla. Zane got in the silver Rolls Royce and I crept a little closer. He drove off last of the three and I pulled out, following him from a safe distance.

A lot of traffic surrounded Golden Gate Fields, especially after the last race, so I knew he wouldn't spot me unless I did something obvious. And I wasn't too worried if a car pulled in front of us. It's not like there were that many Rolls Royces leaving the horse track. A lot more 1996 Honda Civics.

Zane made his way down the hill from the Turf Club. He entered Interstate 80, taking it toward downtown Oakland, then getting in the lane that took you to San Francisco. I continued following from a safe distance.

We made our way to the Bay Bridge, which was pretty backed up, making it easier to follow him without darting in and out of traffic. It took us thirty minutes to travel the eight miles of the bridge. I never got within two car lengths of Zane and I can't imagine he knew he was being tailed.

I instinctively looked over at Alcatraz as we drove across the bridge, as I'd done since moving to the Bay Area. Old habits die hard. I wished they'd reopen it for Charles Zane. Maybe he'd try to escape and the sharks would get him. That would be fitting.

He took a right on Fremont, the first exit after crossing the Bay Bridge. We were now on city streets and I had to be careful. One car drove between us. I couldn't let another car separate us further. On the freeway, you can just accelerate if necessary. If you're stuck at a red light on city streets, you are screwed.

It turned out I didn't have to follow much longer. After taking a left off of Fremont Street, Zane pulled onto Mission Street and entered Millennium Tower. The floors near the top of this famous apartment complex had a panoramic view of the Bay Area. I had no doubt in my mind that Zane's place was near the top. For all I knew, he owned an entire floor.

I couldn't follow in behind him, so I stayed on Mission Street as Zane pulled up to the front entrance. Stuck in traffic, I had time to watch him. He got out of his car, gave a fist pump to the valet driver, and walked through the front door of Millennium Tower.

Part of me was jealous. A life of valets, a place with views of bridges and bays and oceans, a car that cost infinitely more than my life savings.

But the other part of me was excited. Because I now knew where Charles Zane lived. And the time had come to rock the boat even more than I already had been.

24.

All in all, I was happy with how the day went. I got some pictures with Zane and his associates along with finding out where he lived. And most importantly, I was 99% sure he hadn't spotted me.

I spent the night writing. I felt more confident by the day that I was going to be acquitted. Or preferably, they'd drop the charges. I wasn't sure if I'd ever get my job back at the *Walnut Creek Times*, likely not, but I could write a fascinating essay on all that had happened. A lot more interesting than anything I'd written in the last nine years.

I reread the opening paragraph:

It all started with an innocent challenge. An old friend calling me out on my fortieth birthday. Wrestling in the middle of a bar. My head cracking into a glass case. Little did I know, these actions would land me in the same hospital room as a man who'd just killed two people. A man who'd be dead himself within hours. And I'd be thrown into a cat and mouse game with one of the worst criminals to ever call San Francisco home.

It wasn't perfect, but I liked the general tone. It sounded like a mystery, which was what my life had become.

I plugged my iPhone into my printer and made pictures of the men hanging with Charles Zane at Golden Gate Fields. I took the three best pictures and hung them on my storyboard, right below Charles Zane's name. I added a Post-it Note that read, *Associates? Co-conspirators?*

This wasn't a court of law. I didn't have to prove anything. Hanging with Charles Zane was enough for me to consider you suspicious and get you on my wall. I looked at it again. It was a mystery unfolding in real time and the most interesting case I'd ever worked. By far.

I took a picture of the collage. What I wanted to do more than anything was send it to Detective Ray Kintner. But I knew I couldn't. The photos of Zane and his cohorts were probably enough to get me re-arrested. I'd probably lose Gary Rodgers as an attorney as well, on account of him defending an idiot who wouldn't listen.

Couldn't argue with that.

My mind turned to the older lady who lived between Aubrey Durban and James Neil. Annie Ivers.

I recreated our conversation, trying to go through the whole thing. And I realized something didn't feel right. I remembered asking her if anything suspicious happened, and she replied, "Not on that Saturday" or something similar.

Aubrey and James's bodies weren't found till Monday. Would Annie know they had died on Saturday and not Sunday or early Monday? It's possible, but the way she'd adamantly said Saturday stuck with me.

She appeared to be an honest old lady. And maybe she was. But I had become a bit suspicious.

Time to go back and visit her. With a little more skepticism this time.

I didn't think she'd call the cops on me, but considering my face appeared on the news occasionally, I couldn't be sure. I was definitely taking a risk.

But I'd be knocking on her door, and soon. Of that, there was no doubt.

I put on some quiet jazz music to fall asleep, hoping it would calm down my wandering mind. It didn't work, and I was up till 2:00 a.m.

I woke up at 10:00 a.m. and the logical thing would have been to wait until later in the day, when the sun went down. Make it less likely that the Andersons would spot me at Annie's.

But I hadn't been logical in weeks. Why start now?

Arriving in Oakland, I knew I had two options, and neither one appealed to me. I'd tailed Doug Anderson and even though I didn't think he'd seen me, I didn't like having my car on his street. The alternative was parking far away and walking to Annie's house, out for anybody to see. That didn't sound much better.

I decided to split the difference, parking at the beginning of Oakland Avenue, where the Andersons would only see my car if they drove past. They couldn't see it from their home. I still had to walk a good two hundred yards to Annie's house, but I wouldn't be passing by the Andersons'.

I had brought a hat and pulled it down over my head. I wore tan cargo shorts, an LCD Soundsystem t-shirt, and flip-flops. Being unemployed did have one advantage. I could dress however the hell I wanted.

I pulled my hat tighter as I approached Annie's home. If one of the Andersons was peering in my direction, I planned to make it tough for them to see my face. A very good chance remained that they had no idea who I was, but I wasn't taking any chances.

On the third knock, Annie answered her front door. She wore sweats and a stained t-shirt. She didn't look very good.

"Hi, Annie, do you remember me?"

"Quinn, right?"

"Very close. Quint."

She walked a few steps out and immediately looked over toward the Andersons' home. It had to mean something.

"It's cold outside. Why don't you come in?" she said.

It wasn't cold. It was already seventy on what was going to be an eighty-plus day. She acted very suspiciously, but if it was just a ploy to get me out of the Andersons' line of sight, I was fine with it.

"Thanks," I said. No reason to rock the boat. Yet.

She brought me into her home. It wasn't a pleasant sight. Crap lined the floor everywhere. Clothes. Newspapers (uh-oh). Even a few plates and bowls.

She led me to the left, away from the messiest part. We passed by the kitchen and I took a quick peek to see dishes stacked high in the sink. A slight smell emanated from it.

We ended up in what appeared to be a family room. It was the cleanest area I'd seen, but I would hardly call it immaculate. It held a T.V., two recliners, and a rectangular coffee table. She sat in one recliner and pointed me to the second. It seemed odd not to have a couch in the room, but if she lived alone, I guess I could understand why.

"I'm sorry for the way the house looks," she said.

"I didn't even notice." I smiled.

I had to be as charismatic as possible. The newspapers spread around likely included an article about me. I had a hard time believing she didn't know the trouble I was in.

But why would she invite a murder suspect into her house?

"I've been a little down lately. And cleaning up the place just doesn't seem all that appealing."

"I'm not judging. You should see my apartment," I said, even though my place was spick and span.

"Thanks for understanding," she said.

"Of course."

I could tell she had something to tell me and we were just getting the small talk out of the way.

"I know all about you," she finally said.

It was hard to tell whether it was accusatory or sympathetic. Considering she'd invited me into her home, I leaned toward the latter.

"Been a rough few weeks," I said, trying to be vague in case, by some chance, she was talking about something different.

"And I think you're innocent."

There could be no misinterpreting that.

"I am," I said. "That's why I'm here."

"You think the murders of Griff Bauer and my neighbors are related?"

"I do."

Annie didn't seem like the gossiping type, but I had to watch what I said. I had to walk the line between getting information and trying not to give away much myself.

"Why do you think that?"

At this point, I had to give her at least something. "Don't repeat this, obviously, but some people view Griff Bauer as a suspect in the murders here."

She let out a sigh. "Then why would you kill him? Isn't his killer more likely someone affiliated with the murders here?"

"Want to be co-counsel in my case?"

Annie laughed quite loudly, and in that moment, I knew she was on my side. "Hopefully it never goes to trial. I haven't heard much about it lately. What's going on?"

This was certainly not where I thought this conversation was going, but I felt fine with it. I could tell she had something to tell me so I didn't mind this little song and dance we were doing.

"I appear back in court in a few days."

"I'll be rooting for you."

"Thanks," I said and knew this was the time. "Do you know anything that might help my defense?"

She squirmed a little in her chair. "Do you know the real reason my house is a mess? Because I'm a nervous wreck."

I didn't interrupt because I knew she was about to drop a bomb on me. I just hoped it was a big one.

"I've been contemplating going to the police," she continued. "But I'm scared."

I felt it was time to jump in. "What is it, Annie?"

"It wasn't just Aubrey and James. I saw something too."

My heart started beating faster. "What did you see?"

"You have to understand why I didn't go to the cops. My neighbors had been killed for seeing the same thing. I didn't want to join them."

"I understand completely," I said, and meant it.

Annie buried her face in her hands and started weeping. She gained control soon thereafter and looked directly at me. "I saw a young girl running in just her bra and panties out on the street. She looked scared."

"You're kidding me," I said, even though I knew she wasn't. Two people had been killed over what they saw, so I knew it had to be something major. And there was the suspicious "rape van." But still, hearing a young girl had been running away from something made it hit home. In the worst way.

"No. But I thought my eyes were at first. It was probably around 7:00 p.m., just starting to get dark. I was asleep. What can I say, I'm an old lady and sometimes I just fall asleep. I was woken up by the sound of screaming. I got out of bed and saw a young girl running on the street. I didn't turn on my lights, thank goodness. For all I know that saved my life. A few seconds later, Aubrey and James pulled up in their car as the woman passed my house, headed toward theirs. She flagged them down and I saw the three of them talking. At that point, I wasn't as worried. Maybe she was a friend of theirs? If not, I was sure they would do the right thing. There was nothing else I could do at that point, so I went back to sleep."

Annie grabbed a bottled water from the table near her and took a sip. "I didn't think much of it the next day, which was Sunday. I hadn't heard anything and I took that as good news. If I'd seen Aubrey or James I would have asked them. But I didn't see them. Then I woke up early Monday morning and there were cop cars, an ambulance, and the medical examiner's van outside and I knew it had something to do with Saturday night."

I went over the timeline in my head. Aubrey and James see the girl on Saturday night, the same night they are tortured and killed. Obviously, Anderson alerted someone immediately. Time was of the essence and if they called 9-1-1 right away, Anderson was fucked. So the Andersons likely call Griff Bauer to do the job and then he ends up in the hospital after crashing near their home. And by crashing near the murder site, Griff Bauer had become a liability. So he was killed.

Aubrey must have told Tricia what they'd seen before they were attacked on Saturday. Maybe she'd called her immediately, thinking she had to tell someone. Though just a guess, it made sense. And when the killers found out Tricia Knox knew, they had to do away with her.

Annie saw me trying to piece it all together. When I looked up, she had something else she wanted to say.

"Should I have gone to the police at that point? The obvious answer is yes. But I was sure Aubrey and James had been killed because of what they saw. Did I want to be next? No. So I kept my mouth shut. And it's why I lied when we first met."

Who was I to judge? I'd been less than truthful with the police as well. And my life hadn't been at risk. At least, not at first.

"You were in a no-win situation, Annie. No one can blame you for not doing anything. You're probably alive today because of it."

Her eyes began to water again.

"You didn't see the girl come from the Andersons house, though?" I asked.

"No, I just saw her out on the main street. But she was running from the direction of the Andersons'. And the yelling had woken me up. She had to have been fighting with someone."

"Have you ever seen anything suspicious coming from the Andersons'?"

"I've seen that stupid van leave abruptly at weird times of the night. Does that count?"

"Absolutely."

I suddenly regretted coming to Annie's during the daytime. I couldn't risk having the Andersons seeing me here. If my suspicions were correct, she'd be in grave danger. As would I, but I could live with that.

"Can I get your phone number, Annie? I think it might be better if we talk over the phone in the future."

She told me her cell number. "I have a house phone, but if I'm not here, the cell is a better option."

"I'm not going to tell the cops. I'll leave that up to you. But I might have my lawyer contact you over the phone. Would that be alright?"

"That would be fine," she said.

But her body language told a different story.

"Thanks for everything, Annie. I'm going to get out of here, but I don't want to walk out your front door. Do you have a door that opens on the opposite side of the Andersons' home?"

She nodded. I didn't have to explain my reasons why.

"Yeah. There's a door that opens from the kitchen. It heads toward Aubrey and James's home and the Andersons won't be able to see you."

"Good, I'll go that way."

We both stood up from our recliners and Annie instigated a long hug. Ironically, the man accused of murder was now doing the consoling.

"Everything is going to be okay," I said, not sure I truly believed it. But it sounded like the right thing to say.

"I hope you're right."

"I'll be in touch. In the meantime, I'd try to lay low and not interact with the Andersons if you can avoid it."

"Gladly," she said.

She grabbed my arm and led me to the kitchen, opening the door.

"Thank you for everything, Annie. This may just be the information that keeps me out of jail."

"You're welcome, Quint. I'm sorry I couldn't tell you earlier."

"Don't be. You had no choice. We'll talk soon," I said and walked out of her house.

25.

I woke up Monday, the day after my monumental meeting with Annie. I was due in court at 9:00 a.m. the next morning, but had to talk to Gary Rodgers first. I called him and rehashed what had happened at Golden Gate Fields as well as Annie's home.

He reprimanded me to no end, but I could tell part of him was impressed by the lengths I was going to.

"What does this all mean?" I asked as our conversation wound down.

"For tomorrow, it means nothing. They will not recant the murder charge no matter what I stand up and say. However, as far as the bigger picture goes, I would say that you've found yourself mixed up in something much bigger than yourself. It's becoming harder and harder to deny that," he said.

"I just wish I knew what this was all about. What was the underlying crime? I could draw conclusions about the girl running, but I couldn't be positive."

"I'm going to tell you this for the umpteenth time, Quint. You need to stop investigating this. While the case won't be tossed out tomorrow, we have many things in our favor once we get to trial."

"That's great news," I said.

"But it won't do us any good if you're dead."

I didn't respond at first and Gary's words just sat there in the air.

Finally, I said, "I promise I won't do anything before court tomorrow morning."

"It's a start."

And I stuck to my words. I remained in my apartment all day, readying myself for what was to come.

Less than twenty-four hours later, I put on a suit for the first time in several weeks. I chose a dark, conservative one, seeing no need to draw attention to myself as a defendant. I threw on a light blue tie, a brown belt, and some brown dress shoes. On any other occasion, I'd have been pretty excited about how I looked.

I left my apartment at 7:00 a.m., walking down the long hall and taking the elevator to underground parking. I could have taken BART into Oakland, but I didn't want to face the chance of anyone recognizing me, so I drove myself. I arrived a little after 8:00, which was fine as the hearing didn't start until 9:00.

I called Gary Rodgers and told him I was sitting outside the Hall of Justice. He told me he'd be arriving shortly and we could meet at a Starbucks across the street from the courthouse.

I got my half-caf Americano right as he walked in. He carried a huge leather briefcase and wore a dark blue suit and a yellow tie. He looked like your stereotypical lawyer with the briefcase, but I knew he was better than most. I was lucky to have him on my side. For the legal aspect, obviously, but he'd also put up his own home to bail me out. I could never repay him for that.

"Nervous?" he asked.

"I wouldn't be human if I wasn't," I said.

"Well, considering some of your recent actions, I wasn't quite sure you were human."

"It's hard for me to just sit and watch."

"You're lucky to have remained a free man."

"I know."

"We're going to have a huge sit-down soon, maybe tomorrow, and talk more about all that's happened. But today, let's just play it by the book."

"Alright," I said.

"They will call you up and you'll join me. The DA will lay out the evidence they have against you. They won't show their entire hand, but they will give enough so that the judge has no choice but to support the DA's decision. They will set a trial date. We can either ask for more time or ask to expedite it."

"I'd rather expedite it."

"How did I know you were going to say that?"

"I'm innocent. The sooner that people know that, the better."

"You're not guilty." He smiled. "Okay, we'll ask for a trial date sooner rather than later. And once that is done, the DA will turn over some of the discovery they have. More discovery will trickle in over the coming week or two, but we'll at least have a general idea of the case they have."

"Or don't have," I said.

Rodgers smiled timidly, as if he knew people who'd been convicted on less.

"Let's not get too cocky, Quint. They still likely have your DNA, a motive they believe, and no alibi on your end. So let's give the prosecution due respect."

"I understand. I'm not getting cocky. I just know I have the truth on my side."

"That will get you halfway there."

I was going to ask what he meant, but he rose from his seat. "Let's get to the courtroom before the press starts showing up," he said.

That sounded good to me. We walked across the street, toward the gray, impersonal six-story building. We walked through security and took the elevator to the third floor, where the Alameda County Superior Courthouse had their courtrooms.

Lawyers milled around with their clients, just waiting for the doors to their respective courtrooms to open. I noticed a few media members with their cameramen, and a few looks in my direction as I made my way toward Courtroom #23.

My mother and Cara on one of the benches. They stood up as they saw me.

My mother came over and gave me a hug. Spotting one of the cameramen take a picture as we hugged, I gave him a dirty look that surely wouldn't look good when published.

"How are you doing, honey?"

"I've got the truth on my side, Mom. I'm doing okay."

I was tired of saying the same thing, but I felt she needed to hear it.

She slid out of the way and let Cara through to give me a hug and a kiss on the cheek.

"You ready for this?" she asked.

"As ready as I'll ever be."

I hadn't told Cara or my mother the events of the last few days, trying to keep them out of the loop for obvious reasons. The case I'd become enmeshed in had already seen four people killed. The last thing I wanted to do was have my mother or Cara know things that would make them susceptible to retribution or silencing.

We made a few more minutes of small talk and then the doors to Courtroom 23 were opened. Everyone walked in, including some of the local media.

And then I caught sight of Tom Butler. He gave me a nod of the head and I responded in kind. I didn't know if he was there as a friend or a journalist.

It went quicker than I could have imagined. I was the second case called, maybe because the judge realized most of the people in the courtroom were there for me. Getting my case over early was one way of thinning out his courtroom.

The DA, Brent Segal, laid out the case against me, most of which I suspected.

A different judge from the day of my arraignment, this man was a younger white guy, probably within a few years of myself. I imagined there weren't that many forty-year-old judges out there. He seemed fair, but also acted as if he knew this was all a formality. Just as Gary Rodgers had said.

Gary spoke a few times, but mainly let the DA do his thing. *This is a time to learn about their case, not give away aspects of our defense.* I knew that's what he would have told me if I'd had time to ask.

The judge ruled the case had enough evidence to continue and set a trial date for mid-October, three months away.

"Your honor, if it pleases the court, I'd like to ask for an earlier date. My client is not guilty of these charges and would like the chance to prove that as quickly as possible and move on with his life."

The judge looked at the prosecution, namely the DA. "Is a mid-September date satisfactory?"

"That would be fine," Brent Segal said.

The judge looked down at his calendar. Would Monday, September 19th work for both parties?"

"Yes," Gary Rodgers said.

"Works for us," Brent Segal said.

"Then we will reconvene for trial in two months' time," the judge said.

I left the defendant's table and followed Gary Rodgers outside. Brent Segal came up a few seconds later.

"You want to come up to my office, Gary? I've got some discovery for you guys."

"Wait here," Gary said to me. "I'll be right back."

Gary returned a few minutes later with an associate, each carrying a box full of evidence against me. Or at least, what the prosecution viewed as such.

"You're coming with me to my office," Gary said. "Say goodbye to the women."

I gave my mom a big hug.

"I'll come by and see you in the next few days," I said. "Promise."

Cara was next.

"I'll give you a call tonight," I said.

"I'll come over if you feel like you need someone to talk to."

"Alright, no funny business talk," Gary Rodgers said, and we all got a much-needed laugh.

I said goodbye to the two women in my life and followed my attorney to his car.

We arrived at his law office and each took one of the boxes from his car. We carried them past his secretary and back to his office. He set them down on his desk.

He grabbed one of the smaller binders in the first box and handed it to me.

"This is a brief outline of their evidence. Read this," he said.

I grabbed it and started reading. Three minutes in, I felt I hit the mother lode.

Gary could tell.

"What is it?"

"I may have just blown a hole in the prosecution's case."

"How?" he asked.

The binder of potential evidence held a picture of a Starbucks cup. The discovery said it was found at the scene of the crime.

"I didn't have a cup of coffee with me the day I went to Griff Bauer's house. I can promise you it was planted."

"That's excellent. But remember, this is now a court of law, how do we prove that?"

I pointed at the writing on the cup.

"Yeah, so what?" Gary said.

"If I can find out whose writing that is, I can see if they worked that Sunday morning I went to Griff Bauer's. If they didn't, the Starbucks cup is useless."

"You're a genius, Quint. And more than useless, the cup shows you are being framed."

I took out my phone and took a picture of the picture.

"You leaving?" Gary asked.

"I'm going to the Starbucks by where I live. I was there the morning before I went to Griff Bauer's house."

"The absurdity of a coffee cup being found at the scene always baffled me," Gary said.

"It's at least plausible. But no one would ever bring a coffee cup he'd purchased on a different day. That's why finding out who worked that morning is so important."

"I like where this is headed, Quint."

"The officers were looking for anything that would convict me. They jumped the gun."

"You're right about that. Call me as soon as you find out," he said.

We looked at each other like we had a newfound lease on life.

"I will," I said.

I took an Uber to the courthouse, got my car, and drove back to my parking garage in Walnut Creek. I didn't go to my apartment, instead walking up to the Starbucks on street level.

Upon entering, I looked to see who was working. I knew some baristas better than others and would prefer talking to them.

Fatima was there, a woman in her early twenties who had aspirations of becoming an architect. She was a hard worker and I had no doubt she'd reach her dreams.

As I approached her, I realized I hadn't been here since being arraigned for murder. Avoiding being in public even included my favorite Starbucks. I had to assume they all knew my situation, but I didn't care. This was something that could prove my innocence.

"Hi, Fatima," I said, and I could tell by her reaction that she knew. She eyed me coldly, when she was usually very vibrant and cheerful.

"What do you need, Quint?"

"I need to talk to you. It's hugely important. Could I have two minutes of your time? We can talk at one of these tables."

She didn't seem too enthused by the idea, but said, "I'm on break soon. I'll come find you then."

"Thank you so much," I said.

I found a table in the corner and five minutes later, Fatima approached.

"If our manager saw you here, he'd probably ask you to leave," she said.

"I'm out of here after this."

"Fine. What did you want?"

I grabbed my phone and brought up the picture of the Starbucks cup. I focused in on the writing of "Quint" on the cup itself.

"Do you know whose writing that is?"

"It's Sarah's," she quickly said.

"You're sure?" I asked.

"Of course I'm sure. I've worked with her for a year."

I couldn't show my excitement, but it was building inside. I'd gone to this Starbucks enough to have a general feel for their schedules. I had to double-check with Fatima, however.

"And Sarah doesn't work weekends, does she?"

"No," Fatima said emphatically. "She always works four days during the week."

She could tell how important this was to me. "Does this show that you're innocent?" she asked.

"It goes a long way," I said.

"None of us thought you were capable of murder." Her affable personality had returned.

"This information means more than you know. I need one more favor. When will your manager be in? I need to verify that Sarah didn't work on Sunday, June 18th."

"Tony will be in tomorrow morning. But I can already assure you that she didn't."

I bowed my head and felt my eyes starting to tear up. I used all my power to stop them. This wasn't the time or place. But I felt like a five-hundred-pound boulder had just been removed from my shoulders.

"I'll come by early tomorrow. Thanks so much for your help, Fatima."

"This is surreal. I'm glad I could help."

She walked away, leaving me alone. It took a few minutes to gather my thoughts and then I got up to go.

As I passed by the counter where they set your drinks down, something hit me.

I remembered being at this Starbucks a few days before I was arrested. Turning around into a man behind me and almost knocking my drink into him. Finishing my coffee and setting it in the garbage. And then noticing a scratch on my wrist later that day.

Holy shit! Is that how they got my DNA? And the coffee cup?

I tried to think back. I oftentimes had a photographic memory, and the day in question was no different. I could quote my jokes with Laurel and Sarah exactly.

And Sarah had handed me my drink.

Which meant she'd likely written my name!

26.

Euphoric, I almost called Gary Rodgers from the Starbucks itself, but figured I could wait until I got up to my apartment. The charges would surely be dropped. They had a coffee cup that hadn't come from the Sunday on which Griff Bauer was killed. It was from a few weeks later.

I was going on the assumption that the man scratched me intentionally and picked up my cup once I left. My DNA and a "smoking gun": a coffee cup with my name on it. Only, it wasn't. It was now a smoking gun for my innocence.

From the Starbucks, I headed directly to Avalon Walnut Creek, beaming the whole way. I'd outthought the cops. I'd outsmarted the man who'd tried to frame me. I was going to be a free man and boy, did I have a story to tell.

Likely it wouldn't be for the *Walnut Creek Times*, but I'd already moved on from them. I'd broken a few journalistic codes, but after people read all I'd been through, I thought I'd be given a second chance.

Arriving at the downstairs lobby, I pressed the up button on the elevator. It soon arrived, empty. I stepped in and pressed the button for the fourth floor. I continued smiling, thinking my time as a murder suspect was nearing its end.

The elevator arrived at my floor and I got off, taking a right toward my apartment. Every time I walked down the hallway, I realized just how long it was. It felt like being stuck in the farthest room from a Vegas elevator. After a solid forty-five seconds, I arrived outside of my apartment.

I had put the key into the door when I heard a slight noise coming from inside of my apartment. Or was I just paranoid?

A knot in my stomach began to form. Something was wrong. I knew it.

My thoughts turned to Tricia Knox, who'd been killed in her apartment.

As quietly as I could, I removed the key from the lock. I tiptoed back down the hall, hoping like hell whoever was in there hadn't heard me.

After taking about thirty steps backward, I was all set to turn and run, when my door began to open. A tall man—I couldn't see much more—walked out. A gun hung at his side.

At this point, I whirled around and started running as fast as I possibly could. Everything was happening in slow motion, just as the cliché says. I made it another thirty feet before I heard a series of gunshots. I knew in that moment the extra-long hallway was going to be the end of me.

I tried to zig-zag within the narrow hallway, and it must have worked because the first set of shots missed me entirely. Instead, they ripped up the walls around me. I saw the door to the stairwell fifty feet ahead of me and I knew if I made it that far, I'd likely get away.

But I didn't make it that far. Another series of gunshots went off and I felt two bullets tear through me in rapid succession. At first, it just felt like a dull burn, but as I fell to the ground, the acute pain kicked in. And it was grotesque.

If I didn't get to the stairwell, twenty feet ahead of me, my life would certainly be ending. I'd be a sitting duck.

I heard some yelling and just hoped no innocent people would get shot. But I didn't hear anymore gunshots.

I started to get up.

I'd never felt more pain in my life, but I got to my feet and struggled to the stairwell, opened the door, and made my way inside. I assumed he was reloading, but possibly, hopefully, he'd run in the opposite direction to get away.

My life was now at the mercy of the shooter. If he kept coming my way, I'd never outrun him. I could barely walk.

I managed a few steps until I was standing over the stairs that led to the third floor. I couldn't just stand there or the shooter would look directly at me when he entered the stairwell.

I took the first step, and my feet gave out. I fell and started somersaulting down the stairs. Each thud sent a new, intense pain throughout my body. I got to the third-floor landing and the momentum took me into a wall. Pain made me pass out.

At some point, I came to and a tall man stood above me. I was in too much pain to recognize if he was the shooter. I said a quick prayer and everything went black a second time.

27.

It wasn't my turn to die. At least not yet.

Although it was close.

After I was found on the stairwell with bullet holes in my left shoulder and left flank, EMTs feared I might die. I was losing a lot of blood. Luckily, they got me to John Muir Medical Center, a few miles from my place, soon enough to save my life.

But it wasn't easy. I went through two surgeries to repair my left shoulder.

The bullet that penetrated my flank had been a through and through, meaning it entered and exited. Doctors told me I was very lucky, that it came within a few inches of hitting my heart, which would have immediately ended my life.

My mother received a call once I arrived at the hospital and was apparently by my bedside any time the doctors deemed it permissible. For the surgeries, she stayed on the hospital grounds, just waiting to hear how it went.

Cara was much the same. She spent most of her waking hours at the hospital, often looking after my mother. Obviously, I heard about all this after the fact, but if there had ever been a doubt as to how great a woman Cara was, there wasn't any longer. Not that I needed verification. I'd always known.

I was unconscious, or highly sedated, for the first twenty-four hours, and when I was finally weaned off the drugs, I awoke to the smiling faces of my mother and Cara. I was still a little loopy, but realized I was alive, which was a start.

My hospital room was sparse. The bed stood almost flush against the door and two small chairs sat beside it. My left shoulder and arm were raised in a massive sling. I also had a giant bandage covering the wound from the through and through.

I didn't have a roommate, but all the same I flashed back to my time sharing a hospital room with Griff Bauer. Which had started this all. I tried to forget about it.

Cara and my mother both gave me hugs as my eyelids fluttered. Their expressions showed how important this moment was, but I could tell they didn't want to overstimulate me. They were just happy to see me showing signs of life.

Pretty soon after coming to, I started remembering what happened. Hearing a noise from inside my apartment. Taking my key out. Backpedaling down the hall. Seeing someone emerge from my door. With a gun. Turning around and running. Being shot. Making it to the stairwell. Falling down the stairs. Everything going black.

And then I remembered the Starbucks cup. The drugs were wearing off and for all I knew, what I said next was my first coherent sentence.

"Mom. Cara. I need to talk to Gary Rodgers. Or a police officer."

"Now?"

"Yes," I said forcefully, although it still came out as a whisper.

"Gary was here yesterday, but he has court in San Francisco today."

"Then go grab me a cop," I said. "I'm sure there's a few around eagerly waiting to talk to me."

My mother came back a few minutes later with two police officers. With my left shoulder in the sling, it was painful to raise my head, so all I saw of the officers as they walked in was their uniforms. One was from Walnut Creek and the other from Oakland. As my eyes slowly made their way up, I realized the Oakland police officer was none other than Detective Ray Kintner.

"Look at what the cat dragged in," I said sarcastically.

Detective Kintner looked in my mother's direction. "You didn't tell him?" he asked.

"I was waiting until he was totally lucid."

"Tell me what?" I asked.

Ray Kintner took a step closer. "All charges against you have been dropped."

"But how?" I asked.

"Two women from Starbucks. I believe Fatima and Sarah were their names. When they found out you had been shot, they came to the hospital. They approached the first police officer they saw. Told him about the questions you asked them. This was relayed to me and I quickly understood that the coffee cup we'd found hadn't been bought on the day of Bauer's death. We realized we'd made a grave mistake. The coffee cup had obviously been planted. We had no case."

"Case?" I said.

"I phrased that poorly. We think you're innocent, Quint. There's no excuse, but we were under tremendous pressure to arrest someone. And we jumped the gun. There's no other way to look at it."

I wanted to be mad. Furious. Enraged. Apoplectic. This officer had helped make my life a living hell the last few months. But he seemed genuinely apologetic. That wasn't enough in and of itself, but I chose to focus on the positive aspect.

"I'm a free man?" I asked.

"You are. When the hospital releases you, you'll have no more problems with the law. Sure, there's still some small things we could follow through with, but nothing justifies what we charged you with. So we'll drop the lesser charges. You'll be receiving an apology from the entire Oakland Police Department. Myself most of all. I'm very sorry, Quint."

I looked at my mom, who smiled from ear to ear. To her it was a joyous moment and I didn't want to spoil it.

I extended my right hand and Ray Kintner took it in his.

"I apologize for everything," he said.

"Apology accepted," I said.

"This is Detective Steven Declan from the Walnut Creek Police Department."

I realized I knew Detective Declan as well. It's not like there were that many detectives in the WCPD and with me having written about crime for nine years, we had crossed paths.

"Hi, Quint. We've met a few times before."

"Quint Adler. Friends with every cop around," I said, bringing a brief moment of levity into the room.

"Are you up for answering a few questions?" he asked.

"Sure," I said.

Just then, a doctor walked in. She was around fifty and had a quick smile. It amazed me how most doctors were quick to smile after all the things they'd been burdened to see.

"Happy to see you're awake, Quint. I'm Doctor Abbot. I'm aware of your situation, but if you are too tired, you can answer these questions later."

"I just woke up. Might as well get them out of the way.

"If you insist," she said. "I'll come by a little later and explain everything we've done for you. Just so you know, your prognosis is great."

"Thanks so much, Doctor Abbot. I'll talk to you soon. But I've been trying to clear my name forever, so talking to these officers right now is actually a blessing."

Doctor Abbot smiled again. "Alright. I'll come see you soon," she said and walked out.

I responded to Detective Declan's questions for the next ten minutes, going over my trip to Annie's, my date in court, the visit to Starbucks, and finally what I remembered from being shot. Which, surprisingly, seemed to be just about everything. I described the man and Detective Declan asked if he could bring in a sketch artist at some point. I said yes.

At some point in our interview, as the pain in my shoulder began to increase, and I started looking forward to getting back to sleep, someone else walked into the room.

The detectives both took a step aside and I knew a bigwig had entered.

"Nice to meet you, Quint. My name is Devin Moore and I'm the federal agent in charge of the Charles Zane case."

Devin Moore cleared everyone from the room and I was stuck talking to him alone. He was in his late thirties and intense, with a military-type haircut. It may have been stereotypical of an FBI agent, but it was also the truth.

My shoulder was in acute pain, but once I heard the name Charles Zane, I knew I'd make it through it.

He told me before the interview commenced that he was aware of my previous lies and this was the time to come clean. That actually sounded nice. I'd told too many lies over the last several months and they'd taken their toll. While I could excuse each one individually, when I looked at them as a whole, I knew I'd been wrong.

"I know you're the victim here. I'm not trying to trip you up," he said.

So I told the truth. The whole, entire truth. Meeting with Paddy Roark. Talking to Dennis McCarthy. My dad's letter. Tailing Doug Anderson and Charles Zane. I didn't leave anything out.

It felt good, like I was cleansing my soul.

What didn't feel good was my shoulder. The pain became unbearable.

"Mr. Moore," I said, not sure how to address an FBI agent, "I can barely stay awake. My shoulder is killing me."

"Alright, I'll let you go to sleep, but there are still some questions I need to ask when you wake up."

I awoke several hours later, and after a few minutes alone with Doctor Abbot, Devin Moore came back into my hospital room.

"I'm sorry to bother you again, Quint, but this is a very important time in our investigation."

"Have you arrested Charles Zane?" I asked. "I'm sure he's behind this."

"How do you know that?" he asked.

"Because," I said and then paused. "Because it has to be."

Hardly a convincing argument.

"Why?"

I realized, even after all that had happened, I had nothing concrete on Charles Zane. Dennis McCarthy suspected he was sending me the letters. Doug Anderson met him at the horse track. What else exactly did I have?

"I don't know. I just assumed he had to be."

"I'm not saying you're wrong. In fact, we think you're right. Charles Zane is as dirty as they come. But we deal in evidence. We can't just arrest him on suspicion."

"Sadly, I think suspicion is all I got."

"Since you've found yourself immersed in all of this, I'll tell you something I probably shouldn't. We have some warrants being executed within the hour at Charles Zane and Doug Anderson's homes. Hopefully, that will secure us the evidence we need."

"Did I have any part in this?"

"A small part. Although we've been monitoring Zane for a few years now, so this predates you. He's a smart guy and doesn't leave any incriminating evidence. More so than anyone I've ever encountered in organized crime."

"Is that what Zane runs?" I asked.

"Yes, but not in the way you're probably thinking. He isn't some old-school Mafia don."

"So what is he?"

"He's a new school crime lord. Drugs, for the most part. There's millions upon millions to be made in prescription pills these days. We believe Zane has a virtual monopoly on them from Santa Cruz up to Sacramento. He also deals in prostitution. Sells black-market guns. And other terrible shit. The problem is he's got so many subordinates below him doing the dirty work, it's hard to pin back to him. And he's only getting worse. He's been trying to branch out to other illegal activities. Gambling, for example. And if he sent those letters encouraging you to investigate Dennis McCarthy, I'm sure that's why. He was trying to kneecap his opposition, who's been in the gambling business much longer. Dennis McCarthy is in his late sixties. Charles Zane is in his mid-fifties."

"Is Dennis McCarthy part of this investigation?"

"Only on the periphery, as it relates to you."

"Is he dangerous?"

"He's not in the same universe as Charles Zane. The only people with anything to fear from McCarthy are people who don't pay their gambling debts. And he's not a killer."

"Sounds you like have a soft spot for him."

"I'd take a hundred Dennis McCarthys over one Charles Zane. People gamble on their own accord. Opioids are helping to ruin our society."

"Agreed," I said.

"Anything else you wanted to ask?"

"I told you what the next-door neighbor, Annie, saw. Is child trafficking one of his crimes?"

"We don't believe so, but who knows at this point? We'll see what turns up after these searches are conducted. I think the vise around Charles Zane may finally be tightening."

"Had you ever heard my father's name mentioned before I brought him up?"

"No, but that doesn't mean your suspicions are wrong. Just never passed by our radar. After what you told me earlier this morning, I went and read the police report. The SFPD think it was a run of the mill mugging."

I closed my eyes. "There's nothing run of the mill about it for me," I said.

"I'm sorry, Quint. That's not what I meant."

I started thinking about my father and just how much I loved him. The idea that his murderer was still out there enjoying life infuriated me to no end.

"It's alright," I said.

"Your mother and girlfriend are waiting outside. I'm going to bring them back in."

He turned to go.

"Agent Moore?"

"Yes?"

"I know you're the FBI and keep things close to the vest, but if you could just come back and give me a thumbs up or thumbs down after you execute the warrants, I'd appreciate it. The man tried to have me killed, after all."

"I'll see what I can do, Quint."

"Thanks," I said.

My mother came in and I spent the next fifteen minutes with her. I told her I'd met with Doctor Abbot and I was going to be released in a few days.

She asked where I wanted to live. It hadn't even crossed my mind that I would be persona non grata at Avalon Walnut Creek. But I understood her point. Would you want to live next to someone who had been shot at less than a week earlier? I wouldn't. And I'm sure Avalon felt the same way.

They were certainly in a tough spot. If they allowed me to move back in and another shooting occurred, they'd be sued from here to kingdom come.

My mother also expressed concern about the killer coming back after me. She tried to be as delicate as possible, knowing that me being alive was the most important thing. But I could tell it weighed on her. I explained rationally that the last thing the killer wanted to do was come near me. I told her he was probably ten states away. I didn't buy it and neither did she, but at least it gave us a reason to change the subject.

I brought up my ideas on my father, but my mother quickly shot the idea down. The SFPD said he was mugged and that was enough for her.

While she wanted to keep talking about practical things like where I was going to live, I didn't. I asked her, in the most polite way possible, if she could send Cara in. Unoffended, my mother brought her in, telling me she'd wait in the lobby.

"We haven't had much alone time, have we?" I said.

Cara pulled a chair flush against my bed and held my right hand as I talked. My left hand and shoulder continued to be elevated in the massive sling.

Cara's hair was dirty and up in a bun. She had no makeup on. And she still looked beautiful.

"Probably be a little painful for you," she said.

I laughed. "Not the alone time I was talking about. That can wait."

She smiled. "Agreed. Let's get you healthy first. We'll have plenty of time to fool around once you're out."

I laughed and she squeezed my hand tighter. I couldn't wait to fool around with Cara.

"Do your parents know what happened?" I asked, deciding to change the subject. They lived in Marin County, just north of San Francisco.

"Quint, everyone within a hundred miles of the Bay Area knows what happened. The man accused of killing Griff Bauer is almost murdered and then the police drop the charges against him. It's big news."

"Probably a good thing I've been out of it the last few days."

"Gary Rodgers has been on the news a few times."

"Good for him. I hope he uses the publicity to his advantage. He put up his home for my bail, after all."

"He's talked about suing the Oakland Police Department for arresting you with such little evidence."

"He's not wrong," I said. "But I'm not sure I want to sue anybody."

"They made your life a living hell."

"They did. But I made some mistakes as well. I'm just hoping someone will allow me to be a writer again. I'd take that over some money in a lawsuit."

"No one has to allow you to be a writer. You can always write. And it doesn't have to be for some boring paper."

"How dare you!" I said, through a smile. "The *Walnut Creek Times* is second to none."

"Speaking of which, I saw Tom Butler at court the other day," Cara said.

"Yeah, so did I. Have they been covering my shooting?"

"In yesterday's edition, you were front and center."

"I guess I can't blame them. Too bad the best crime story to come around in years involves me. I'd have preferred writing it as opposed to being smack dab in the middle of it."

"Can you believe it's been less than two months since your birthday?"

"Feels like a lifetime," I said.

I adjusted my body and let out a scream.

"Are you alright?" Cara asked.

"If I move the wrong way, I get this shooting pain through my shoulder. It's agonizing."

"Do you want to go back to sleep?"

I hadn't been awake long, but the pain was getting unbearable. Again. "That's probably a good idea," I said.

"I love you, Quint."

"I love you too, Cara. I've been an idiot at times over the years, but I've always loved you."

"I know. Now get some rest. I'm looking forward to our time together outside of the hospital."

She said it in a very seductive voice.

"You're going to have to do all the work," I said. "My shoulder is useless."

Cara managed to laugh. She kissed me on the forehead and walked out of the room. I was asleep within a few minutes.

Agent Moore returned to my room that night.

"You wanted an update," he said.

"Yes."

"You know this is only for our ears. No one else's."

"I understand," I said.

Moore paused, giving weight to what he was going to say next.

"I don't think you have to worry about Charles Zane anymore."

I'd seen the Stones live. And Radiohead. I'd listened to Miles Davis's Kind of Blue on vinyl. And yet, these ears had never heard anything more beautiful than the sentence just uttered.

"Fantastic," I said, unable to come up with a better adjective. "What did the warrants turn up?"

"Those are being executed as we speak. But we got one of his associates to admit on a wiretap that he tried to frame you for murder."

I lay there dumbfounded. It was all coming together.

"There's more," he continued. "The associate admitted that Zane became concerned after you followed him from the racetrack. And that's when he put the hit out on you."

So he had seen me. I wanted to kick myself for being so stupid.

"And there's one last thing," Moore said. "This one is going to sting. A lot."

"I can take it," I said.

"The associate pretty much admitted that Zane had your father killed."

Although I had my suspicions, I had never gathered any concrete evidence. So for an FBI agent to tell me that my father had been murdered still came as a shock.

I wanted to say something. Anything. But nothing would come out. My father, my hero, hadn't died in a random mugging. He'd been murdered.

"I can tell this is an emotional moment for you," Moore said. "I'll let you be and come visit you later."

"Thanks," was all I could muster.

"Charles Zane is as good as over. I'm going to get him for all those he's done wrong by. Including you. And your father. He's going to be spending the rest of his life in jail. He's on borrowed time, he just doesn't know it yet."

Lying in a hospital room, suffering from two bullet wounds, I'd never been more content. I thought of Tricia Knox. I thought of Aubrey Durban and James Neil. I even managed to think of Griff Bauer for a moment.

Someone could have handed me a million dollars and it wouldn't have made me as happy as what Agent Moore had just told me.

But he was wrong.

PART III: OUT TO SEA

28.

(one month later)

And when I say he was wrong, Agent Moore was wrong about everything. Charles Zane wasn't charged with my father's murder. Or my attempted murder. Or even arrested. He was as free as I. Actually, technically he was freer, because the Oakland Police Department hadn't gotten around to dropping their final charge against me: withholding information in the course of a criminal case. It was in the process of being dropped, but the fact that I had a charge pending while Charles Zane walked the streets free drove me up the fucking wall.

I'd been released after a total of five days in the hospital, three days after Agent Moore told me that Charles Zane was on borrowed time. But it didn't turn out that way.

Moore had made many assumptions, most of all that someone would turn on Charles Zane. While they did have a recording of one of his subordinates saying he'd murdered my father and attempted to murder me, the subordinate lied when questioned. He claimed he was joking and the FBI had no firsthand evidence of anything he'd said.

And while they still believed he had told the truth, they couldn't prove any of it. A case built on hearsay was no case at all.

The warrants proved to be a bust as well. Nothing out of the ordinary was found at Doug Anderson's home. Or the three homes that Charles Zane owned, including the high-rise I'd followed him to. His computers turned up nothing. And none of his subordinates who were arrested said a single word to the police. They asked for lawyers and then kept their mouths shut.

The FBI had been outfoxed.

After I got out of the hospital, Agent Moore wouldn't return a single call of mine, so I heard all of this through Gary Rodgers. He was a man with a million connections, and that included knowing someone working the Charles Zane case. I'd almost wished he didn't. The updates were always so discouraging, like someone punching me in the gut.

Adding insult to injury (literally), they didn't have any suspects in my attempted murder. They had scrubbed my apartment and couldn't find any DNA or prints. Ironic that they found my prints at a murder scene when I wasn't even there, yet couldn't find any when someone tried to murder me.

They tested the shell casings and the bullets fired at me, to no avail. They assumed the gun was bought on the black market. Which, according to Agent Moore, was one of Charles Zane's illegal business activities. They also believed the shooter used gloves when entering my apartment, as well as when he escaped from the complex. A few people said they saw a tall man hurriedly leaving Avalon Walnut Creek around the time of the shooting and the local police hired a sketch artist. The resulting picture looked like a stick figure I could have drawn in fourth grade. I knew it was worthless.

As for myself, I was on the mend and improving every day. My mother and Cara had both offered me a place to stay. I told them I wanted to move back into my old apartment. I acted a bit hypocritically in this regard. I tried to argue with Avalon Walnut Creek that there was no threat and I should be allowed to move back in. In turn, I told my mother and Cara it was just too dangerous for me to move in with them. I tried to have it both ways.

Avalon Walnut Creek wasn't having it, telling me "it wouldn't be conducive to a friendly atmosphere" if I remained. Whatever the fuck that meant.

It's like I was a victim all over again. I'd been charged with a murder I didn't commit and now I was being uprooted because someone had tried to kill me. I know life isn't fair, but this was beyond the pale.

I found a singular apartment a few blocks from Avalon Walnut Creek. I signed a six-month lease and hired a moving company to move everything for me. My shoulder was healing, but I still had a very limited range of motion, and I couldn't lift anything over about twenty pounds. I'm sure Avalon Walnut Creek was plenty happy not to have me on site when my furniture was moved.

Both my mother and Cara continued to worry that the man who tried to kill me might try again. I wasn't that worried. When you have information that the police don't have yet, you are a threat, and thus a target. Once you go to the police, there really is no point in killing you.

It's not like I could testify to any firsthand evidence I had. Just suspicions. Of which I had many.

So I settled back into day-to-day life. I was still on meds for the shoulder, but they got less and less powerful. I hated the groggy feeling the powerful ones gave me and I told my doctors I preferred dealing with a little pain, which continued to subside.

Of everything going on, what drew my utmost ire was that Charles Zane had my father killed. I, like the FBI, felt sure what the subordinate said on their wiretap was the truth. Just because they couldn't prove it didn't change anything.

I wanted the man dead. Call it an eye for an eye or vigilante justice, but if I saw Charles Zane on the street, I'd have bludgeoned him to death. And that was just for my father. The fact he'd tried to have me killed was almost secondary.

And it was becoming all consuming.

So while I recovered, the case was never far from my mind. Some of the loose threads had been tied together. Maybe not in a court of law, but by what Gary Rodgers had been able to find out.

Griff Bauer was low on the food chain, but appeared to have worked for Charles Zane. Likely as a drug dealer. They assumed Bauer was commissioned to carry out the murder and torture of Aubrey Durban and James Neil after they saw the young woman running away. When Bauer got into a car accident after finishing the job and was taken to the hospital, he became a liability. And was killed the next morning. When Bauer tortured Aubrey and James, he likely found out that Aubrey had told Tricia Knox about what they had seen. However, Tricia Knox was on vacation at the time, so she wasn't killed until several days later. And finally, when they saw me poking around and then following Zane home from the horse races, I became a liability and they tried to take me out.

That covered all of the murders and attempted murders. Except for one. My father's.

All I had to connect him was the note he'd written about Mason Anderson. Could my father have gone to the Andersons' and seen something he wasn't supposed to? Possible. Could my father have brought up the potential child abuse to Mason Anderson, who relayed it to his father and they decided to do something? Also possible, but I thought unlikely.

I understood most of the case, but my father's involvement remained the missing link. And one more question was of consequential importance as well. What had the young woman been running from? Agent Moore didn't think Zane trafficked women, but what did that mean? It's not like the agent had a good track record with me after nothing happened to my would-be killer.

Whatever happened, Charles Zane and Doug Anderson were good at covering their tracks. Gary Rodgers held the opinion that once I was admitted to the hospital, they started scrubbing their computers and cleaning their homes of any potential incriminating evidence. They knew I'd share my suspicions with the police and warrants would likely be procured.

It made sense. How else could the FBI find nothing?

It was frustrating beyond words.

One thing that survived my attempted murder was the collage/storyboard I'd had in my room. The wannabe killer likely never made it to the room, waiting closer to my front door. Otherwise he probably would have torn it all down, considering its many references to Charles Zane.

I asked the movers to keep the storyboard in mint condition. And they did. Once I received it, I put it up in my new apartment. On the wall, directly across from my bed, so I'd see it every night as I went to sleep.

An attempt on my life had done nothing to stop me from wanting to find out the whole truth. I no longer trusted the FBI or my local law enforcement. All they had gotten me was a bullshit murder charge and my hopes up that they'd arrest Charles Zane. Which hadn't happened.

Stop me if you've heard this one before, but it was time to take things into my own hands.

Once again.

29.

"A cockroach has fucking nothing on you," Paddy Roark said.

I took it as a compliment. And he said it with a glint in his eye, as if, after all I'd been through, I now had his respect.

Roark had whisked me into the back office as soon as he'd seen me at Boyle's Grocery Store again. I had gotten the big Transformer-looking instrument off of my shoulder a few days before. I still had a sleek, padded brace that hid under my clothes, but for the most part I looked normal. The gunshot to my flank had healed nicely, despite the huge scar it left in its wake. So far, only Cara had the "pleasure" of seeing it.

"You've got a soft spot for me," I said to Roark.

His smile gave him away.

"People who shake the tree of Charles Zane usually don't last this long."

"My father was one of those who didn't last," I said.

I filled Paddy Roark in on what Agent Moore had told me.

I didn't have many other people to talk to. My mother didn't want to hear about my father. She preferred to think he died in a mugging. I intentionally left Cara in the dark for her own peace of mind. The FBI was done with me and even though I had accepted Ray Kintner's apology, I could never trust him again.

So here I was talking to Paddy Roark, a criminal like Charles Zane. No, he wasn't on the same level as Zane, but he wasn't a saint either. But I decided to befriend him. Like the old saying goes, the enemy of my enemy is my friend.

That's how I viewed Paddy Roark, and by extension, Dennis McCarthy.

Plus, and I know this may sound weird, I had a certain camaraderie with Roark and McCarthy. I trusted them. In the brief time I'd spent with both, I felt a mutual respect. And they worked in the gambling business, not the drug business. As I said, not saints, but nothing approaching the evil of Charles Zane.

So I dealt with them.

"I'm sorry about your father. I really am. But what do you think we can do?" Paddy Roark asked.

"You can tell me where Zane is vulnerable."

"I'm not sure what you mean."

"An old ally who wants revenge. An ex-wife. A family member of someone he killed. I'm ready to shake the tree harder than it's already been shook."

Paddy Roark stroked his non-existent goatee. I guessed that meant he was thinking.

"Or you could go to more extreme measures."

"I'm listening," I said.

"Can you come back tomorrow?"

"Why?"

"Because I've got an idea, but I have to clear it with the boss man."

"I'll be here," I said.

I returned the next day, Tuesday. As had become protocol, I was escorted to the back of Boyle's by Paddy Roark. This time, when we got back to his little office there a third man waited for us. Dennis McCarthy.

I took a seat. As did Roark. Dennis McCarthy remained standing.

"Paddy informed me that Charles Zane killed your father and law enforcement are doing nothing about it."

"That's right," I said.

"And you want to do something yourself?"

"Right again."

"I think we might be willing to help you out. But, and I shouldn't have to say this, if you ever went to law enforcement, we'd never deal with you again. And deny everything."

"I would never. I'm done with them."

"That's what I figured. Just making sure."

No one said anything for ten seconds.

"So what have you got?" I finally asked.

"Have you heard of the Cliff House?"

"Yeah, the restaurant on the water out by Ocean Beach."

"Correct. Well, Charles Zane eats there every Friday for lunch. And we know one of the valets. I don't think our friend would be above putting a recording device in Mr. Zane's car."

I hadn't expected something so big. A potential game changer.

"How does this work?" I asked.

"We'll give you a cell phone and stream the audio through that."

"This is more than I ever expected," I said.

"Just so you know, if he finds out about this, your two little bullet wounds will feel like a Swedish massage."

My mind wandered to Charles Zane feeding his employee's body parts to the sharks.

And yet, I said, "I'm in."

"Alright, I'll talk to my guy. Come by Friday afternoon and I'll let you know if it was a success."

"Thank you so much, Mr. McCarthy."

"Call me Dennis, since we're officially friends now. But don't be thanking me. We may come to regret this. All of us. I told you that Charles Zane used to work for me, right?"

"He did," I said, nodding to Roark.

"Well, he's the type of guy who wanted to do the collections. He enjoyed roughing people up if it ever came to that. Me, I'm a businessman at heart. I hated that aspect. But Zane enjoyed that shit. I think he really would have broken kneecaps if he could have. He was too much of a wild card, and that's why we let him go. And he went off on his own."

"From what I've gathered, he's used your business playbook. Surrounding himself with people he trusts, having subordinates way down the totem pole."

Dennis McCarthy stared at me and I knew I had crossed a line.

"Maybe it's better we don't discuss things of this nature. You got that, Quint?"

"I'm sorry. Of course not," I said.

"Just be vigilant. You are fully on Zane's radar and he'd like nothing more than to succeed in killing you this time."

His warning sat there in the air.

"Well, I guess I'll see you Friday," I said, not sure what else to say.

"See you then, Quint. Not a word to anyone."

"Of course not."

I shook their hands and walked out of Boyle's Grocery Store.

The next three days sailed by. I had my daily phone calls with my mother, which had become less to talk and more for her to make sure I was unharmed. And on Wednesday night, Cara came over and we Netflix'd and Chilled. And chilled. And chilled.

If Cara had any misgivings about hanging out with me, she didn't express them.

Friday afternoon came and I drove into the city. My new place was only three blocks from a BART station, but I'd become somewhat of a local celebrity these days, and I didn't like the attention. I preferred to drive myself than deal with the potential "fans" that might see me on BART.

I made my way into Boyle's for the third time in five days, heading right toward the back. There were cameras littered throughout the store and Paddy Roark must have seen me walk in, because he appeared almost immediately. He didn't have to say a word and I followed him to the office where I was now a regular.

This time, Dennis McCarthy was seated and I joined him. Paddy Roark took the chair behind the desk, making him look like the boss. But that was Dennis McCarthy's position no matter what seat he was in.

"Our friend did what we asked of him," he said, getting right to the point.

"That's great news," I said.

"Yeah." McCarthy sighed, signaling he wasn't so sure.

"We've gotten you a burner cell phone," Paddy Roark said. "Never use this phone for anything else."

"I won't."

He handed me a beat-up iPhone. "You see here on the main screen where it says CZaudio?"

"I do."

"When you click on that, you'll hear the audio from Charles Zane's car."

"Wow, you guys made that simple."

"We've got some young people to aid us in technical support when necessary," McCarthy said.

"Let's see if we hear anything." Paddy Roark pressed the CZaudio button.

No sound came from the phone.

"He's not in his car right now," Roark said. "Even if he's driving, but not talking, you'd still hear the noise of the car moving."

"I understand," I said, thinking the less I spoke the better.

They had gone out on a limb for me, surely for their own selfish incentives as well, and I didn't want to give them any reasons to reconsider the arrangement.

"This is an iPhone 7, so go get a charger if you don't have one. Wouldn't want you to run out of juice when listening to something important."

"I'll get one today."

Dennis McCarthy stood up. "And this is where we say goodbye, Quint. We feel for all you've been through and have decided to help, but we don't need you coming around all the time. You just never know if Charles Zane is watching."

"I'm grateful for all you've done," I said.

"We hope this helps you get what you're looking for. Remember, no cops and no friends. This is just for you. It's not like it would be admissible in court."

"After all that's happened, I don't put much stock in cops or courts."

Roark and McCarthy smiled at me.

"Thank you, guys. For everything."

"We have our personal reasons for wanting to see Charles Zane go down. But you're welcome," Dennis McCarthy said.

"Hopefully my body isn't turned into shark food," I said, hoping to lighten the moment.

It didn't work. They both stared at me like I had a death wish.

Maybe I did.

30.

As I listened to the audio from Charles Zane's car, which produced nothing fruitful over the first few days, I thought about my father often. All the great teaching moments he'd given me over the course of my life. And his.

One stood out.

In 1990 I was ten years old, playing for a traveling soccer team. I had been the best player on my local team, but I was average, at best, on this new team that took all the best players from in and around Seattle.

I didn't get much playing time and it affected my attitude. I was *being a snot,* as my mother used to say. Complaining. Sulking. Focusing on the negative.

At the time, my favorite sports team in Seattle was the SuperSonics, the local NBA team. They had just drafted Gary Payton, who everyone immediately knew was going to be a generational player. I watched the Sonics every night and Payton quickly became my favorite.

He grew up in Oakland and was its hometown hero. Little did I know at the time, my life would eventually lead there.

My father decided to ask a friend for a favor. One of the assistant coaches for the SuperSonics had a son in my father's class and the two men had become friendly. One day, my father brought up to him that I wasn't handing my soccer experience very well and asked if there was any chance he could introduce me to one of the Sonics.

A week later, my father surprised me and said we were going to the SuperSonics game that night. We left an hour and half before the game started and I couldn't understand why we'd gotten such an early start.

I soon found out.

As the players warmed up for the upcoming game, my father walked me down to the court. He saw his friend, the assistant coach, who brought Gary Payton—GARY PAYTON!—over to meet me.

"Hi, Quint!"

"Hi, Mr. Payton," I said, dazzled by the moment.

"I heard you're having a tough time with your traveling team. I'm going to tell you about a guy who went to college at Oregon State. He got bypassed by all the big teams. North Carolina didn't come calling. Or Kentucky. Or Indiana. So he had to go to a little small school and work his butt off. But he didn't give up. He kept practicing and trying harder than the other guys. Because he knew in the end, his work ethic would pay off and he'd be better than those guys at the big schools. And it has. That little guy was me and now, and I'm not trying to be cocky, I'm one of the best players in the NBA. So keep working hard, Quint. Don't worry if you're not getting the playing time. You'll surpass them all if you work hard!"

And then he leaned in and gave me a hug.

I wish I'd seen my face in that moment. It might have been the most exciting, unforeseen moment of my whole life to that point.

"Thanks, Mr. Payton," I said.

"You're welcome. But my name is Gary," he said and smiled as he walked back to the court to warm up.

I didn't know in the moment just how much my father had in making this happen. But it changed my attitude for the whole season. It's still one of my favorite memories.

And no, I didn't become some great soccer player, but that's not the point of the story. It's to show just how great a man my father was.

I missed him all the time.

I got a call from Tom Butler out of the blue one day.

"Quint, how is your recovery coming?"

"Hey, Tom. I'm getting better. My shoulder is getting more of a full range of motion every day."

"That's great to hear. You know, I tried to call you a few times after what happened. I even went to John Muir hospital, but they only allowed a few people to see you."

"Yeah, it was just Cara and my mother. I saw you called, Tom. As you can guess, I had tons of people reaching out and it was tough to get back to everyone."

"I understand. I just wanted to make sure that you know that I care. So does Krissy. And the rest of the staff at the *Times*."

"Thanks, Tom. I appreciate that."

"We'd love to have you come by the office one of these days. Krissy and I have even talked about potentially bringing you back on board."

Listening to the audio of Charles Zane's car wouldn't be possible at the office, so that was a non-starter.

"I'm so busy right now with physical therapy that it's probably not the best time."

"Of course. Just thought I'd throw it out there."

"Thanks. I miss you guys too. I'm sorry for my actions."

"No need to apologize. You've suffered much more than you deserved."

"You mean a few white lies doesn't deserve a few gunshots?"

"Very funny, Quint. You know what I mean."

"I do. Just trying to get back to our old tête-à-tête."

"I miss you, my friend."

"I do, too. But now is not the best time for me. Can we talk in a few weeks or a month?"

"Of course. And if you'd like to come by the office, stop in at any time. Everyone would love to see you. Maybe Crystal could set up another little party."

"That was a fun night. Until I was arrested the following day."

"You've been through a lot."

"Yeah. Oh well," I said.

"Last thing, Quint. Remember when you came to my house and I said I knew a lot of people in the publishing business?"

"I remember."

"I wasn't just blowing smoke. I really do. And I've talked to a few of them and they've expressed interest in your story. You have to admit, it's pretty wild."

With a few more chapters to be written, I thought to myself.

"That's great, Tom. Thanks."

"Anyway, let's talk soon and I can put you in touch with them. You can flex your writing muscles."

"That would be great. And thanks for looking out for me."

"You're welcome. Stop in the office soon."

He'd mentioned it three times. I knew it was important to him.

"I will. Take care, Tom."

"You too, Quint."

I'd had the audio to Charles Zane's car for five days, and it had still produced nothing. It wasn't like he didn't talk in his car. He did. But it was usually in code.

Did you take care of that thing? Yeah, talk to that one guy. We'll deal with that other thing soon.

It was smart, leaving nothing you could pin back to him. He likely worried about a tap being on his phone and not in the car, but regardless, he watched his words.

I started to presume my greatest potential lead to this point was going to amount to nothing. Like seemingly everything else involving this case, I was wrong about that as well.

31.

My first lead occurred on Friday, one week to the day that Paddy Roark and Dennis McCarthy had stuck their necks out for me.

I was sitting in my new apartment, as had become the norm, when I heard the car start up on the audio. I instinctively got excited each time this happened, despite being let down time and time again. I was one of Pavlov's dogs, foaming at the mouth, just waiting for some information from Charles Zane.

Nothing happened for the first fifteen minutes and I started doing a few dishes that had been left in the sink. The burner phone was never far away from me, however. I had the volume at its max as I scrubbed down the pan in which I'd made chicken piccata the night before.

Usually I'd do the pans right after dinner, but I'd gotten a little lazy as of late, I had to admit. I discovered that having more free time actually worked against you getting things done. It seemed counterintuitive, but I'd found it to be true.

As I towel-dried the cleaned pan, Charles Zane's voice came to life. I could always hear his end, but would only hear the person he talked too if he had his phone on speaker, which he rarely did. He must have used a Bluetooth or equivalent.

This time was no different. He spoke to someone else, but I only heard his end of the conversation.

"Hi, Doug."

That grabbed my attention.

"You're fucking kidding me."

Pause.

"How the fuck did that happen?"

Pause.

"What do you mean, that's not it?"

Pause.

"Jesus fucking Christ. Well, we have to get them both out of there. And toss them in the ocean."

Pause.

"Too risky during the daytime."

Pause.

"I'll send someone over there at 10:00 p.m. tonight."

Pause.

"Goodbye."

There was then a five-second pause, followed by the loudest *"FUCK!!!"* I'd ever heard. It reverberated through my apartment.

This was a crucial moment in my investigation of Charles Zane. In my life, if truth be told.

I went back over all I'd heard.

I had to assume Zane was talking to Doug Anderson. And at 10:00 tonight, I would be outside of his house. Of that, there was no doubt.

I was parked on Oakland Avenue by 9:30 p.m. Not with my own car, however. Certain that Charles Zane and his associates knew what kind of car I drove at this point, I wasn't going to risk them easily identifying me. I decided to rent a vehicle. One with tinted windows.

I went to a rental company and picked out a black Ford F-150, mostly because the windows on that particular truck were darker than most. It didn't appear that you could see someone sitting in the driver's seat. Especially at night. I rented the truck for a week, knowing this probably wasn't going to be the last time I'd need an undercover vehicle.

I parked twenty feet down on the opposite side of the street as the Anderson home. Good thing I arrived early. By 9:45, a van had pulled up to the Andersons'. It was the same make and model as the "rape van" parked in the back of the house. I wondered if it was the same guy Anderson had met when I'd tailed him.

I looked down at my cell phone and made sure the flash was off. That would have been catastrophic. I started taking pictures of the van. I didn't have an angle on the license plate, but figured I would at some point.

Doug Anderson approached the vehicle a few minutes later. The driver got out and the two men headed toward Anderson's house. They bypassed the front door and walked around back. The other man was short and squat, but I couldn't see his face well.

I continued to snap photos until they were out of view. The pictures probably wouldn't turn out well in the dark, but I still took as many as I could.

I looked over at Annie's home. She'd told me she went to sleep early, so I wasn't surprised to see every light out. I held out hope she wouldn't turn any on if she heard them walking outside. Like me taking a picture with the flash on, it could be catastrophic for her.

About five minutes later, the men returned to the van, carrying something approximately four and a half feet long and barely over a foot wide. It almost looked like a small carpet, but blue masking tape covered the whole thing.

I felt sick. I knew it wasn't a carpet. And if my fears were true, this wasn't an adult. It was too small.

Grief and anger overtook me in equal measures. If I'd had a gun, I might have stepped out of the car at that very moment and shot the two of them. Of course, these were just suspicions on my part, but from what Charles Zane had said, I had no doubt it was a body. What else do you throw in the ocean?

They set their parcel (I didn't know what else to call it) in the back of the truck and went to the back of the house a second time.

This time, when they emerged, they were carrying something wider and longer. It could have been a full-grown adult. My stomach had tied into complete knots. I instinctively looked over in the direction of Annie's home, hoping beyond anything that she was sound asleep. It killed me thinking the second body could be hers.

I continued taking pictures.

They set it down in the back of the van, shut the doors, and Doug Anderson got in the passenger side.

I debated whether to call 9-1-1. I wanted to with every ounce of my being, but I'd ended up at the house illegally. We'd set up an (also) illegal audio device in Charles Zane's car. It was all likely inadmissible. I'd also be selling out Dennis McCarthy and Paddy Roark, to whom I'd promised to keep my mouth shut.

But Anderson might get away with murder. I decided I had no choice. I had to call. However, I couldn't let them identify me, because then my evidence would be tossed out in a court of law.

Maybe I could make this work.

I looked down at my burner phone. It was a better alternative than calling from my own.

The van started pulling off the curb. After it got about one hundred yards down the road, I started my Ford F-150 and set off behind them, keeping my headlights dark until they were farther on.

At the same time, I picked up my burner phone and called 9-1-1.

"9-1-1, what's your emergency?" a young woman's voice said.

"I'm on Oakland Avenue and there's a dark van driving a hundred m.p.h. Or more. Ignoring every stop sign. He's going to kill someone if you don't pull him over."

"Did you get a license plate number?" she asked.

I didn't have a chance. It was dark and when the van drove past me there was no time.

"No, I didn't. But he's about to take a right from Oakland Avenue onto Harrison Street. He almost just hit a pedestrian, you better hurry."

I slowly approached the truck as it was about to take the right. I could now see the license plate. But the truck sat there a few seconds too long.

I feared they saw the LED from my call to 9-1-1. While the side windows were tinted, the front windshield wasn't, and they might be able to see the illuminated phone.

"Send someone quick," I yelled, turned the phone off, and tossed it on the passenger's seat.

I couldn't risk staying on the line even to give them the license plate number.

The van took the right turn very slowly. I started breathing again. But once they straightened out, they gunned it and accelerated off into the night. I took the right and sped up, but they were already way down the road. I'd been made.

It was over and I knew it. I'd failed again.

I just hoped the police were sending someone in their direction. And soon. Because if they didn't arrive in the next minute, and that van made it to the freeway, my phone call to 9-1-1 was all for naught.

I decided I had to do one more thing. I'd deal with the repercussions.

I restated my burner phone and called 9-1-1 again.

"9-1-1, what's your emergency?" an older male said. I was happy to hear a different voice.

"I was just parked outside of 254 Oakland Avenue and two people put two separate packages in the back of a van. I don't want to jump to any conclusions, but they almost looked like bodies."

"Please hold, sir."

"I can't stay on the line, but I'd send someone to that address now."

I hung up. And I drove home.

My life had become pure insanity.

32.

I turned on the news the next morning and saw nothing. My 9-1-1 call had happened pretty late at night, but I'd still hoped for something.

I grabbed my phone and went through my contacts. I found the number Annie had given me.

It was only 8:30, but considering how early Annie told me she went to sleep, I assumed she was an early riser. I called and it rang five times before going to her voicemail. I tried again five and then ten minutes later. Same result.

The knot in my stomach had never left from the night before, and it only tightened with each successive call.

What card did I have to play? Detective Kintner and I had somewhat patched things up, but if I called asking about Annie, he'd immediately be suspicious. For good reason.

I looked down at the burner phone and wondered if the police could trace it to my house. It wasn't registered to me, so I wasn't sure. I'd have a million more questions to answer if they showed up. I half-expected a knock at my door.

I picked the burner up and clicked on the icon with the feed of Charles Zane's car, but there was just silence.

I didn't know what the fuck to do!

I tried Annie again, but still received no answer.

That's how Saturday went. I'd watch the news or check the internet, trying to find out anything. And call Annie periodically. Nothing developed on either front.

I went to bed early that night, but didn't sleep well. I still was expecting that knock at the door from the police.

But it never came.

Early Sunday morning, I went directly to my couch and turned on the news. A few minutes in, a young, bespectacled woman appeared on the screen saying the following:

"If anyone has seen or heard from Annie Ivers, please call the Oakland Police. She's been missing since Friday and authorities haven't been able to find her. She's sixty-eight years old. Authorities are not sure what she was wearing when she went missing."

A picture of Annie came up on the screen. I'd seen her recently and the picture was from several years ago. But it was close enough.

I'd learned that Ivers was her last name. I don't think I'd ever known. Not that it mattered. She was dead now. I had no doubt in my mind.

I felt the world closing in around me. This was somehow worse than being shot. At least in the hospital, I had law enforcement around to protect me.

And I'd had my mother and Cara. Now, I didn't want to be anywhere near either one of them. I was radioactive. People in my vicinity just ended up dead. I couldn't put them at risk. I vowed to not meet with either one of them until this was all over.

I wondered if I was back on Charles Zane's radar. Or if, in fact, I'd ever left. Could they have suspected me as the truck behind the van? Was I in mortal danger again?

Just then, I heard a noise outside. It turned out to merely be a tree rustling, but I still jumped. My mind was going to overreact to any noise from here on in. I had to accept that.

Despite my anxiety, I knew I would proceed. I wanted Zane dead more than I wanted to be alive. For Tricia Knox. For Annie Ivers. For myself. And most importantly, for my father.

No, I still didn't know exactly why he'd killed my father, but I knew what the guy said on the wiretap. And that was enough for me.

In that moment I decided, if I could trade my life for Charles Zane's, I would.

Give me the chance!

I called my mother and told her I was going to Las Vegas for a few days. I wasn't sure if she believed me.

I called Cara and told her the same story. I know she didn't believe me.

But I was on my own for a few days. Which was what I wanted.

Little more about Annie Ivers appeared on the news that day. I found a tiny article online, but didn't gain any more information. There was no mention of Doug Anderson, his home, or the van on either the T.V. news or the internet.

And there was nothing from Charles Zane's car all day. I hoped he hadn't discovered the wiretap and turned it off.

Be just my luck.

33.

Monday arrived and I realized I hadn't been out of my apartment since coming home Friday night. Well, that's not entirely true. I'd stepped a few feet outside of my apartment to collect some deliveries from DoorDash.

My face had become a mess of facial hair. I tried to remember the last time I shaved, but I couldn't place it. And it wasn't the cool kind of facial hair with straight lines and contours. It was a hot mess.

Not that I cared.

My only concern on earth was getting Charles Zane. It's all I thought about.

I got an incoming call early that morning. It was Detective Kintner.

"Hi, Quint."

"How are you, Ray?"

"Can we talk, man to man?"

"Of course. What's up?"

"I know when you came clean to the feds you talked about meeting up with Annie Ivers. Have you heard she's missing?"

I suddenly knew why he was calling. "I heard. And I'm heartbroken. I've tried calling her, hoping by some miracle she picks up and is safe."

"You see, that's the funny part, Quint."

I knew nothing funny was upcoming.

"Oh yeah, why is that?"

"Because the first time she was reported missing was on Sunday morning, but you called her eight times on Saturday."

There was no excuse that would make sense. And that was okay. I'd grown tired of lying.

"Are you free later today?" I asked.

He ignored me.

"There were also two calls to 9-1-1 on Friday night. I have a sneaking suspicion you know about those as well."

"Are you free later today?" I repeated myself. He heard me this time.

"Yes. You better have a good explanation. I don't want to arrest you again, but if you leave me no option, I will."

"Maybe, just maybe, this time I'll be arrested for a crime I actually committed."

"I deserve that," Kintner said. "Look, I'm giving you more rope than I would to most. Because of all that's happened. But don't leave me without options."

"I'll call you in a few hours and we'll meet. You'll know everything I do," I said.

And I really did plan on meeting with him.

But then everything changed.

Again.

After getting off the phone with Detective Kintner, I turned on the audio to Charles Zane's car. There was nothing, but I kept it on just in case.

About an hour later, I heard the engine roaring to life.

A few minutes later, I heard Zane's voice. As usual, I only heard his end.

"*I need something, Max,*" Charles Zane said.

Pause.

"*I want my boat.*"

Pause.

"*No, the big one.*"

Pause.

"*Because they are getting too close. Especially after this latest incident. I need to get out of Dodge for a while. Maybe be out at sea for the next six months. Shit, maybe dock at some place in South America and never come back.*"

Pause.

"*No. I don't want a captain. I don't want any deckhands. I don't even want a cook. I'm trying to get away from people. Can't you understand?*"

Pause.

"*I've captained many boats. I'll be fine.*"

Pause.

"*Ninety minutes. I can feel different varieties of pigs bearing down on me. Local, FBI—shit, maybe I'm on the CIA's radar. I need to get the fuck out of here and let things calm down.*"

Pause.

"*It's docked in the Berkeley Marina, isn't it?*"

Pause.

"No, keep it there. A little less conspicuous than San Francisco."
Pause.
"One more thing, Max. Since I'll be commandeering this myself and I don't know for how long, make sure you give me enough of everything. Gas. Food. Supplies. Etc."
Pause.
"Thank you. Tell the others that I will be calling them once I'm off the coast with instructions for while I'm gone."
Pause.
"And let them know there's an extra bonus if they kill that Quint fuck. He's behind all this, I just know it. And tell them to make him suffer."
Pause.
"Thanks, Max. I'll see you soon. And only you."

I was out of my apartment before having time to consider what I was doing. Before I'd fully digested everything he'd said.

It's like I was being forced to leave my place by some foreign entity. But I knew it was all me. I wanted this. To end it once and for all with Charles Zane. Hopefully with him being dead, although I knew I might well be me.

I took the rental truck. The tinted windows could come in handy again.

I'd spent some time by the Berkeley Marina over the years and knew it pretty well. It lay only a few short miles from Golden Gate Fields, but it felt like a different world.

The marina was home to some of the most beautiful boats imaginable. If Golden Gate Fields was a boat, with the exception of the Turf Club, it would be a paddle boat.

Despite a little traffic, I arrived in less than an hour. I entered and parked along the marina itself, getting as close to the water as I could, finding a spot in the last row of cars. I wanted to walk the shortest possible distance to Zane's boat. Or ship. Or ocean liner. Whatever it was, I felt sure it was going to be extravagant.

I hoped Zane's boat was parked on the dock and I didn't have to take a dinghy or swim out to it. That would present its own set of likely insurmountable problems.

And what exactly was I going to do even if I got on the boat? Hit him over the head with an oar? Execute a citizen's arrest? I was so far out of my league.

I'd acted so instinctively that I hadn't had time to organize any sort of plan. I just knew that if Zane was trying to flee the country, I couldn't let it happen.

I looked at the time. It had only been an hour since Zane had said ninety minutes. I had a little time. I knew this was going to be painful, but I had to call my mother. In case I didn't make it out alive, I at least owed her that.

She answered on the first ring.

"Quint, how is Vegas treating you?"

"I'm not in Vegas, Mom."

"I thought you said…"

"I lied."

I hated interrupting my mother, but I had to. I couldn't let her hijack the conversation.

"Why?"

"Because I'm going after Dad's killer. I know you don't like to talk about it and you still want to think it was a mugging. But it wasn't. And the killer is still out there, walking around and probably enjoying fine wines and good food. I can't have that."

"You're scaring me, Quint."

"Mom, I just want to say how much I love you. And how much I loved Dad. It's why I have to do what I'm about to do."

"Quint, slow down. Listen to me. Let the cops do their job."

I had to get off the phone soon or I never would.

"Mom, I've got to go. Just know I did this because of how much I care about our family."

"Quint. Quint…"

"Bye, Mom. I love you!"

And I hung up. I'd never felt more guilty in my life. With all my heart, I wanted to call her back and apologize. But I couldn't.

Next, I called Cara. I didn't look forward to this call either, but I knew it wouldn't be as emotional as the call to my mother.

"Hey, baby," she answered.

"You know how much I love you, don't you, Cara?"

"I do. You may not say it all the time, but I know."

"You and my family. Those are the two things that I love the most in this whole world."

"Well, thanks," she said, but I could tell she was suspicious.

"And if anyone ever did anything to you, I'd seek revenge no matter what the consequences."

"Nothing is going to happen to me, Quint."

"Yeah, but something happened to my father. And I now have a chance to avenge his death."

"Please don't do what you are thinking about doing," Cara said, starting to stammer.

An astute woman, she could tell how consequential this moment was.

"I have no choice. Listen, if I somehow don't make it out of this, I want you to look after my mother."

"No! No, no, no, no! You can't put that on me. Come back to Walnut Creek. Come by my place and let's talk."

"It's too late for talking," I said. "I have to do this."

I didn't know if it was the intensity of my own voice, or her realizing she couldn't change my mind, but I was shocked by what she said next.

"Well, if that's the way it's going to be, then do a good fucking job of it. And come back safe to me."

"I will," I said.

"I love you, Quint."

"I love you, Cara. Goodbye."

"For now! It's goodbye for now! Okay? I'll see you soon,"

"I'll see you soon," I said and ended the call.

There was one more phone call I had to make. For this one, I grabbed the burner phone, knowing it would be tougher to trace.

"Detective Kintner speaking."

"It's Quint."

"What time are you coming in?"

"I'm not."

"But…"

"But nothing. Just listen to me, Ray. If you don't, I will hang up the phone."

"Alright. Speak your piece."

"I was the one outside of the Anderson house on Friday night. I'm the one who called 9-1-1. Doug Anderson, and another man, a short, squat guy, carried two long packages out of the Andersons' house. They were duct taped, but I'm almost positive they were bodies. One was the size of an adult. The other was smaller, maybe a teenager."

I heard Kintner sigh on the other end.

"They saw the light from my phone when I called 9-1-1 and they sped away. I'm scared that the adult body might have been Annie Ivers's. That's why I called her so many times Saturday, before the media had released that she was missing. Because I suspected it from the moment I saw that bag being carried out of Anderson's house."

"Can I interrupt for one second, Quint?"

"Yes, what is it?"

"We found blood in Ms. Ivers's home. A lot of it. I'd be shocked if she's still alive."

If I wasn't careful, I easily could have gotten choked up for another senseless death. I had really liked Annie Ivers. And while my soul ached for her, I knew I had to remain as composed as possible for what lay ahead.

"Charles Zane is a monster. So is Doug Anderson. Annie was a very nice woman. Listen, Detective Kintner. Ray. I'm going to get off the phone soon, but I just wanted to tell you this. Charles Zane knew about the two murders. He told Doug Anderson to throw the bodies in the ocean. You don't want to know how I found this out. But I'm telling you the truth. And I can't sit idly by and let this continue to happen."

"What are you planning on doing, Quint?"

It was the third time I'd been asked that in the last several minutes. For good reason, obviously.

"Avenging my father," I said.

"How? Where? Give me a clue, maybe I can help."

I couldn't risk the police showing up. They'd fucked this thing up way too many times along the way. But if I ended up being murdered somewhere in the middle of the Pacific, I wanted to at least give them a reference point that might lead them back to Zane.

"Do you know Charles Zane's nickname?"

"I don't think so."

"It's an old one. It's not used much anymore because he murdered the person who originated it."

"What's the point of this?"

"I'm giving you your hint."

"But I don't know his nickname."

"Well, if you did, and I told you that I was going to fight him on his own turf, you'd make the connection."

"I'm lost," Ray said.

"I'm not. I finally know what I have to do," I said.

He knew I was getting off the phone.

"Good luck, Quint. Hope this isn't goodbye."

I thought of Cara.

"Goodbye for now," I said.

34.

The next twenty minutes felt like two hours. More than anything, I wanted to walk around the docks and ask which boat was Charles Zane's. But I had to be inconspicuous. I couldn't be roaming around the marina when he arrived.

And I still didn't have any worthwhile plan. I didn't even have a weapon if the chance to take down Zane ever presented itself.

I was winging it. At the worst time possible.

One small thing weighed in my favor. Zane had said he didn't want anyone else on the boat. It gave me a fighting chance. If, by some small miracle, I was able to get on it without him seeing me.

But then what? Knock him out, torture him, and threaten to feed him to the sharks? As much as I wanted Charles Zane dead, and to find out the truth about my father, I'm not sure I could go to those extremes.

As my mind wandered, something caught the corner of my eye. Two men had just stepped onto the docks.

I looked over. One of the men was Charles Zane. It all hit home in that moment, the seriousness of my actions. This was finally going to be decided. One way or the other.

They were walking in my direction and would pass by my car from my left side. If I rolled down my driver's side window, they'd see me. So I rolled down the passenger side to try and hear what they were saying.

They approached.

"As you can see, ZANY is docked about three boats down. It's truly a spectacular boat, Charles. It was an honor driving it, even if only to bring it to the dock itself. I've already gassed it, but there are some other supplies I haven't had time to load. Since you wanted me to do this all myself."

They were about to walk right by my car, but the window was only halfway down, and unless they turned around and looked directly through the passenger window, they wouldn't see me.

"You've done a great job, Max. I want to get out of here ASAP, so let me help you bring some of those supplies down. How many loads have we got?"

"Probably two. Three max. And then you're ready to go."

They stopped walking, likely because they would be doubling back to get the supplies.

"Well, let's get to it," Zane said.

They turned around and walked back up the dock. When they were far enough away, I got out of my car, and headed along the waterfront. I was looking for a boat called ZANY. The narcissistic nature of the name was somehow perfect. I expected nothing less.

I found it at the end of the dock. And I immediately knew why they put it there. It was twice the size of any other boat around, and parking it between two others would have been next to impossible. Really, calling it a boat was like calling a stretch limo a car. It was a yacht. And it was the most spectacular one I'd ever seen. It was like a mini cruise ship.

Probably fifty feet long, it stood higher in the water than any yacht I'd ever seen.

ZANY sprawled in huge navy-blue lettering on the stern. The rest was a breathtaking shiny white that looked like it had been painted that morning. Or more precisely, glossed. Zig-zagging lines of the navy blue played well off the shiny white.

I'd guess it would have fit twenty-five people, maybe more, on its three levels. On the bright side, there would be places to hide if need be.

The bow of the yacht held two small tables and padded seating from which you could look out on the ocean ahead of you. It was a different life, that's for sure. I would have been jealous. If it hadn't been built on the blood of others.

On the side of the yacht, in small cursive, I read *Ferreti Yachts: Model 920.* I didn't know much about yachts, but I did know Ferretis were world famous. I'd guess the yacht cost millions of dollars. It was spectacular in every sense of the word.

I started to realize I was ogling. Not the time.

I had to make a decision. And quick.

Looking up toward the top of the marina, I didn't see Zane and his friend walking toward the dock yet. But it could happen at any moment.

It was time to make up my mind. And then I saw my father's face, and a lifetime of memories flashed before me. I knew there was no turning back.

I stepped onto the back of the boat and realized I had to get below deck immediately. If they saw someone walking along the docks, their suspicions wouldn't be aroused. Seeing someone standing on the yacht was a different story entirely.

I surveyed the three levels: the top, where the helmsman/captain would drive the boat, the main level where I'd entered, and the below-deck area. Which is where I needed to be.

I climbed the elegant teakwood ladder down to the luxury sleeping quarters. This would be where people would stay if Zane took them out for the night. Which wouldn't be the case today since there was only one other passenger. Me.

I saw two doors and opened each. Both guest cabins had a sizable bed that dropped down from the wall. I also found a bathroom and a small kitchen area.

Some voices came down the docks. I recognized Zane's immediately. I'd spent too many hours listening to him in his car over the last week.

He had a confident, intense voice that I'm sure women went nuts over. I had come to despise it.

They were quickly approaching the boat. I didn't have much of a decision: either one of the two small rooms.

I chose the one farthest away from the ladder. The room was small, but with the bunk beds still in the wall, I had enough space. I shut the door behind me.

A glass window, about two feet wide by one foot long, offered a view just a little above the water. Even in the sleeping quarters, this yacht had thought of everything.

Hearing the two men walk onto the boat, I tried to remain completely silent. Even the slightest noise might have been a death sentence.

They were walking down the ladder a few seconds later.

"And I checked the hot plates. They're working fine," the man named Max said.

"Good."

"You've probably got enough food for a month if you need it."

I heard them set some boxes down. The sounds came from the other side of the bottom level.

"I said I might be gone several months. I didn't mean I'd be sailing in the middle of the Pacific the whole time. I'm sure I'll head landward well before a month," Charles Zane said.

"Where do you think you'll go? If you don't mind me asking."

"Probably better I don't tell you, Max. Just in case."

"I understand, Charles."

"But maybe I'll hit up some coastal town in Mexico. Live on fresh fish and young women."

"Wish I could join you."

"Not this time. Need to keep my distance for a while."

"Of course."

"I'm putting you in charge while I'm gone. I'll still be checking in when I have the ability to. But you've been with me long enough. Do what I would do."

"I will."

"And I'm serious about Quint Adler. Please make him suffer. He's been a pain in my ass for the last few months. Don't make it easy like we did on his father."

It took all of my power not to break down the door and attack Charles Zane. But I had to bide my time. Two on one was a losing proposition. In fact, so was one on one after what I heard next.

"We won't make it easy, like with a gun. Speaking of which, I've left a handgun for you. I'm sure it won't be necessary, but just being cautious. It's in the glove box on top, right next to the ship's wheel."

They shuffled some boxes.

"Maybe I'll shoot a few tuna. Have some fresh sushi," Zane said.

Max laughed too hard. "You'll find a way to eat well even out on the ocean."

"Alright, let's go back up and get that final load. I don't think we'll need a third trip."

"Me either. We'll put it in one of the rooms. You don't want too many loose boxes down here."

I heard them go back upstairs and start walking down the dock.

Logically, being in the room farther away, it was less likely they would set the supplies where I was. But that wasn't calming in the moment as my mind visualized them opening the door and finding me there. I tried not to imagine the pain they'd inflict on me.

I started wondering what the hell I was doing. I could have been back in Walnut Creek, making love to Cara. Instead, the idea of vengeance had taken hold of me, and I found myself in the most compromising position imaginable.

I told myself I could still leave. They would be gone at least five or ten minutes. Now was my chance to get out of this.

And yet I knew I wouldn't run.

I braced my feet against a wall, making them less likely to make noise if the boat started rocking. I just wanted to get out into the open water. I still thought I stood a fighting chance. In fact, I was younger and bigger than Charles Zane. And with all of my pent-up anger, I knew I could take him. But he did have a gun, which could tilt the odds in his favor. Hopefully, he'd leave it in the glove box.

They came back on board several minutes later, quickly going below deck.

This was the moment of truth.

I pleaded to no one in particular: *Please have them choose the other room!*

And they did. I heard the other door open and knew I was safe. For the moment.

"I packed three life vests. Probably overcautious, but you never know. The sea can be a pretty unforgiving place."

"You can never be too safe," Zane said.

"I packed steaks and some chicken in the freezer. Maybe have a filet with those tuna you shoot. Little surf and turf."

"You missed your calling, Max."

"Standup comedian?"

"Something like that."

They continued setting boxes in the other room until they slammed it shut. I heard a boat docking close by, causing a slight ripple in the water as it swayed a little bit. For a brief moment, my shoe started to slide off the wall. It didn't squeak, but my heart jumped in my mouth for a horrifying second.

"Is there anything else you need, Charles? You've got food, life jackets, some nice bottles of wine. A gun. And two fully powered burner phones, although I don't know how well they'll work the farther out to sea you get."

"You've done enough, Max. Thank you."

"Alright, I'll release you from the dock."

"One last thing. Tell Doug Anderson that he's on borrowed time. He's been a valuable asset, but this is one too many fuck-ups. We can't kill him right now with everything going on around him, but we can scare the shit out of him."

"Consider it done. What do I tell the cops if they come calling about you?"

"Nothing. But spread the word I'm in Europe. I'm sure it will somehow get back to them. And they'd be more likely to believe it than if someone told them directly."

"You got it."

"Let's go above deck and get me out of here."

They walked back up the ladder and I finally exhaled.

A few minutes later, the motor started up. It was loud, the sound of a massive engine coming to life. It didn't hurt that I was likely lying right above said motor.

Voices spoke and I thought I heard a *"Goodbye,"* but it was hard to make out with the engine purring below me.

Finally, I had gotten what I wanted. We were headed out to sea.

Time approaching for the one on one battle I'd desired.

The yacht moved efficiently, effortlessly gliding through the marina. The motor now made a small noise, barely audible. It was like a lion who had already roared. We knew its power, it didn't need to remind it us while it went navigated through a harbor at five m.p.h.

I looked out through the small window, in awe of all of the boats we passed, despite knowing I was on the nicest of them all.

There would be some horrific moments to come, of that there was no doubt. I didn't even want to imagine what would happen between Zane and myself. But in that moment, I managed to enjoy looking out on the marina.

Once we made our way through it, Zane increased the speed and we moved smoothly through the waters off of Berkeley and Oakland. We were not yet the ocean, but still in the bay in a no-wake zone, so he couldn't just gun it.

Out the window I could see the Bay Bridge, but I knew we wouldn't be driving under it. That would just lead to more of the Bay, ending when you got further south near San Jose.

No, I knew where we were going.

And we'd have to pass under one of the most famous bridges in the world to get there.

I continued looking out of the window, fascinated in spite of myself. I watched as we passed the Bay Bridge and around fifteen minutes later, we approached the span of the Golden Gate Bridge.

Always a spectacular sight, but even more so when you saw it from sea level. It was massive and looking up at it made it all the more breathtaking. We cruised past sailboats and I'm sure they held the same opinion. Truly one of architecture and engineering's grandest feats.

Before you knew it, we were passing under the massive bridge, and it got dark for a moment as it blocked out the sun. When we passed it, I tried to turn around and get one last look, but the small window no longer supplied me the opportunity.

A minute later, we started accelerating. We must have just passed the m.p.h. checkmarks. The sheer force of the yacht finally took hold. We moved faster and faster through the ocean water.

The irony was not lost on me. With a name like Quint, how could it be?

In *Jaws*, the majority of the movie takes place on land, until Brody, Hooper, and yes, Quint, head out to sea to get their shark.

Life was imitating art.

I guess it had to end this way.

Quint vs. the Shark. At sea.

Charles Zane must have pushed the throttle down to flank speed, because we quickly accelerated in one more burst and I was sent sliding from one side of the room to the other.

I'd gone well past the point of no return.

We were headed out of the bay and into the Pacific Ocean.

35.

It was time to formulate a plan. Ten minutes had become twenty, which had become an hour. Once we'd hit the Pacific Ocean, we'd taken a left and started heading down the California coast. The guest cabin was on the port side of the boat and I could see the coast through the small window.

We were slowly getting further out to sea, but for the most part we followed the coast. If I had to, I'd guess we were approximately a half-mile from land. I wasn't sure exactly why, but all things being equal, I preferred it. The further out you got, the more you'd have to brave the elements.

I'd run through my options and narrowed them down to two. One, I could bide my time and wait until Charles Zane came downstairs. There was a hidden little inlet once you took the stairs below deck. I considered waiting there and finding something to bash him over the head with as he stepped down the ladder.

The problem with that plan was, how long was I willing to wait? I couldn't just stand there for four hours. Six hours. Eight hours. A day.

A second option was to wait until he went to sleep. I assumed he'd stay close enough to shore where he'd be able to set an anchor down. I couldn't imagine just floating haphazardly in a yacht worth millions of dollars.

And when he slept, he'd probably come down below deck.

And then something hit me.

They'd put boxes in the other room. He'd probably be expecting to sleep in the room I was in.

Fuck!!!

But as I thought more about it, I realized maybe I could use that to my advantage. There wasn't much space to hide in the room, but if I heard him about to open the door, I could set my feet and be ready to bum-rush him.

None of the options sounded good.

Being with Cara in Walnut Creek sounded good.

Talking with my mother sounded good.

But those were no longer options. Thanks to my thirst for revenge.

I didn't hear any noise from above. Not that I should have expected to. Was he just going to start talking to himself?

It did get me thinking. What did a terrible man like Charles Zane think about when he was by himself? Did he ask for forgiveness? Did he relish in memories of all the people he'd murdered? For a shit-fuck murderer like him, I'd think being alone with your thoughts would be the worst place to be. But then again, I had morals.

I grabbed one of the two phones from my pocket. It was 3:45. We'd been out to sea for a little over two hours at this point. Now in early September—where had all the time gone?—and the days were getting shorter. If I wanted to go after him while there was still light out, it had to be in the next few hours.

I started going over my options once again.

I had to decide soon. No more flip-flopping.

And once I committed to a plan of action, there was no going back. I had to commit 1000%.

Ten more minutes passed. I considered pulling down the wooden bunk bed, breaking off two pieces of wood, and using one to sharpen the other into a weapon. Making too much noise posed a huge risk, but I thought it was worth it.

I stood up and cautiously started pulling the bunk bed down. It was very quiet and I thought this just might work.

As I slowly, deliberately, finished setting the legs on the floor, the door suddenly opened.

Charles Zane stood before me, a gun in his hand. I was six feet from him, the base of the bunk bed still in my hands. I couldn't jump at him. I was defenseless.

He moved the gun upward and took aim at my chest.

I tried to think of something nice, knowing my life was ending. I remembered a picture that was framed in my parents' family room. In it I, probably three years old, sat on the laps of my mother and father. It was our favorite family picture.

Cara then came to mind and all of our great times flashed before my eyes.

"Get on the floor!" Zane said.

If I'd been closer to him, maybe I would have leapt. But that was suicide at this point.

I sat down.

Charles Zane moved a step closer, now standing directly above me. I readied myself for a gunshot, to the head or chest, but it didn't come. Instead, he grabbed my left arm and fastened a handcuff around it. He took the other cuff and fastened it to one of the little metal handrails the room had.

If I tried to make any sudden move, I knew he would have killed me. I didn't have much choice but to obey.

Next, he leaned down and started going through my pockets.

He took out the two cells, mine and the burner Dennis McCarthy had given me.

Charles Zane took a step back and kept the gun pointed at me.

"You didn't think you were going to get off that easy, did you?" he said.

And then he walked out of the room and shut the door behind him.

I heard him walk up on deck. The yacht took a quick right turn and accelerated. Looking out the little window, I saw that we were heading away from the coast and further out to sea.

Zane wanted me alive. I initially shuddered at the reason why, then tried to avoid thinking about it. Instead, I vehemently shook the handcuff, hoping the rail might give way. No luck; it was strongly bolted to the wall. I didn't give up and kept attempting to yank it out. After my fifth attempt, I realized it was a lost cause and stopped wasting my energy.

I tried thinking of anything that might give me a chance to fight back. I came up empty.

I wasn't giving up, but the thought of my body being fed to the sharks was never far from my mind. I couldn't go through that.

Of course, it might not be my choice.

Another twenty minutes passed. I could no longer see the shoreline. The sun was still out, but definitely on its way to setting. It got a little less bright by the minute. Heading further out to sea only expedited it, as the lights from shore were no longer visible.

I decided to shake the handrail a few more times, but it still wouldn't budge.

I leaned back and just hoped the end would come quick.

But I knew better.

The engine under me came to a halt. We were now miles and miles from the coastline, so I knew there's no way that he could anchor the yacht. We'd just be drifting.

I heard Zane take the ladder and come below deck. He didn't go straight to my room, but instead he rustled about, probably grabbing things.

Then the door opened. He had a knife in his hand. Along with a little bag of food. He moved quickly to my left side, where I was defenseless, my hand still being cuffed to the rail.

He took the knife and sliced across my thigh several times. He hadn't cut deep enough to rupture anything, but it did lead to a lot of bleeding. He grabbed some of the food he'd brought in—the raw chicken and meat Max had packed for him—and started coating it with my blood.

"I'm not sure this will be enough blood to attract any sharks, but I figured what the hell, let's give it a try."

And he smiled at me.

I was so dumbfounded by how evil this man was, and how much I was at his non-existent mercy, that I couldn't think of anything to say.

He made a point of shutting the door as he left, not that it mattered.

As terrible as everything had been up to this point, I knew it was only going to get worse.

36.

I didn't have to wait long for Charles Zane to come back.

He opened the door and said, "I think we're all set. Hope you're ready for this."

I still hadn't said a word to him. And I wasn't sure why.

He approached me and pulled a piece of rope from his back pocket.

Zane started trying to tie my feet together by the ankles. I kicked at him and connected to his mid-section, sending him back against the opposite wall.

A second later, he brandished the knife.

"If you don't let me do this, I'll take out an eye," he said.

And pushed the knife within a few inches of my left eye to illustrate.

I'd likely be dead soon, but there were some things I couldn't deal with. Losing an eye was one of them.

He finished tying my ankles together. And I had to let him.

Then he brought the gun back out.

"If you don't do exactly as I say, I'm going to shoot you in the groin."

I couldn't even imagine the damage.

"I'll do what you say," I said, horrified.

He walked to my right side, making a point to aim the gun down toward the region he'd mentioned.

"I'm going to remove the cuff from the handrail and you are going to slide your right hand through it. I don't have to remind you what I'll do if you don't."

He had a knife in one hand and a gun in the other. My feet were roped together. I hated having to do what he said, but I had no choice.

Zane set the knife down and released the cuff from the rail.

I slid my right hand through it.

204 | Revenge at Sea

I was now roped and handcuffed. But I had my private parts and my eyes.

And if, by some miracle, I got out of this, I wanted to do it as a full man.

The only thing he hadn't done was put a piece of tape over my mouth. When you're dozens of miles from shore, sitting in the middle of the Pacific Ocean, I guess a guy screaming doesn't really matter.

"We're going above deck. If you resist, I'll gladly follow through on one of my threats. Please, I'd like to."

Each line Zane said made me realize just how diabolical he was. I'd been over my head from the very start. Not that I'd deserved what was coming, but I never should have gotten involved with this monster.

Sadly, I'd come to this realization too late.

Zane led me to the ladder. I had to take many small steps since my feet were roped together. It reminded me of the perp walk by shackled men in the movies, headed to their execution. It didn't take a genius to understand the similarities.

Zane set me down at the stern of the boat. There was a little metal bar on the deck which I assumed was meant for attaching knots. While pointing the gun at my groin, he quickly unhooked one of my handcuffs, slid it underneath the little metal bar, and then reattached it.

If I'd made the slightest motion, he would have shot me. But I began to think maybe that would have been preferable.

I was now defenseless. In every sense of the word.

I was lying on the stern of the boat, my ankles tied together. My wrists were handcuffed behind my back and solidified by a metal bar.

I finally spoke.

"You're going to do what you want to do. I'm powerless to stop it. Just tell me why you killed my father. Please, it's all I've ever wanted to know."

It was weird saying the word "please" to the monster in front of me. And it wasn't to get into his good graces. I knew I was a dead man. I just spoke out of instinct. My parents had raised me to be polite, and even in this, the last minutes of my life, I couldn't avoid it.

"I have some questions of my own," Charles Zane said. "I'm fine with a little Q & A before we get down to the squeamish stuff."

I'd do anything to avoid thinking of what he meant by *squeamish*. So I kept talking.

"How did you know I was on the boat?"

Technically, it was a yacht, but I wasn't going to give him the satisfaction. What a weird, tiny thing for me to care about. I'd say please, but I wouldn't say yacht.

"I got a call from my friend Max about thirty minutes ago. He was walking around the dock when a man started asking about this here *yacht*."

Zane emphasized the word in a way that showed he was offended I'd said boat. My aversion to him magnified.

He continued, "The man asked whose yacht this was and Max knows to be coy, so he just said an old friend's. The man then said, and I'm paraphrasing, 'That's a huge yacht, is it just the two of them?' To which Max asked, 'What do you mean, two of them?' Apparently, the man had seen you step onto my boat."

He paused for a few seconds.

"I think I'm going to get that man something special when I return," Zane said.

I couldn't believe my bad luck. Despite the gun, I surely would have had the upper hand over Zane. I had the element of surprise and could have used that to my advantage.

But no. Some guy had to see me get on board.

I wanted to scream, "FUCK!!!!" at the top of my lungs, but what was the point?

Zane went downstairs and came back up with more meat. He took a two- or three-pound piece and wiped it on my thigh, trying to coat it with blood, even though most of it had dried at this point.

He took the meat and nonchalantly tossed it in the ocean.

I don't think it mattered to him the blood was dry. This was more to make a point than anything else.

"Supposedly, there's a lot of sharks fifteen to twenty miles off the coast of Santa Cruz. Did you know that, Quint? That's quite a name, by the way."

He wasn't being subtle and I knew mentioning both Quint and sharks was not an accident.

"I know your old nickname," I said.

Zane took a step back. That I was in on his sick little joke genuinely seemed to shock him. I could tell he was trying to figure out how I could know.

He went back downstairs and reemerged with a chair. He set it next to me and took a seat. And smiled down at me.

"Ah, I got it. Had to be Dennis McCarthy. How is that old asshole?"

"I think we both know he didn't kill Griff Bauer."

"Shit, I almost forgot. My letters to you are what got this all started," he said, seeming to enjoy the moment.

I looked past Zane and saw the sun was probably thirty minutes from setting. Not that it really mattered. Sunup or sundown, the handcuffs weren't going to magically disappear.

"What exactly did you expect me to do with the bullshit info you fed me?" I asked.

"In all honesty, not much. But on the slight chance you mentioned McCarthy as a potential suspect, I thought it was worth it. Even if it was just your shitty paper."

I didn't take the bait. "How did you find out who I was?"

Zane smiled at me, amused by this all.

I looked up at the human version of a pit bull. Not all that big, but strong, ugly, and ferocious.

"I generally like to drive around an area in which I've commissioned a crime. After the fact, and before the police show up, obviously. I'm not that dumb. Make sure nothing stands out that could get us in trouble. So I was loitering around the home of Griff Bauer on that Saturday morning when I saw you looking in the house."

I was listening to every word he said. But I was also trying to slowly, subtly wiggle my feet around. The rope felt tight, but not immovable.

"And then," he continued, "I drove by the next day and you were talking to some cops. Now, that made me more than just a little suspicious, so I found out everything I could about you. Your name. Your parents. But we'll get back to that later."

My thoughts turned to my father. But I tried to remain focused. I had to keep Zane talking. I wasn't sure exactly how it could help me, but at the very least, it would delay the inevitable. "And that's when you started sending me the letters?"

"That's right. Once I found out you were a journalist. Seemed like a fun game to play."

"Wasn't that risky?"

"Not really. I wore gloves. And dropped the letters in the *Walnut Creek Times's* mail slot late at night. No post office or anything to narrow down where or who the letter had been sent from."

"You don't leave much to chance, do you, Mr. Zane?"

"No, but that doesn't mean I'm infallible. I mean, if I hadn't gotten that phone call from Max, it might have been me who was tied up."

"Want to switch?"

Charles Zane laughed, surprisingly loudly.

Then he said, "Stop being funny. It will make it harder to cut you up and feed you to the sharks."

At that moment, he looked over the side of the boat.

"Nope, not here yet."

He took another piece of meat and tossed it overboard.

"More than likely, we won't see them until I start throwing pieces of you overboard."

A shiver went up my spine. I tried wiggling my feet, but the rope still would barely budge. His chair sat near my upper body, so he didn't have a view of my feet.

Still, I had to wiggle them very delicately so he wouldn't notice.

It gave me an idea. It was a thousand to one, but what else did I have?

At some point, when he stood up, I'd swing my feet at his legs, trying to take him down with a blow from underneath. Hopefully, he'd be unprepared and hit his head on the fall backward. Then, when he went to the deck, I'd raise my feet up and repeatedly kick him over the skull with my roped-together feet.

A heel crashing down on a face could do a lot of damage.

So while it was a long shot, I didn't think it was impossible.

I had to wait, however. His chair was a bit too far away at the moment. And knocking him from a chair wouldn't do much, anyway. From a full standing position, damage could be done.

"I got it, Zane. You've got the upper hand and you're going to feed me to the sharks. Can I at least find out all that's happened first?"

"What if I decide to just start killing you now?"

"I think you want to tell me. So you can gloat."

"You're a smart man, Quint. That's exactly what I want. But I have more questions first."

"Go ahead," I said. I wanted to say *fuck off*, but being polite might give me more time.

"Why did you go to Dennis McCarthy?"

"I didn't. He came to me when he found out I was asking questions at Boyle's Grocery Store."

"Ah, yes. Paddy Roark. Quite a disagreeable gentleman."

I ignored him. A deranged killer calling someone disagreeable.

"So, McCarthy found me and told me he assumed you were the one writing the letters. Trying to make him look bad."

"Dennis was always a smart guy. And he recognized me as a different breed from day one. It's amazing I lasted a few years with him."

"I've got a question."

"I'm all ears," he said in a mocking tone.

"Did you kill Vern Coughlin?"

I was expecting a quick denial.

"Not personally. But yes." And he laughed.

"Why?"

"The same reason I sent you the letters. To create trouble for Dennis McCarthy. You don't fire Charles Zane without paying for it."

"Vern Coughlin was an innocent man."

"If you are trying to get me to develop some morals, you're about fifty-six years late. I was the kid tripping other kids at school. Leaving small pieces of glass in the sandbox. Killing a neighborhood cat occasionally. For a while, I thought I was going to be a serial killer. I just hated everyone. But I loved the finer things in life. I wanted wealth. Beautiful girls. Yachts. So I thought about trying to get rich at the expense of other people's addictions. Gambling came to a dead end once Dennis McCarthy fired me. But drugs have worked out just fine. You probably feel sad for all the opioid addicts these days. I see a prospective client. These drugs help ruin lives, ruin families, and meanwhile, I'm getting rich off of it. That's perfection in my mind. Sometimes, if I see someone I know who has an addictive personality, I'll have one of my subordinates give them a few pills for free. Get them a little taste. It's a good investment, if you know what I mean. The money will come back to me tenfold."

Charles Zane started laughing controllably.

I'd never heard a more disturbing statement in my life. You could argue he was worse than a serial killer. Who knows how many thousands of lives Zane had ruined? And the fact that he took pride in it disgusted me to no end.

"Why did you try to frame me for murder?" I asked, needing to change the subject. "I'm assuming it's you who planted my DNA and that Starbucks cup."

"It sounded like something fun to do. I've done a lot of crazy things, but never framed anyone for murder. It was a challenge."

"And you hired someone to run into me at Starbucks and scratch me to get some DNA?"

"Wow, you've gotten a lot correct. Truly impressive, Quint. Yes."

"And you had the guy pick up a cup I discarded?"

He looked down at me. Some form of admiration crossed his face. "Right again. And I had him take skin he'd scratched off of you and leave it around Bauer's apartment. Best part is that a little skin might make it look like Griff Bauer was trying to scratch you. A defense wound."

"You're diabolical," I said.

"Thanks," he said.

I didn't bother saying it wasn't a compliment.

"And then had someone call the police?" I asked.

"Yeah. From a pay phone. Hard to find one of those these days. I had my subordinate call and say they were in Summit Hospital on the Saturday night in question and heard two people arguing. I knew Griff Bauer's room number, so obviously we said that's where the arguing came from. When they found out Griff's roommate at the hospital was you, they'd immediately go back to the crime scene. And now they'd find your DNA."

He'd literally thought of everything. Some sort of demonic genius.

So much of the puzzle was coming together. Sadly, there was no way to relay it to the police.

I continued slowly, subtly, rubbing my feet together.

"And when did you decide it was going to be easier to just try and kill me?"

"After you were bailed out, a few of my connections told me the DA's office and police weren't convinced it was an airtight case. And then I saw you at Golden Gate Fields a few times and I just figured it would be easier to kill you."

"You almost did."

"I'm curious, how did you manage to get away?"

"I heard a slight movement from my apartment as I put my key in the door. It gave me a fighting chance of getting down the hallway."

A smile crossed his face. "Your demise is inevitable, but I've got a lot of respect for you, Quint."

I wanted to keep him talking. The more time the better. Maybe he'd have a heart attack. Anything to give me a sliver of a chance.

"You had Griff Bauer kill Aubrey Durban and James Neil?"

"Yes," he exclaimed, continuing to enjoy telling me all that happened. "Griff was a drug dealer for us, but he had a big batch stolen from him. He knew he was in deep. So we gave him an option."

"And he found out that Aubrey had told Tricia Knox?"

"Yes, so she had to go."

"She was a very nice person," I said.

"I'm sure she was. As you may have gathered, that's not going to affect me. It was just business."

"Torture shouldn't be part of business."

"If you have to find things out, it's sometimes necessary."

"You plan on torturing me. I've got nothing to give."

Zane smiled again. "You caught me. Sometimes I torture if someone has caused me an excessive amount of aggravation."

"Like the man who nicknamed you Shark?"

"Precisely."

I wanted to change the subject.

Zane was still seated and too far away for my legs to swivel and strike him. But I waited for the moment.

"I've got another question for you," he said.

"Okay."

"How did you know, and I'm assuming it was you, to go to Doug Anderson's home last Friday night?"

He saw me pause. "If you don't want to talk, we can get right to the torturous part of our scheduled program."

God, I hated him. For a million reasons. Even his smugness made the list.

"I went to Paddy Roark and Dennis McCarthy. I told them I wanted something on you. An ex-wife. A disgruntled employee. Something to use against you."

"And..."

"And they didn't have anything in that regard. But they told me they had a friend who worked at the Cliff House and he'd be willing to put an audio bug in your car."

He shuffled his chair as if this shocked him. "When I grabbed your phones earlier, I saw one had no apps except the link for 'CZaudio' on the home page."

"That was it."

"So you listened to me for days?"

"Yes."

"Probably didn't get much info. I try to keep quiet. But I trust, or I should say, I used to trust Doug Anderson. I felt comfortable talking to him. When I told him I'd send someone there that night, you showed up?"

"I did. And saw the two bodies get taken out. Annie Ivers was another very nice lady."

"Collateral damage," Zane said.

"I have a question." I knew we were getting down to the nitty gritty. "Why have there been young girls running from Doug Anderson's house? That's what Aubrey and James saw as well, right?"

"You don't pull punches, Quint. I respect that."

"If you respect me so much, why don't you let me go?" I asked.

He laughed. "Sorry, but we're past the point of no return."

I figured there was no need to go down a road that led nowhere.

"Were you guys trafficking women?" I asked.

"God, no. A little prostitution now and then, but no trafficking. Doug Anderson just has some peculiar habits. He likes young women. Although I guess, technically, they are girls. I can't prevent all of my subordinates from partaking in their worst fantasies."

"There's a difference between liking young women and having them run from your house." I paused. "Or being taken out in a body bag."

"Doug is a tough case. He's literally my number one dealer in the Bay Area. Any housewife within fifty miles who is doing Oxy or Vicodin or any of a number of other pills is either getting them from Doug or one of his subordinates."

"A subordinate with his own subordinates."

"Makes it much harder to get to the man on top."

"Your business plan is similar to Dennis McCarthy's."

"Where do you think I came up with the idea? We're both surrounded at the top by guys who would never turn on us. And the people near the bottom barely know they're working for us. Take Griff Bauer for example. He never met me. Maybe he had an inkling he worked for me, but would never have any proof if arrested. And yet, I authorized hiring him. I gave the go-ahead to have him kill the couple on Oakland Avenue. And I'd even sanctioned his murder."

I didn't need to hear him toot his own horn.

"I'm assuming the girl that Aubrey and James saw is dead."

"What do you think? We sent someone to that house almost immediately. Luckily, they hadn't called the cops yet. Apparently, they were consoling the young woman. She was disposed of immediately. Just some runaway no one would miss. These Aubrey and James people were different. We had questions for them."

"And let me guess, you disposed of the young woman's body in the ocean?"

"Yes."

"How many bodies are there in the water around the Bay Area?"

"Over the years?" He seemed to be pondering the question. "If I was still a gambling man, I'd set the over/under at twenty-five."

He started laughing. I was disgusted.

I continued to move my feet back and forth, hoping to cause friction on the rope. If I kept him talking, maybe, just maybe, I could slowly wear it down. But, even then, I'd only have my legs free. I would have to do more.

"Who was the man who came to Bauer's hospital room that first night?" I asked.

"You were there?"

"Yes, I thought you knew."

"It's the one part I couldn't figure out. What brought you to his house the next morning?"

"I overheard him arguing with someone in the hospital. I took a picture of his address. And went there the next morning, hoping it would lead somewhere."

Neither one of us said anything. It wasn't necessary because we both knew where it had led me.

Defenseless, handcuffed to a boat, drifting on the Pacific Ocean.

"Your stitches were visible those first few days I saw you," Zane said. "I should have put two and two together."

"So who was the man who came to the hospital?" I repeated.

"That would be Max, the man you just saw me with at the Berkeley Marina. If I had anything close to a second in command, it would be him."

"And he killed Griff Bauer?"

"No, no, no. I don't ever have someone that close to me commit the murder itself. We hire someone down the totem pole, so if the jackass is caught, he has nothing of importance to tell. But once we heard Bauer was in the hospital, we knew we had to get him out of there. In case the police found out someone had crashed near a double homicide. They'd probably want to ask a few questions. So I sent Max to get him the hell out of there. Glad I did."

He gloated. He loved to show how smart he was.

"So who killed Griff Bauer? Was it the same man who tried to kill me?"

I saw Zane genuinely thinking about it. "As a matter of fact, it was. He did such a good job on Bauer, we gave him a second job. He wasn't as successful with you. So he's probably on borrowed time himself."

"When does it end?" I asked.

"I'm hoping with you." He smiled again.

I didn't give him the satisfaction of smiling back.

"So all these murders happened because of Doug Anderson's propensity for young women?"

"This latest round of murders. But trust me, there have been many bodies over the years with nothing to do with Anderson. And it's almost never me doing the actual killing."

A decent-sized wave rocked the boat. Zane had to regain his footing and sat back down.

"You still order the murders," I finally said.

"Semantics. And if it makes you feel any better, once the attention around Doug Anderson's house subsides, he'll be meeting a bloody end as well."

"You need to be stopped."

"Yeah, you're probably right. But it's not going to be by a guy with no free arms or legs. With a knife wound to boot."

I started to sense that Zane was getting tired of talking. Once that happened, I was a dead man.

I needed to play off his ego. Praise him. I knew he loved that.

"So how did you have my father murdered without anyone ever suspecting anything other than a mugging?"

"You're ready to get down to it?"

I knew how hard this was going to be for me. But I needed to keep him talking. And I had to know.

"I'd at least like to know what I'm going to die for."

Charles Zane adjusted his seat, now facing me straight on. He slid his chair back a foot, which put him potentially in range for me to sweep my feet under him. But I knew I had to wait. A fall from a few feet wouldn't have any chance of incapacitating him.

"Sadly, it's not all that great a story. I wish I could tell you your father infiltrated my criminal enterprise and was talking to the CIA, but that's not the case. He just asked questions one too many times. And I'm not one to take chances."

"What questions did he ask?"

"Well, now we have to go back a little bit. As I assume you now understand, Doug Anderson is a wild card. And not the good kind that you want in your poker hand. He had many vices, the young girls only being one of them. And these would be exacerbated when he dabbled in his own drug supply. He'd get touchy. And not just with the women. His daughter and his son were on the receiving end at times. Not sexually, but physically. The kids missed school all the time for 'being sick'. But they weren't really sick. They'd gotten the wrong end of the belt or Doug Anderson's fist. I know you think I'm a monster. Rightfully so, I might add. But I'm not the punch-your-kids-in-the-face type of monster. So I tried to get Doug to stop. The problem was that Doug was good, no, Doug was great for business. It's like a professional sports league. If you commit a serious crime, you'll be let back in the league, but only if you're a great player. They have no time for someone who doesn't produce. Well, Doug produced for me. Made me millions of dollars a year. Helped buy yachts like these."

Zane extended his hands toward the boat, as if I hadn't noticed how extravagant it was. Being stuck on the deck, I couldn't see out to the ocean, but I could tell the waves were getting slightly bigger. The boat had started to move back and forth a little more.

"And it's hard to just get rid of someone that valuable," Zane continued. "Trust me, I thought about it. Would have worked out better for you if I had. Your father as well."

The anger I'd been trying to suppress suddenly rushed back to me. "You murder the good people and let a rapist child beater live. You better hope there's not a hell."

"Sorry, but there's no afterlife that levels everything out. Some people are just dealt a shitty hand. Like your father."

I tried to relax. I couldn't risk being this close and not finding out.

"So what exactly happened?"

"You really want to know? You're surely going to be disappointed."

"I don't want to know. I need to."

"Alright. I'll tell you," he said, shuffling his chair even closer. "So, Doug's son Mason was a student of your father's. I guess this all started about eighteen months ago now. As was the norm with the Anderson kids, they missed school occasionally. As I'd said, it was because Doug would lay a hand on them. The problem was, some parents in the Oakland school district were clients of Doug's. You think drugs and you think some homeless guy on the street, but it's not always that way. There's plenty of parents hooked on the shit. A housewife's party used to involve a bottle of wine. Now they throw in a few pills for fun. I'm sorry, getting off track a little bit. The point is, Doug had too many clients in Oakland and I didn't like them crossing paths so often. So I suggested he send his son somewhere else for his junior year of high school. And Mason transferred to Northgate. That's when he got your father as a teacher. And your father proved to be a very intuitive man and sensed something was up. He asked Mason if there was a problem with his home life. Mason, knowing the beating he'd take if he told the truth, told your father no. But your father wasn't convinced. Apparently, he started calling the Andersons' home, leaving several messages. Doug came to me at this point and told me all that was going on. I told him Mason had to drop out of your father's school, which he did, even though they were only a few weeks from the school year finishing. We thought that would be the end of it. But your father was dogged. I never met the man, but I can safely say it's a trait he passed down on to you. Your father kept calling."

I was gaining more respect for my father by the second. This story was going to end in grief, but I already knew that. I tried to focus on the bravery that Dad had shown.

Since he watched me, Zane could tell I was proud of my father's actions. He continued, "Doug finally returned your father's call and told him that Mason was a klutz and always falling around the house. That was the reason he'd have bruises or the occasional black eye. He also informed him that Mason dropped out and was transferring schools to be closer to home. Being a few weeks before the end of the year, I'm sure your father knew it was bullshit. Of course, Mason wasn't going back to any school. I told Doug it was too big a risk. He could homeschool him if he wanted. Apparently, this wasn't enough for your father. He kept calling even once the year had finished. I think he was actually worried about young Mason's well-being. Very admirable. He found out the Andersons' address and showed up at their house one day. He was a persistent little fuck, I'll give him that.

"Doug answered the door and your father demanded to see Mason. Doug wasn't going to let him. You see, Mason had a fresh black eye. But apparently, Mason heard the commotion at the front door and started walking down the hallway. Your father looked past Doug, saw Mason, and noticed the brand-new bruises. At this point, your father took out his phone and said he was calling child services. Doug hit the phone out of your father's hand and shoved him against the wall. No punches were thrown, but it got physical. Your father asked for the phone back, but Doug saw his life flashing before his eyes. He refused. Your father shouted that he was going to Child Protective Services and then the police, and he stormed out the door. Doug immediately called me. I told him we had too much to lose. He knew what that meant. And since your father was about to drive away, it was something that Doug would have to take care of himself.

"He told Mason to wait inside. He put on a long jacket, grabbed a large knife, and ran to his van. Started following your father. Doug told me later he was surprised that he headed into San Francisco. Your father worked in the East Bay, so it was unlikely he lived in the city. But that's where he drove. With Doug following him. Another surprise was him parking just a block above the Tenderloin. Not exactly the best spot for old white guys. But Doug knew it might be the perfect spot to get away with what was to come. He parked his car and when he saw your father start walking up Jones Street, Doug went to the next parallel street and sprinted up two blocks. He then walked back across to Jones Street and darted into a little alley that your father would have to walk by. Your father approached the alley and…"

"Stop!" I shouted. "I don't want to hear any more."

It was too much. I didn't need to hear how it ended. I already knew that part.

I started sobbing. For my father. For myself. And for my mother, who was about to be all alone in this world.

Despite all my grief, I knew I couldn't let it get the best of me. I had to stay focused.

I quickly gathered my emotions and began to think about all that Zane had told me.

One thing that had always bothered my mother and me was why my father had been in San Francisco that night. I now had a good guess. Gary Rodger's law firm was about four blocks above the Tenderloin. Parking is always impossible in the city and my father must have seen an open spot and decided to walk the remaining blocks.

If you don't know San Francisco, it's hard to understand. But a lousy area like the Tenderloin can turn into a nice area, perfect for a law firm, in a matter of a few city blocks.

Of course, I could never be sure, but it made perfect sense. He'd just had his phone taken and been thrown up against a wall. Not to mention the fresh black eye he'd seen on Mason Anderson. He probably wanted to talk to Gary about his options. My father knew Gary kept long hours and probably assumed the office was open.

I took a deep breath. Charles Zane didn't say anything, showing a rare moment of compassion. Or he just enjoyed my misery.

It was a lot to take in. It explained many things and despite my own dire circumstances, I was glad to find out. And I felt my dad died a hero. He was trying to protect one of his students. He was doing a heroic deed. Of that, there was no doubt.

It was hard to not think about how it ended for him, though. Walking up Jones Street when Doug Anderson jumped out and…

I tried to push it out of my mind. I wanted to remember him as someone looking out for his students to the very end. That's what he'd want.

I bowed my head. "I've found out everything I wanted to know. Let's get this over with," I said.

"That's it?"

"You can't let me go, so what's the point?"

"I can't let you go. You're right."

"Then let's get on with it," I said.

I was playing possum, not ready to concede death. I was going to fight till the very end.

I just hoped my little charade would get him to let his guard down. Even just a little bit.

"I've gained respect for you, Quint. It's not going to save your life, but I don't have the stomach to torture you."

He started to bring the gun out of his sweatshirt. My life was about to end, unless I could pull off my improbable plan.

I'd only have one chance, so I had to time it perfectly. I couldn't attempt it too early. I had to wait until he stood up. The legs of the chair were currently between my legs and his. They'd soften the blow too much to cause any damage. Plus, a fall from that short distance wouldn't knock him out, and knocking him out was my best chance.

My feet were tied together, but that wouldn't prevent what I had to do: sweeping my legs into his with the utmost ferocity.

Zane began to rise. He grabbed the chair and started to slide it away from where he stood. His eyes turned away from me for a brief moment.

The next few seconds would determine whether I lived or died.

I swung my legs out to the left to gain some momentum. And then, with all the force I could muster, swung them back in the direction of Charles Zane…

37.

And connected with more power than I could have ever expected.

The back of Zane's head was facing me and he didn't see it coming. My legs connected with full force and took both of his feet out from under him.

He started falling backward toward me. Before he hit the deck, I had my legs raised again, ready to pounce.

Zane hit butt first, but it happened so quickly that the whiplash sent his head backward, striking the boat's rigid floor. He hit hard and I prayed it had knocked him unconscious, but I had no time to wait and find out.

Before he had a chance to gain his bearings, my feet came down full speed on his face. I hit him flush in the nose, blood exploding from it immediately. I made sure to crash down with both heels, the hardest parts of my feet.

I raised my legs as high as I could and brought them down once more.

I did it again. And again. And again. And again.

The rope started to loosen, so I moved my feet around, trying to get free as I raised them between kicks.

I brought my feet down together four more times in rapid succession, alternating between his nose and his forehead.

Zane was conscious, but barely. The effect of hitting his head on the hard floor combined with my repeated blows had him in bad shape. But he was still making noises.

And I couldn't take any chances.

I brought the heels of my shoes down on his face one more time, with as much force as I could exert. I focused primarily on his nose, which was collapsing into his face. It was grotesque, but I was fighting for my life. I didn't have a choice.

And finally, mercifully, the knot came undone. I kicked the rope off and my legs were free.

This made it easier. I started rotating between my left heel and then my right heel, bringing them down on Zane's face and head.

I did it again. And again. And again. And again. And again. And again.

His face was starting to looked like a smashed tomato. Not that I cared.

I couldn't risk having him stumble away or I was a dead man.

As I continued to bring my legs down on his face, I looked for the gun. I saw it. He must have dropped it when I initially took out his legs. It was directly behind his back.

To be safe, I brought my feet down five more times on to Charles Zane's head. I heard a few barely audible, shallow breaths, but he was now struggling for air. And for the first time, I exhaled. He was not going to be getting up anytime soon. If ever.

I now had to concentrate on getting out of these handcuffs. My plan with Zane had worked to perfection, but if I remained cuffed in the middle of the Pacific, it might all be for naught.

I swung my right leg over his body and slowly brought my foot down on top of the gun. It was a pistol that looked like it took six bullets. I pushed it in my direction, careful not to move it much. I didn't care if it took five pushes to get me, I just didn't want to accidentally shove it too far past myself.

After four small pushes, I brought the gun directly next to my butt. I raised my backside to push the gun toward my wrists.

I heard another belabored breath from Charles Zane, so I brought my right foot down three successive times on his nose. There was an odd silence after the last kick. I couldn't be sure, but it seemed like life was leaving his body.

I didn't celebrate. Despite him being a murderous thug who deserved anything he got.

It was time to concentrate on my own survival.

Another moment of truth had arrived. I had a little room to wriggle my wrists around. My goal was to lift up the gun and shoot through the handcuffs, breaking them to free myself. It wasn't going to be easy. How do you shoot through a little chain link? I'd have to get lucky.

The other option would be to try to shoot out the metal bar that my handcuffs were wrapped around, but it lay right at the base of my spine. Any deflection could paralyze me. Effectively a death sentence considering my situation.

I reached for the gun and was able to pick it up rather easily. I couldn't tell by the weight how many bullets were in it. But considering the difficulty of what was to come, I hoped it was fully loaded. I'd likely need more than one bullet.

Now for the tough part. I had to shoot the gun from behind my back. And not only that, I had to break the chain link that connected the handcuffs.

I positioned my wrist and leaned the handcuffs into the nozzle of the gun, which I made sure pointed away from my body.

"Here goes nothing," I said.

And fired the pistol.

There was a noise as it hit through the deck and ricocheted. But I was not freed from the handcuffs.

"Fuck!!!" I screamed.

There was no telling how many bullets remained in the chamber. Maybe an experienced shooter would know, but I had no idea. If, by chance, there had only been one, I was screwed.

I spent a good thirty seconds repositioning the gun in my grip. I tried to feel for a bigger piece of the chain. Once I did, I put that flush against the pistol.

And fired again.

More noise as the bullet deflected toward the bottom of the boat. But I wasn't freed.

"Dammit!!!"

A terrifying thought came to me. What if the bullets penetrated the bottom of the yacht, causing a leak? I'd be stuck in the middle of the ocean on a sinking boat.

But it's not like I had a choice. No one was coming to my rescue.

I had to get out of these handcuffs.

Even if I risked creating more holes in the boat.

I repositioned the handcuffs, spending a good minute trying to line up the greatest surface area against the nozzle of the gun.

I fired. But once again, nothing happened.

I decided to take a few seconds and collect my thoughts.

And that's when I started to smell the smoke. Here I was, worried the bullets would puncture the bottom of the boat. Instead, I'd hit the gas tank, or a gas can, or a fuel line. Regardless, I'd started a fire.

Somehow, against all odds, I might have a fate worse than drowning to death. Burning alive while handcuffed.

I repositioned the gun in my grip for what seemed like a tenth time. It wasn't easy. My wrist was behind my back and I had to shuffle it around to make sure I wasn't shooting back up toward my own body.

"Please work this time," I said to myself.

I fired again. Nothing.

There were two bullets left. At most.

The smoke now came up from below deck. It was no longer just a smell; I could now see the black flumes rolling past me. I coughed a few times when the wind sent it in my direction.

I had been trying to shoot off the chain link, and it had amounted to nothing. So I decided to try something different. I put the cuff around my left wrist flush up against the pistol that my right hand held. There was a chance I might be blowing my left hand off, but I had to risk it.

The other way was just too difficult, with so little surface area to hit. Especially shooting from behind my body.

I positioned the cuff at an angle where I thought the bullet would be headed away from my wrist. Assuming it wasn't redirected.

I didn't waste any time and fired the pistol. The noise was different than the one I'd heard on the first four shots.

I began to raise my hands from behind my back, figuring I'd be met with the resistance that had accompanied each previous attempt.

But this time was different.

I raised my hands up without being met by any impediment.

I was free!!

I could see the clear gunshot entry point through the cuff on my left wrist. It had opened the hinge that locked it in place. The handcuffs now dangled from my right hand.

"Yes!!" I yelled.

And I stood up.

I never could have imagined what a great feeling that simple motion would bring.

My attention turned to Zane. Maybe I'd seen too many horror movies, but the bad guy is never dead. And I was ready to finish him off once and for all.

But as I looked down at him, I knew it wasn't necessary.

Charles Zane was dead.

His face looked as you'd expect after forty or fifty kicks. It was a bloody mess with his cheeks, nose, and forehead almost inseparable.

But you could clearly see his eyes. They were bugging and not going to blink. Ever again.

His face looked similar to Griff Bauer's when I looked through the hinges of his door. This had all come full circle.

After one last look at Zane, I headed toward the ladder that took you below deck. My worst fears had come true. The fire was already out of control.

I searched for a fire extinguisher, but couldn't find one. It was likely below deck and going down there was now an impossibility.

The flames were giving off a crazy amount of heat. I wouldn't be able to stay on the boat much longer.

What were my options? I didn't have many.

Then a terrible revelation struck me. The life jackets had been below deck.

I walked back to the ladder and looked down. In the inferno, the bottom of the ladder had burnt away.

Surely the life jackets were gone as well.

And it's not like I could jump down there anyway. I'd be burnt to death in seconds.

There was no way around it. In a very short time, I was going to enter the remorseless Pacific without a life jacket. I was a dead man.

Making matters worse, the sun had begun to set over the course of the last several minutes. Most light came from the fire. When the boat went down and the water extinguished the fire, I'd be all alone in the pitch black of the Pacific.

One last chance remained. I walked up to where you helm the boat.

I found a radio on the side of the steering wheel and picked up the transmitter, which was really just an old-school walkie talkie.

"Help!" I yelled.

But there was no answer.

I saw a little plaque and found the section I was looking for.

It read: *In case of emergency, go to Channel 16 and transmit "Mayday. Mayday. Mayday."*

I switched the radio to Channel 16 and picked up the transmitter.

The smoke was getting worse and making it tougher to breathe. I had to be quick.

"Mayday! Mayday! Mayday!" I yelled. "Is anyone there? I'm on a boat that's on fire. In the middle of the Pacific."

I realized how stupid that sounded.

I heard a voice on the other end.

"This is the Coast Guard. What are your coordinates?"

"I have no idea." Then I remembered something that Zane had said. "Wait. I think we might be fifteen miles off the coast of Santa Cruz."

"Your coordinates will be on the boat's GPS. If you are on the radio, you probably have them on the screen in front of you."

I found them and relayed them to the dispatcher.

"How long do you have?" she asked.

"I don't know. A few minutes max. The smoke is getting worse by the second."

"Do you have a raft or anything to get off the boat in?"

"No."

"At least make sure you throw on a life jacket."

"Those burnt up."

Her silence said it all. She knew, like me, that I was in deep, deep trouble.

"I'm sending someone from the Coast Guard right now. I hate to tell you this, but we don't have patrols that far out. It could be twenty minutes."

"I'll be dead in half that time," I said.

"Do what you can. Stay on the boat until the last possible second. Then try to grab on to something that will keep you afloat."

"Thanks. I have to go."

"Good luck."

I walked back down from the helm, and the heat became nearly unbearable. The flames had overtaken the lower level and were starting to appear on the main deck.

As I looked out onto the Pacific, I noticed two shark fins breaking the surface, parading around the boat. Clearly, they'd been attracted by the flames, noise, or the vibrations of the boat, but after all that happened, it sure didn't feel like a coincidence.

I heard a deafening pop. It sounded like an oxygen tank or something similar had exploded. I had to get off the boat.

"Shit! Shit! Shit!" I said.

The flames were my immediate concern, but the boat was going down soon. I didn't have much else I could do.

Hopefully, by some miracle, the Coast Guard would arrive before I drowned. But the odds were stacked against me.

As the boat continued to disintegrate, one end rose higher in the water. The angle forced Charles Zane's body down toward the blaze.

I watched as it caught on fire. He was lucky to already be dead. I guess I should have been happy that at the very least, I had taken him with me. Avenging my father's death. But that didn't give me any solace in the moment. I had myself to worry about.

The heat was becoming too much and I knew I had to get in the water.

It was a horrible choice to have to make, but I'd take drowning over burning alive.

The boat took on water as the lower deck sank. I went to the farthest point from the fire, waiting for the last second until I entered the Pacific.

I looked out on the horizon for a boat. Surely, if there was one in the vicinity, they'd head toward something burning. But I saw no one. So far out in the ocean, the idea of having another boat close by was a pipe dream.

And the Coast Guard was still at least fifteen minutes away.

The water now came over the edges of the boat.

I saw Charles Zane's lifeless, burnt body get swept overboard.

And then, as if on cue, the two shark fins headed toward Zane's body. Tooth-filled maws started tearing him to shreds. It was vicious, primal, and over in a few seconds.

I probably would have enjoyed the irony if I wasn't about to enter that very same water.

Cracking noises sounded from the bottom of the boat. It must not have been able to take the pressure of the fire anymore.

Then, with a huge crack, one portion of the boat broke off from the other. We were going down.

In a mere five seconds, I'd gone from ten feet above sea level to the inevitably that I was about to enter the Pacific Ocean.

This was it.

The boat sank quickly. As my last line of protection gave way and I first touched the ocean water, it was even colder than I expected. My stab wounds immediately stung from the salt, but I thought being in shorts actually gave me a fighting chance. It would be nearly impossible to move around in wet jeans.

Still, lasting until the Coast Guard arrived would be a long shot. And that's assuming they found me. I was no longer on a boat, just an individual floating at sea. They might never see me.

As I entered the water, I was able to hold on to a rather large piece of the boat. It offered my best chance of surviving, considering I had no life jacket. I was a good swimmer, but surviving the Pacific Ocean was something entirely different from swimming laps at my apartment complex.

I remained holding the wreckage for a minute.

But just when I thought I might get out of this alive, a huge wave slammed me from behind and I lost my grip. A few seconds later, I slid back down the other side of the wave, but couldn't see any fragments of the boat.

How had it vanished from my line of sight so quickly? I was amazed at the power of the ocean.

Which was going to be my final resting place. I knew that now.

I was all alone in the Pacific Ocean without a life jacket.

And it's not like I was near the coast with reasonable swells. I was miles and miles from shore and the waves were massive.

Another took me by surprise and dragged me under for a good five seconds. I struggled to get back above water and catch a breath. I made it, but knew I couldn't last much longer.

I'd be lying if I said the image of the sharks ripping Zane's body apart hadn't entered my mind. I visualized them swimming below me, but did all I could to push that picture out of my mind.

And despite the menace of the sharks, I knew I was more likely to drown.

It was dark out. I was in the unrelenting ocean. And each wave sent my head underwater for several seconds. I couldn't imagine a more frightening scenario.

A minute passed and I don't know how I survived it. It felt like an hour.

The Coast Guard was still at least ten minutes away. Likely more.

Another huge wave passed over, sending me under. As I fought to get to the surface, I realized if I just opened my mouth and took in a huge amount of water, it could be over soon.

No!!!

I was going to fight to my very last breath.

Which might come at any moment.

My whole body started to shiver.

I looked up toward the heavens.

"I'll be joining you soon, Dad. I love you."

I thought of my mother and of Cara. I'd let them down. I just hoped someday they'd forgive me.

Another wave came over me, and it was an immense struggle to get above water and take in a breath. Something smacked my head from behind, likely a piece of wood from the boat. It almost knocked me out.

Maybe that would have been for the best.

Before I could grab the floating piece of boat it had slipped out of my reach. Seaweed had wrapped itself around my left shoulder and slapped me in the face.

Another wave took me under. I once again thought swallowing a lot of water might be the easiest way out.

But I couldn't. I had to fight. If I lost my life, it was going to because of the elements, not from giving up.

I looked around for anything to hold on to, but it was too dark. I saw nothing.

The biggest wave yet carried me up and then sent me underwater. It was too powerful and I wasn't going to be able to get to the surface. Just when I'd conceded the inevitability of death, I saw a light shining through the water.

I had to fight!

I used all the energy I had to get above the surface, taking in a huge breath once I did. I'd been seconds from dying. Of that, there's no doubt.

I looked around for the light and saw a boat. I took another deep breath, knowing I needed more oxygen if I was going to yell.

"I'm over here!! I'm over here!!"

I screamed louder than I'd ever had before. But I could only muster the two screams. My low oxygen level wouldn't allow me any more.

The waves went over me every few seconds. When I had a brief respite, I spent all my energy trying to yell, even if it wouldn't last long.

"I'm over here!"

The boat continued in my direction. And I kept trying to yell.

"Quint?" I heard a voice yelling from the boat.

I didn't have time to consider how they knew my name. I was just ecstatic to hear it.

I took the deepest breath I could. "I'm over here!" I shouted, using all the strength I could muster. "I'm over here! I'm over here!"

And somehow, the boat heard me. Or saw me. I didn't care. I just knew they were now coming directly at me.

Fifty feet away. Forty feet. Twenty feet.

I was exhausted. My muscles were failing. But no way could I go back underwater. This was my one shot.

The boat came within ten feet and a man looked in my direction.

"I see him!" he yelled.

The boat came up next to me and the man reached down, grabbing me by my shoulders, and pulled me onto the deck.

Immediately, someone at my side threw a jacket over me. He had me sit down.

"How long have you been in the water?" he asked.

"Ten minutes, I'd guess," I said.

"With no life jacket? And in that unforgiving ocean?"

I nodded, it taking less energy than speaking.

"Truly amazing," he said.

I looked out upon the ocean, still in a bit of shock it wasn't going to be my grave.

The man looked down at my thigh.

"Knife wounds," I said, my breath slowly coming back.

"Jesus, what happened to you?"

I didn't know how to answer.

"Don't worry about it," he said. "You just rest for now."

Someone brought over a huge blanket and laid it over me.

I was beyond exhausted, but getting fuller breaths. The man gave me a minute as I deeply inhaled air several times.

"How did you guys get here so soon?" I finally asked. "The dispatcher said it was going to be twenty minutes or more."

"We had a head start on our patrolling Coast Guard brethren," the man said and nodded in someone's direction.

A familiar face approached me. Ray Kintner.

He came and put his arm around my shoulder. And started smiling.

"You know, we could have been here sooner if you'd just told me you were going to be on Zane's boat instead of giving me some fucking riddle about his nickname."

I don't know why, but it was one of the funniest things I'd ever heard.

For a moment, Ray and I shared a laugh, but then I started coughing uncontrollably.

"Save your breath," he said.

And then he hugged me.

We sat there for a while before he spoke again. "I'm sorry for all that happened," he said

"Don't be," I said. "You just saved my life."

And then, once the moment passed, I broke down and started crying.

It was all too much. I cried for my dad. For what happened on the boat. For almost having died at sea. For what my mother was likely going through.

"I'm sorry," I said, once I'd got ahold of myself.

"No need to apologize," Ray said. "Zane is dead, I assume?"

I nodded.

"I'm sure you have quite the story to tell."

"You have no idea."

"It can wait. Rest up."

38.

I was largely left alone for the next ten minutes.

One of the Coast Guard came over and bandaged up the knife wounds on my thigh. He then took my temperature and smiled at the reading.

But that was it.

They obviously thought rest was best.

I had a jacket on and a huge blanket covering me and my body was warming up by the minute.

Ray Kintner walked back over right as we glimpsed the coast for the first time.

"Quint, are you feeling up for a five-minute conversation? Once we get to the hospital, the doctors will take over, but you could give me some vital information right now. It could be time sensitive."

"I can talk," I said.

I only had time to give Ray the bullet points, so I summarized what Charles Zane had divulged on the boat. I mentioned Anderson and his murders, the man who'd successfully killed Bauer, but not me, and Max, who'd helped load the boat.

I told him that Zane said Max was his second in charge. He'd be vital.

We were approaching the shore when I asked to borrow his phone.

"Hello? Who is this?" my mother's voice said.

"It's your son, Mom. I'm fine," I said.

She started crying on the other end. Tears of joy, to be sure. I figured she'd be finding out about my ordeal shorty, so I didn't want to alarm her.

"And I found out that Dad died a hero," I said.

This was too much for her and she began crying louder. Our family had never been the most emotional group, but that sure had changed.

"When can I see you?"

"I'll call you later today. Just know I'm safe."

I called Cara, who didn't answer, possibly because she didn't recognize the number. I left her a voicemail.

Ray took his phone back.

"How did you think to sweep out his legs?"

"I didn't have many options," I said and smiled wryly.

"I guess not."

"And my hands were indisposed in the moment."

"If I was a gambling man, I'd have said you were a hundred to one to get off that boat alive."

"I told myself a thousand to one."

"A bookie could go broke taking bets against you."

I laughed. "Thanks, Ray."

He called ahead to a hospital in Santa Cruz, telling them he was bringing a patient in.

"We'll try to get you a single bed this time," Ray said.

I laughed again. "You're funnier than I remember," I said.

"Thinking about throwing my hat in the stand-up ring."

"Cop Comedy. Somehow don't think that's going to catch on."

"Yeah, I guess not."

A member of the Coast Guard walked up to us. "Mr. Adler, we are pulling in to the Santa Cruz marina. We have an ambulance ready."

The Guardsman, or "Coastie" as some called them, smiled at me. I owed them a great debt, but it must have been fulfilling on their end as well. They had saved a life.

"Thanks so much," I said. "I'll never be able to repay you guys."

"You're welcome."

The Coastie smiled and left Kintner and I be. I made a note to get these guys' names and send them something special.

"I can't wait to hear how you found out Zane's nickname and how that led you fifteen miles off the coast of Santa Cruz," I said.

Ray Kintner looked out onto the approaching dock. "I'll fill you in on everything later. But let's just say, if we weren't able to ping your cell phone, we'd still be near the Berkley Marina. It's what gave us a fighting chance. To be continued. We're pulling in."

The Coast Guard parked its vessel and one of the Coasties escorted me off of the boat. I thanked them all a second time.

An ambulance waited less than fifty feet from the dock.

"Here, let me help you get there," Ray Kintner said.

We arrived at Santa Cruz's Dominican Hospital, a huge white building with blue lettering. I was given my own room, where they started conducting a series of tests.

My main doctor was a polite, red-headed woman in her forties. Her name tag read Doctor Rhonda Grimes. The way she looked at me made me think she knew who I was. It seemed too early for my rescue to already be on the news. Of course, having been accompanied to the hospital by a police officer might have alerted her. Or my name itself, which had been on the news way too much in recent weeks.

Doctor Grimes told me the knife wounds on my right thigh were mainly superficial. "Probably just some stitches."

Stitches seemed to be the bookends for the wild ride of the last three months.

She said I had no hypothermia and that overall I'd been pretty damn lucky.

"How long does it take to get hypothermia?"

"With that temperature it could take up to an hour. You would have drowned before hypothermia set in." She smiled. The doctors I'd encountered all seemed to have an odd sense of humor.

"How long do I have to stay?"

"We'll probably keep you two days for observation. You went through a crazy ordeal, Quint. Detective Kintner informed me what happened. We've also got several psychologists on staff if you feel you need to talk to someone."

"For now, I'm good. But if that changes, I'll let you know."

"Alright. I'm going to let you go back to sleep now," she said. "It's a wonder you're in such good health after all you've been through."

"Thank you, Doctor," I said.

Rhonda Grimes walked out of the room.

Looking at the clock, guessed I'd been at the hospital for about ninety minutes. But I couldn't be sure. Time had blended together once the sun went down and I'd entered the Pacific.

I heard some voices talking outside of my room, but they were whispering and I couldn't make them out.

A minute later, Cara and my mother walked in. Ray Kintner trailed behind them.

"Was this you?" I asked him.

"I may have secretly texted the two numbers you called."

"You guys just set a record time in getting to Santa Cruz," I said.

"I may have broken a law or two," my mother said, making us all laugh.

She leaned in and gave me the longest hug of my life.

"Three hospital visits in three months," she said. "Can this be the last one?"

"This is it. I promise."

Cara leaned in and whispered, "You are going to need a lot of TLC."

"Doing nothing has never sounded so good," I said. "I wouldn't be alive right now if it weren't for this gentleman," I told the two women, nodding to Ray Kintner.

My mother hugged him.

"Does this make up for incorrectly arresting him in the first place?" Ray laughed.

"Everyone is a comedian today," I said.

At some point, I'd need to address all I'd been through. Being stabbed, being tied up, being handcuffed, being forced to shoot off the handcuffs, and then being alone in the mighty Pacific Ocean. It wasn't something that would just go away. But I wasn't ready to deal with everything yet.

Laughter and bad jokes were just fine at the moment.

"Your doctor said we should give you some time to sleep," Ray said.

The phone call which led me to the Berkeley Marina seemed like a week ago. But it had been a matter of hours, not days.

"Yeah, I think that's a good idea," I said. "Will I see you all in the morning?"

Cara and my mother nodded.

"I imagine work will come calling for me," Ray said.

They started to walk out, but he stayed a second longer.

"A lot of arrests are going to happen tonight. All because of you. You've done a great service to the Bay Area. We'll talk tomorrow, Quint. Sleep well."

"Thanks, Ray."

And I was left alone. The longest day of my life was about to come to a close.

Two days later, I was released from Dominican Hospital.

Different types of law enforcement had descended on me the morning after I was admitted. And after answering questions for a few hours, I went back to sleep. And continued sleeping for the majority of my duration at the hospital.

My test results had all come back normal. I'd even spent an hour with a psychologist, who'd said he was amazed how well I was dealing with all the adversity I'd gone through.

He made me promise to go see another psychologist if it all became too much to handle. I promised.

Doctor Grimes was there to say goodbye, which meant five of us were in my small hospital room. Ray had been working diligently on the case, including asking questions of me that next morning, but he came back to Santa Cruz the day I was released. Cara and my mother had only left to sleep at a local hotel each night.

I said goodbye to the doctor and I left my room. They'd offered me a wheelchair, but I told them I felt fine. It was the truth.

We approached the front entrance to Dominican Hospital. The handful of media had left the previous day, not willing to wait me out. My recovery could have required a week for all they knew. So there would be no reason to use the back door. We'd exit out the front.

Ray and I went to open the doors for the women. But the doors opened automatically.

We stood there, looking like idiots, as the women walked through the opened doors.

"If there was ever a debate about who is smarter between the two sexes, it's now been decided," Cara said.

We all shared another laugh.

And I walked out of the hospital.

39.

"Mr. Adler, this is Agent Devin Moore of the FBI."

The call came the day after I was released.

My old phone was now a piece of evidence somewhere and I'd only purchased a new one that morning. I began to wonder how the FBI already had my number. I'd texted Ray Kintner a heartfelt thank you. Maybe that was how. Or maybe not.

It's not like the FBI didn't have their ways.

"The guy who wouldn't return my calls last time I got out of the hospital?"

"One and the same," he said. "I'm sorry."

I sure was getting a lot of apologies from law enforcement lately.

"All's well that ends well, I guess," I said.

"I'd like to talk to you."

"I'm recovering. Can it wait?"

I looked over at Cara, who had spent the night and was sticking to her promise of looking after me.

"I think it would be mutually beneficial if we met today," he said. "I'll come to you."

At least I didn't have to move.

"I'm in Walnut Creek. 4182 Treat Avenue. It's a little apartment with its own address."

"I'll see you soon."

A knock came at the door less than an hour later. Cara answered it and led Agent Moore to my bedroom.

My legs were elevated, as per the doctor's request. I felt fine and thought it unnecessary, but if it meant more doting by Cara, I could live with it.

"Nice little setup you got here," Moore said.

He had a jacket with *FBI* printed across the front. This was obviously official business.

"It was all her," I said, pointing to Cara.

"Listen, I hate to be a jerk, but this conversation has to be private."

Before I could say anything, Cara spoke: "I wanted to get some fresh air anyway. I'm going to go for a walk."

"Thanks for making it easy," I said.

She came over and kissed me.

"This shouldn't take too long," Agent Moore said. "Can you give us a half hour?"

"Sure," Cara said, and walked out of the apartment.

Agent Moore took a chair and pulled it up next to me. I hadn't taken down the collage I'd made and his eyes scanned it over. He gave me a nod.

"Impressive," he said.

"Thanks."

"Detective Kintner called me from Santa Cruz after all that happened. We've been apprised of your interviews with law enforcement, but the Bureau would like to hear it from your mouth. I was too busy serving warrants and arresting people to make it to Santa Cruz myself."

He took out a little recording device. "Do you mind?" he said. "Save you a trip to one of our field offices."

"Then I'm all for it," I said.

I spent the next fifteen minutes explaining everything that happened leading up to me getting on the boat. Followed by the experience on the boat itself. Moore expressed admiration at a few points. And exasperation at others. He couldn't understand how I could take everything in my own hands at the exclusion of the police.

I didn't bother telling him that I'd been fucked over by the police a few times, which had weighed on my decision. Of course, they were back in my good graces after Ray Kintner had effectively saved my life.

I finished by telling him of being admitted to Dominican Hospital.

"Truly remarkable, Quint."

"Thanks. Now you said this was going to be mutually beneficial. I'd love to hear what you've got," I said.

"I'm a man of my word," he said.

He cleared his throat and continued. "Charles Zane's criminal enterprise is no more. And this time I mean it. Once I got the call from Detective Kintner explaining what had happened on the boat, we raided all associates of Zane. We arrested Doug Anderson and he broke down within minutes. I was there for that. We told him Zane was dead and what you'd seen outside of his house. Once he cracked, he started admitting everything. The young girl was a prostitute. She was seventeen. Apparently, Anderson likes to do S&M, but not the consensual kind, and that's probably why more than one girl had fled his house. This one temporarily escaped, but Anderson ran her down and brought her back to his house. While doing this, he saw Annie Ivers peering out her window. The prostitute told Anderson she was going to tell the police she was held against her will, and he panicked and killed her. Then he went over to Ivers's house, where a fight ensued in which he threw her against a wall, killing her. He claims it was an accident. It doesn't really matter. Going over to Ivers's house is what ensured her death."

I started wondering if it wasn't Doug Anderson who was the real villain. He was the one who'd killed my father and had a propensity for young girls. He'd also killed Annie Ivers, a woman I'd come to view as more than just an acquaintance.

And yet, Charles Zane was the one who allowed this to keep happening. All because Anderson was good for business. I decided there was more than enough blame to go around.

"Anderson also gave up Max Crowder," Agent Moore continued. "We arrested him by the Berkeley Marina where you saw him. He lives in a boat down there. We haven't had time to go through everything, but we hit the jackpot when we arrested him. He had several laptops with information pertaining to Zane's business. I have a sneaking suspicion that when they initially feared they were going to get raided, Zane and Anderson gave Max Crowder anything self-incriminating."

I tried to absorb all of the information coming in rapid-fire style.

"He didn't break as fast as Doug Anderson, but he eventually did. Once he found out that you had killed Charles Zane on the boat, I think he realized life as he knew it was over. Then it was just a matter of time. Finally, a little after midnight last night, he broke and told us everything. I won't bore you with all of it, but it's pretty much as we suspected. Zane made the majority of his money from drugs, but they sold weapons, employed prostitutes, took bets, and many other things. This was a full-on criminal organization. I can tell you all about it at a later time. But there was one thing Max Crowder told me that I knew would interest you."

"I'm not sure I can process any more," I said.

Moore smiled. "I understand it's a lot to take in. But you'll like this."

"What is it?"

"We arrested the man who tried to kill you at your apartment complex. His name is Kenneth Fields. We took him into custody at 2:00 a.m. in San Leandro."

If this was Moore's big reveal, it didn't impress me all that much. I felt happy they had caught the guy. Obviously. But I was more interested in getting the people at the top. Like Anderson and Crowder. That gave me a lot more satisfaction.

Still, they had arrested the man who tried to kill me. That should mean something to me.

"Well done," I said. "I'm assuming he was low on the totem pole."

"It looks that way. But he still had $100,000 of drugs at his house. Even the grunts of this operation dealt in high volume."

I'm sure there were a million other questions I'd think of over the coming days. But I couldn't think of any in the moment.

"Thanks for all you've done," I said.

"We're only getting started. There will be more arrests in the days to come. There's no telling just how deep this goes."

"Did Anderson admit to killing my father?" I finally asked, not sure why I hadn't broached it earlier.

"Yes. Anderson said he told Zane that he didn't want to kill your father. Anderson said Zane told him to follow your father and kill him. And if he didn't, Zane would kill him instead."

"Do you believe him?" I asked.

"He admitted to several murders. He's going away for life. Why would he lie about this one thing?"

Oddly, this comforted me. Doug Anderson was a murderous, reprehensible human, but the true evil was Charles Zane. After all that had happened on the boat, I preferred it that way.

"What's next for me?" I asked.

"A few more interviews. But you're not going to be charged with Charles Zane's murder, if that's what you mean."

It was nice to hear. But not unexpected.

"Anything else?" I asked.

"A big thank you. Because of you, we are bringing down a crime syndicate that's brought a lot of disorder to the Bay Area."

"Disorder?"

"Yeah, I guess that's not a strong enough word. Murder. Mayhem."

"That's better."

"And I'm truly sorry about your father. Detective Kintner told me how much justice for him meant to you."

"Thanks."

"Even if it was a bit of vigilante justice."

I laughed.

"If it's any comfort, his going after Anderson led you to do the same," Moore said. "And that helped bring down this murderous organization. The Bay Area owes a debt of gratitude to your father as well."

For what felt like the twenty-third time in the last several months, my eyes started to water.

"You'll never say anything more meaningful to me. Thanks, Agent Moore."

"You're welcome. I'm going to show myself out. But I'm sure we will be talking again soon."

"Take care of yourself," I said.

"You as well."

And with that, Agent Moore left. A few minutes later Cara was back and joined me in bed. This was recuperation at its best.

Two days later, I was back at John Muir Medical Center, having the stitches from my leg removed. I was given a clean bill of health and the doctor ordered me to start avoiding hospitals for the foreseeable future. I promised to try.

It was time to start a new phase of my life. I was forty years old and three months. I no longer worked for the *Walnut Creek Times*, but after all that had happened, I was going to be a desirable free agent. If Tom Butler had been right, there was definitely interest in a tell-all book from yours truly.

Quint and The Shark sprang to mind as a possible title.

That could wait, obviously. I was just happy for all I had.

This included a girlfriend who loved me and a mother who was grateful I was alive. I had a father I saw as heroic. I even had a lifelong friend in Ray Kintner.

There'd be some interesting times ahead, to be sure. Arrests. Trials. Questions about my father. Questions about me.

But I'd get through it all. After everything I'd already experienced, what was to come would feel like a vacation.

For the first time in a while, I looked forward to what the future held.

I walked out of the hospital and the sun shined directly in my eyes, blinding me momentarily. I reached for my sunglasses.

Which brought to mind the title of a cheesy song from the '80s that my father used to play. It seemed apropos:

"The Future's So Bright, I Gotta Wear Shades."

THE END